D0426565

FAMILY TERRORISTS

Books by Antonya Nelson

The Expendables

In the Land of Men

Family Terrorists

FAMILY TERRORISTS

//////

A Novella and Seven Stories

Antonya Nelson

Houghton Mifflin Company

BOSTON   NEW YORK

1994

For information about permission to reproduce selections
from this book, write to Permissions, Houghton Mifflin Company,
215 Park Avenue South, New York, New York 10003

Library of Congress Cataloguing-in-Publication Data
Nelson, Antonya.
Family terrorists : a novella and seven stories / Antonya Nelson.
p.   cm.
ISBN 0-395-68679-2
I. Title.
PS3564.E428F36 1994
813'.54 — dc20   93-45825
CIP
Printed in the United States of America
BP 10 9 8 7 6 5 4 3 2 1

Book design by Melodie Wertelet
Printed on recycled paper

"Loaded Gun," "Dirty Words," and "Naked Ladies" first appeared in *The New
Yorker*, "The Ocean" in *Alaska Quarterly Review*, and "Her Secret Life" in *Story*.
"Dirty Words" was also published in *Prize Stories 1993: The O. Henry Awards*,
and "Naked Ladies" was included in *The Best American Short Stories 1993*.

For my family,
the first one and this one

I WOULD LIKE TO THANK

Ehud Havazelet, Don Kurtz, Anne Marie Mackler, Eva McCollaum, Kevin McIlroy, Daniel Menaker, Paula Moore, Bonnie Nadell, Rita Popp, David Schweidel, John Sterling, and, especially, Robert Boswell.

CONTENTS

Loaded Gun / 1

Dirty Words / 25

The Ocean / 49

Naked Ladies / 65

Crybaby / 91

The Written Word / 115

Her Secret Life / 137

Family Terrorists / 167

LOADED GUN

—— ++++++ ——

"I'M GOING TO TELL YOU SOMETHING YOUR MOTHER doesn't know," her father said. Edie was fifteen; she didn't want to hear such things. Her older sister's warning came to her, too late: "Whatever you do, don't get in the car with Dad. That's where he traps you when he wants to talk." She braced herself, watching the Kansas winter landscape go by, her shoulder belt like a leash at her throat. They had been discussing Edie's cousin Tara — Terrible Tara, Edie and her brother called her. They'd been laughing, her father pursing his lips as if he were a pigeon to imitate Tara's cooing voice, shifting his rear on the seat to suggest her undulating hen-like bottom.

"Your mother doesn't ever want to hear bad things about her family," Edie's father went on, stern now. He steered as if throttling the wheel, as if it might leap away, and he never went faster than fifty miles an hour.

"Tara is living with her father," Edie's father told her. Edie nodded, waiting for the part her mother didn't know. Though Tara was thirty years old, she had yet to live on her own. For a while she had stayed in Edie's family's basement. Edie's father looked away from the road at Edie's profile. "I mean, they're *living together*," he said, the last two words like the title of a dirty movie.

She found herself gargling something at him, her face reddening like a bloodstain.

"Don't tell your mother."

She shook her head.

Cousin Tara couldn't be contained. Every memory of her Edie had was ugly. Whenever Tara saw Edie she'd say something like "So here we are, Eeds, the black sheep of the family." It was true that Edie had been caught shoplifting the year before. Also true that she'd stolen some of Tara's Valium. But Tara always intimated that there was more to it, that they were *close,* that they *understood* each other.

In the car, Edie had been trying to tell her father about the times Tara had insulted their family, but it was hard to explain. Tara was sly, and you could mistake her meanness for joking. It was *supposed* to be joking. "She's jealous," Edie's mother always replied, to the same information. She didn't feel angry, just sad. For a while Edie would try to feel sorry for her cousin, who couldn't finish school, who couldn't keep a job. Poor Tara. Her parents had been teenagers, reckless and foolish, and she'd grown up at her grandparents' house, Edie's grandfather embarrassed by her.

But Edie's pity wouldn't last. Under some quack advice, Tara would drag their grandmother to a therapy session and call her names. Or she'd steal morphine from the hospital where she used to work and get written up in the newspaper. A few years ago, she had made Edie's mother drive all the way to Topeka to pick her up from the drunk tank after her motorcycle had been impounded. Edie could so perfectly see Tara's face, that rubbery, sloe-eyed expression — as if she were permanently high, flirting, unrepentant, insinuating. "Pren," she would say to Prentice, Edie's shy

brother, "you old egghead, lemme yank your chest hair."
Worst of all was that Edie's mother refused to see Tara for
who she was. Edie wanted to know why the family couldn't
disown her; she tried to explain that Tara was *evil,* and
probably contagious, but her mother always provided a forgiving explanation for it all: poor childhood, Tara's mother's
death, lack of luck.

"Your mother's loyal," Edie's father said. "She never wants
to assume anything bad about anybody, especially someone in the family, like Tara."

Edie's mother was naive; even Edie, the baby, knew
that. "Mom's a chump," Edie told her father glumly.

He gave her a lengthy look before saying, "Someday it
might be you who needs her forgiveness."

They swung onto a dirt road. Ahead was the old mill
where he bought flour and cornmeal. In the last year he'd
begun baking bread — every Sunday, listening to opera on
public radio in the kitchen, wearing an apron and drinking
red wine, slamming a heavy armful of dough on the For-
mica — and he insisted on driving the forty miles from
Wichita to Harkins' Mill to shop for ingredients. The mill
still ran with a water wheel. Edie's sister had said, "Beware
those long trips when you can't even roll down the window.
You know he's going to say something you don't want to
hear."

At the mill her father parked and set the emergency
brake. The building looked like a giant's house, with huge
double doors and a turret on either side. It was February,
freezing cold; smoke puffed from a black chimney on the
roof. The water wheel wasn't revolving because the stream
had turned to ice. "How do they work the mill without the
wheel?" Edie asked her father as they stepped from the
Mustang.

"What?" he said, fingers to his deaf right ear.

"No wheel," Edie said, pointing to the Gothic structure. Icicles hung from its wooden cups.

"There's a regular electric generator," her father told her. He fitted his cap on his head and cleared his throat, then asked Edie if she was coming inside.

"I'm going to just walk around," she said. "I'm carsick."

He nodded and moved off toward the eight-foot wooden doors.

Edie climbed down the incline behind the mill, down among the wrecked cars the owners either collected or tolerated. There were a half-dozen rusting vehicles, one from each of the past six decades, Edie decided. She peered through the empty space where the windshield should have been on an old farm truck, then crawled into the back seat of what had once been a plush sedan. Springs coiled where the cushions used to be; the piled beer cans on the floorboard were probably forty years younger than the car. Edie crouched, sitting delicately on a wooden frame. She wondered when they quit using wood in the manufacturing of automobiles.

This car's windshield was also missing, and the wind blew through. Edie's feet were so cold she couldn't feel her toes, as if her legs ended in points, like big pencils. She studied the dashboard, thinking of Tara. It was impossible to imagine her cousin having sex with her father — a man with porkchop sideburns whom Edie had met just once, long ago — without also imagining herself having sex with *her* father. For a few seconds Edie didn't realize she was staring at the car's steering wheel — her own father, for God's sake — and then she blinked to clear her mind. In the hard plastic, at the top of the circle, was a perfect curve of teeth where the driver's mouth had been hurled into the wheel. Edie sucked in her breath and scrambled out of the wreck. Her own teeth ached suddenly with a sharp bitterness, like cavities. The front end of the car was smashed and pleated, with rust growing in the folds, taking over the pretty fifties turquoise. She glanced once more through the driver's window, reached her fingers in and ran them over the marks, eight cold little indentations on a pristine arc.

Her father stood waiting at their car, his shoes touching at the heels and pointing in nearly opposite directions. The cloth bags of flour sat in the back seat like small passengers leaning into one another. Edie climbed in the front and switched the heater to high. Her father got in and cleared his throat, probably to remind her not to tell her mother about Tara, and Edie turned the radio on. All the way home they listened to the golden oldies station Edie's mother liked, the one Edie and her siblings called K-BAD.

*

Tara came to dinner in March and brought her new boyfriend, Claude — a name she pronounced as if it rhymed with *cow*. Tara and Claude drove over in Edie's grandmother's LTD, the two of them in the front while Granna sat meekly in the back. When they arrived, Edie's father had to go help her get out, and the stereo speaker was so loud the door vibrated. "Oh, shame on us," Tara proclaimed, laughing her slutty laugh. The noise of her tall white heels on the concrete driveway made Edie's cheeks ache. The new plan was for Tara to move back to Granna's. Of course, this was Edie's mother's idea.

Claude was supposed to be a French chef. "From Canada," Tara told them all. Claude didn't say much, glancing around the house as if casing it, sneering down his large nose at Edie's family. He wore completely mismatched clothes, as if he'd set out to look as foolish as possible. His pants were plaid, his shirt flowered, his suit jacket a brown and olive pattern like office wallpaper. Tara was speeding, chattering a mile a minute while she gaily flung together her contribution to dinner — a salad of overripe fruit, stuff marked down for quick sale at Food Land. Her hair had been dyed a dull beet color and she'd lost some weight.

Edie's mother pretended nothing was peculiar. She smiled so hard it looked like it hurt; to whatever anybody said she responded with a woofy laugh. She bustled from kitchen to dining room carrying baskets and bowls and utensils, stopping to offer drinks or give orders. Whenever there was even a hint of uncomfortable silence she launched into one of her stories, which never had anything that you might call a point. Prentice was home from college but staying out of the way, avoiding the onslaught of chores and errands — "projects," their mother often called them — she would surely hand him. And though Edie liked Prentice, his hunger — his literal need for food — was so powerful that he didn't see the weirdness around him. Edie had told him what her father had revealed about Tara and Tara's father, and Prentice hadn't commented. Their older sister would have wanted to believe it, but Prentice was skeptical about most things Edie told him. She'd used to be a pretty big liar.

And besides, Tara had brought her boyfriend. Maybe she didn't actually sleep with her father. This made Edie appraise her own father. What had he been talking about, anyway?

At dinner Tara sat next to Edie and said in a whisper, "If I'd made this chili, I would have used lean beef instead of ground round."

Edie looked down at her bowl, where a clear layer of

bright orange grease floated on the chili. In it she could see her reflection, eyelashes and nostrils.

"Don't eat," she told Tara.

Instead, Tara stuck the corner of her napkin in the chili, then wadded the soiled cloth into her fist. "Prentice," she called across the table. "Yoo-hoo, Earth to Prentice." Prentice looked up from his food, which he had been steadily shoveling in, completely oblivious of everyone. "Help me move tomorrow? Over to Granna's?"

Cornered, Prentice had to say yes. Edie wondered what would happen with Tara's father, if he would simply slide out of the picture the way he had in the past.

When she was seven or eight years old, she used to spend the night at Granna's house. Tara was living there between dropping out of nursing school and enrolling in beauty school, and Edie had to sleep in the upstairs bedroom where Tara also slept. In the night Tara sometimes got into bed with Edie. "You be the man," she would say, rolling Edie on top of herself. Edie only vaguely knew what that meant. While Tara bounced beneath her, Edie would try to hear her grandparents downstairs, Granna in one room, Gransir in another, their distinct but noisy breathing like big kind animals in the night. Tara was twenty-two or -three; she whispered in Edie's ears the frightening news of what would happen to Edie soon, what future her body held in store. Then Tara would return to her own twin bed, leaving Edie to stare at the dire photograph of her great-grandmother on the wall, the rounded glass of the picture distorting the room and hallway like a fisheye lens.

At dinner, with her lips too close to Edie's ear, Tara said, "And this iceburg lettuce has absolutely no nutritional value. It's like eating that plastic grass in an Easter basket."

"Don't eat," Edie repeated.

Claude picked at his chili with a fork and drank beer from the bottle, even though he'd been given a frosted glass, which now sat empty beside his salad bowl, sweating onto the tablecloth. After dinner, he and Tara loaded the dishwasher together, laughing, crashing plates around carelessly in a way that Edie or Prentice never could have gotten away with. Edie's mother had made a chocolate cake for dessert, but Tara and Claude insisted on frozen yogurt, taking Granna's car to go get it. They were gone for an hour, and when they returned — the thump of the bass like a heavy heartbeat in the driveway once more — they'd forgotten the yogurt.

On the back porch, as they were leaving, Tara turned to Edie's father and said, "Didn't I see you down at the Holiday Inn lounge the other night?"

Edie's father said no.

"Oh, I thought I did," Tara said, grinning, tipping her head back to look through lowered lashes at Edie. "With a redhead."

Edie hugged Granna goodnight, holding tight in case Tara and Claude wrecked the car on the way home and she never saw her grandmother again.

*

Just after Easter, Edie caught mono from a boy she barely knew and missed two weeks of school. They'd kissed at a party for the East High boys' swimming team. He was a senior, a diver named Mark Anthony. Edie knew there was something slick and ironic about his name, but she hadn't taken the time to research it yet. She enjoyed kissing, and he had been content to keep it at that, which made her like him all the more. A week later she felt sick.

When Edie was young her mother didn't have a job, so

whenever anyone stayed home ill, she was there to make soup, switch TV channels from one game show to another, heat or cool washcloths, read stories, or simply sit on the sickbed and sympathize. Her children's illnesses used to make Edie's mother mournful. Edie had liked that. Now her mother worked at the Department of Motor Vehicles, and Edie had to stay home alone, get her own aspirin. Her friends called at lunchtime to see if they could bring over their boyfriends and a couple of six-packs. Edie told them she expected her mother home early even though she didn't. Around three in the afternoon her mother called to find out how things were with Edie and what they'd gotten in the mail. Bravely Edie talked, her throat sore, her feelings hurt.

Over Easter, Tara had moved away from her father to Granna's house. Edie was lonely and would have called Granna, but she knew Tara would answer the phone. It made Edie furious, how Tara was taking advantage. She'd begun using Granna's car to go to bars, coming home late, drunk, bringing men to stay with her in what had been Gransir's bedroom before he died. From Edie's mother Tara borrowed things and never returned them — sweaters, jewelry, shoes. If Edie mentioned them to her mother, her mother would get annoyed. "Don't you have more important topics to occupy you?"

By herself in the house, Edie became curious. Her mother believed in privacy, but Edie was a snoop. One morning she ransacked her mother's bathroom, looking for her birth control. Whatever they used, they'd hidden it well. Edie found nothing but an ancient electric massager, probably for her father's bad back, sitting in a drawer full of scarves. She switched it on and let it jiggle her hand for a while.

Ten days later, when she went back to school, she was hopelessly behind in all her classes, and Mark Anthony passed her in the halls without seeming to recall who she was.

*

A black man named Dick Stubbs took care of Edie's family's yard. When he wasn't doing yards, Stubbs lived in the bus depot downtown. He had, thanks to Edie's parents, a small storage shed behind the Trailways building, containing gardening tools, and a used golf cart someone from the Wichita State Shocker Club had given him, in which he drove from yard job to yard job. Sometimes Edie saw him putt-putting down Douglas Avenue, wearing wraparound shades. Edie's parents, especially her mother, had what Edie considered foolish faith in people's general goodness. Every Christmas for twenty years they had hung an enormous lighted peace symbol from the attic window, as if the traffic passing it might be inspired instead of amused. It was a rare moment when her father displayed his more sinister pessimism, as he had concerning Tara. Most often they were busy doing the right thing, like hiring Stubbs, a homeless man, three years ago to bail pine needles from the rain gutters. Now this man felt he could give Edie advice.

"Smile," he ordered her on the first day of spring. He'd come over to prune roses. Someone was always telling Edie to smile, as if she didn't have a right to surly thoughts. She was also constantly given the baffling instruction "Be yourself."

"Why do I have to help him?" she'd yelled at her mother earlier. "What do we pay him for, if not to pick up our trash?"

Her mother had slapped her face. "Don't make me ashamed of you," she'd said, sending Edie to collect the winter's debris in the yard.

Theirs was a corner house on two busy streets. Everyone threw litter into their yard — school papers, cheap wine bottles, fast-food wrappers. Edie filled three grocery sacks with the limp mulchy mess, still smarting from her mother's slap. She was popping bagworms, using her heel to press open their crusty little larva sacs, hoping this was the way to infect all the yard's trees, when she found a gun. It lay beneath a brown cypress in a nest of dead needles. She drew the gun out and held it in her palm, recalled suddenly to the peril everywhere around her.

"I wish I'd found that," Stubbs said when she handed it to him. "Wouldn't have showed you."

"You can have it," Edie told him.

He took the gun and banged it against his wrist; the cylinder fell open. Stubbs snapped it closed and looked left and right, then lifted the gun and pointed it at Edie's nose. She inhaled. Now wouldn't her mother regret trusting Stubbs, when she found Edie with her face blown off, lying here among the rest of the litter? Stubbs lowered the weapon, pinched open his loose, sweaty khakis, and fitted the gun into the hollow beneath his ribs. "Thank you," he said, patting it lightly.

Edie was furious with him for scaring her, furious with her mother for making her work with him, but what could she do? She wished now she'd kept the gun.

Around the block came the ice cream truck, on this year's maiden voyage, its warbling tune ringing out. In her mind, Edie heard her mother's voice singing along: *Playmate, come out and play with me.* The tune would stick with her for hours.

"That thing is constantly going around our block," she told Stubbs peevishly.

"The driver makes deals in the park," he said. "I've seen him buying weed over there."

"Really?" They listened to the tinkling tune grow loud and distorted as the vehicle passed, the driver lifting a hand to wave at them, then fade quickly as he rounded Second and headed toward Hillside.

"High as a fucking kite," Stubbs said, then added, "I think you ought not to bring up this gun thing with your parents."

"Don't worry," Edie told him. The ice cream song tinkled in Edie's brain like the soundtrack from a horror movie about psycho children with scythes. She felt full — to the point of nausea — of knowledge she couldn't do anything with.

*

Edie made straight C's on her final report card. "Average," she told her parents, who merely looked sorry for her, not surprised; she wasn't like her brother and sister, who'd actually cared what grades they received, but neither were Edie's parents the same people they'd been back then. They didn't have the enthusiasm to push her the way they had pushed the two others, sitting at the kitchen table and suffering over logarithms or metaphors.

Her cousin Tara had never finished school, she kept remembering with panic.

Summer brought the spreading malaise of humid hours. When she grew tired of lying in the sun listening to FM radio, Edie decided to get a perm in her mousy, fine hair. One of her classmates' fathers was a hairdresser and offered discounts to his daughter's friends. Edie didn't think of herself as a friend but got a deal nonetheless. The daughter washed Edie's hair in a plastic sink that held her neck like a cattle yoke. A little girl — her classmate's sister, Edie guessed — chased a fly around the salon with a tea strainer. "I don't want to kill it," she kept wailing as she waved the strainer ineffectually over her head.

The father had photographs from Washington, D.C., on his walls, pictures of himself with famous women newscasters from the early seventies. He'd been some kind of semi-celebrity back then; all the photos were signed by the women, "With love and gratitude," etc.

"Jessica's dead," his daughter told Edie, pointing at a smiling blond woman with Cleopatra eye makeup. "He did her hair for years."

Edie had no idea who the woman was; history, besides her own, lapped unknown around her like a dark sea. The father permed her hair in such a way that she couldn't really tell she'd had a perm. Somehow he'd made her hair simultaneously shrink and plump out, like the hair of a cheap doll. She'd imagined corkscrews falling wildly to her shoulders, but what she saw in the mirror was a blow-dried version of the same hairdo the women on the wall had, only brown instead of blond, coarse instead of sleek.

"I'm growing out my hair," she pleaded as the father snipped off some bangs.

"Get this fly away," he said to his daughters, ignoring Edie altogether. His girls giggled.

"You smell good, Papa," the older one said, "that's why he's bothering you." Her father waved his clippers at the fly.

Edie said, "I sort of like the natural look," but he'd already sprayed hairspray, lacquering everything solid.

When she paid, filling in the blank check her mother

had given her, the fly landed beside her fanny pack on the counter. Despite the odds against it, Edie smashed him with a well-placed slap. She flicked him to the floor. The little sister was crying when Edie walked out.

*

For her summer project, Edie's mother decided to learn Spanish. "It's a crime not to know another language," she told Edie and her father at dinner, as if reprimanding them for not wishing to join her. Her class met every day for two weeks at the university and then flew to Mexico City for some hands-on experience. For those last two weeks, Edie hardly saw her father. He took up smoking again — something he hadn't done since before he'd gotten married — and he began sleeping in Prentice's room. Meanwhile, Edie was reading dirty books. These consumed a shelf in her father's study, resting there as if they were as innocent as *Bleak House* or *Jane Eyre*. There were different types: sex a long time ago, sex between men and women, men and men, women and women, people alone, people being watched. Occasionally an animal was involved. There were virgin girls, thermometers, cucumbers, birch twigs, tongues, fingers, teeth. There were stories with a lot of driving around — in carriages or cars or trains — and getting hardly anywhere, and then there were stories that went straight to the point, again and again. Edie couldn't get over the books — their frankness, their effect on her. When her father disappeared in the early evening during the two weeks her mother was gone, Edie retreated to her bedroom, paperback in hand. She lay awake for hours, thinking, worrying, dazed and chagrined. In the morning she would slip downstairs, passing Prentice's closed bedroom door, her mother and father's wide queen-size bed and its undisturbed red, white, and blue quilt, and return the book she'd chosen to its place on the shelf.

Edie spent the Fourth of July night at her grandmother's house. The two of them sat in La-Z-Boys watching reruns of *Murder, She Wrote,* Granna's favorite show. They had cold cereal and low-sodium grapefruit soda for dinner. Afterward they played robin rummy and ate butter mints. Tara and Claude were out in the car. Edie called home just to hear the phone ring in the empty hallway. She kept picturing the little green Post-It notes her mother had attached to everything in the house: *la mesa, la silla, el teléfono.*

"Hosannah," Granna said at nine-thirty, "I'm a-whupped. Had an x-ray yesterday and I'm still worn out."

"An x-ray of what?"

"My liver, my spleen, my gizzard." Granna lifted herself daintily from her chair. She was big but always seemed light, like an air-filled sweet pastry, her skin dusted with powder. She walked tilted sideways, and Edie heard the bed in the next room sink as Granna sat on it.

In a few minutes, her grandmother called her. Edie found her in her underwear, still sitting on the bed.

"Hon-hon?" she said. "I need some help."

Edie located her summer muumuu, a thin flowered garment smelling of lavender. Granna didn't stink the way Edie's mother did, of Chanel No. 5 or Arid. Granna smelled like a baby. She didn't even have to shave; hair just didn't grow on her legs or under her arms. Edie sat beside her on the bed. Edie's mother always praised Granna for being "so chipper," an expression that made Edie think of squirrels. She and Granna looked in the huge round vanity mirror at themselves. "I'm afraid I might be leaving this world," Granna told Edie's reflection.

Edie began to cry. Granna reached out as if for her hand but didn't seem to have the energy to take it. "I don't want you to tell your mother I had x-rays, you hear?"

"Why?"

Granna tipped over slowly away from Edie, resting her head on a pillow as if she might never lift it up again. "Oh, well, you know your mother," she said vaguely.

"Hmm," Edie said, curious for a moment about the truth of that. Then she added, "You should sleep." Granna lay limp on the bed while Edie worked the spread out from under her, rolling her body from side to side until she was beneath the sheets. She switched off the light as she went out. Outside she heard distant firecrackers, the *pop pop pop* like crossfire. A few hours later, while Edie was staring at music videos, Tara came home, banging the front door open into the back of Edie's chair.

"Eeds, Eeds, what's the story?"

"Be quiet. Granna's in bed. You reek."

Tara swung the front door closed. "I reek?"

"Where's Claude?"

Tara squinted at the TV over Edie's head. "You like them?"

Edie turned to watch four skinny guys in leather pants bend over and swing their long hair in circles like propellers as they played guitars and shouted. "I guess," she admitted.

"Oy." Tara headed for the kitchen, where she stood before the open refrigerator eating from a turkey carcass. However hateful Edie found Tara, it was still good to have someone younger than Granna in the house. Edie had been afraid to go listen at Granna's door, afraid she might not hear breathing. Didn't people always die on holidays?

Now she followed Tara to the kitchen. "What's wrong with Granna?" she asked. "Why did she have an x-ray?"

"What's wrong with Granna is she's old. Old people get paranoid about every little thing. So her side aches? So does mine. It comes from laying around the house."

"Oh."

"Fucking Claude went up to Hutchinson."

"Why?"

"Because in Hutch you can score."

Tara brought out a jar of olives but couldn't get the lid unscrewed. "Those are really ancient," Edie told her. "Like fossils. I saw them here last year and the year before."

Tara put the jar back in the refrigerator.

"Aren't those my mom's boots?" Edie asked.

Tara looked from the lighted refrigerator to her feet. "So?" she said, glaring now at Edie. "Isn't that her ring?"

Edie grabbed her left hand; her mother's opal ring was on her pinkie.

Tara snorted, slamming the refrigerator door. The eggs rattled in their holder. "And guess what else, Edie?" Tara reached into her bag and produced a Baggie full of something that looked like heavy silt and pieces of shells.

"What's that?"

"Ashes," Tara said. These would be her own mother's ashes — Edie's aunt Regina, who had died two years before, of cancer. They belonged in a Blue Willow ginger jar in Edie's mother's bedroom, on the mantel with everyone's school and wedding photos. Most alarming to Edie was the idea of Tara in her family's house when they were gone.

"Go ahead and tell your mother — I dare you," Tara said. She pushed past Edie and headed for the bathroom. "And be sure you tell her you saw me piss on them before I flushed them away."

The bathroom door closed, and a few minutes later water ran through the pipes. All night Edie woke up on the couch feverish from nightmares and images, worried that someone would walk through the living room door, sit down on her, say something, do something.

*

On the day her mother returned, Edie and her father cleaned. He threw away his rolling papers and tobacco pouch; Edie made her bed for the first time since her mother had left. They opened windows and switched on ceiling fans. In her parents' bedroom, Edie opened the ginger jar and looked in. Half her aunt's ashes were still there. It was possible her mother would never notice. Together, she and her father cooked lasagna and French bread and listened to opera. Edie felt happy to be back to normal, to be a kid with parents.

At the airport, her mother arrived sunburned and smiling hysterically at Edie and her father, as if she hadn't smiled in weeks. She walked from the plane beside a dark-haired, bearded man who was earnestly telling her something.

"Who was that?" Edie's father asked as they left the airport, a suitcase hanging from one hand and a garish woven basket stuffed with newspaper-wrapped curios from the other. Edie's mother was babbling away about what she'd brought them and appeared to have to think for a moment to figure out what her husband had asked.

"Oh. Duane," she said, dismissing him with a shake of her head. "He's a reporter at the *Eagle,* a very interesting man, but a little lonely."

"He seemed to like you," Edie's father commented.

"Oh, he's one of those people who need a nurturing older woman to listen to their woes." Edie was reminded of how her mother always had to categorize everybody, "one of those people who."

Duane was standing pathetically at the curb outside, trying to hail the single taxicab waiting at the Wichita airport. Edie watched her father watch him, noting his perplexed frown. Her mother waved, shouting something in Spanish, to which Duane nodded, either grimacing or smiling.

"We could give him a ride," Edie offered, so content at having her mother home that she was trying to think like her.

"Oh," her mother said lightly, still walking, leaving Edie's idea behind her somewhere.

At the dinner table, Edie was allowed to drink champagne with her parents while her father served the food and her mother prattled on about her trip, inserting occasional Spanish words, her mouth working so hard at forming them it was as if she were disgorging golf balls. Though the lasagna had scorched and was leathery, she complimented it a hundred times. Edie regretted helping her father hide his and her own messiness during her mother's absence. She wished the smell of smoke still lingered. She was on the verge of saying or asking something. She could feel her thoughts circling busily in her brain, crowded and confused, the champagne working like lubricant. But they were ugly things, her thoughts, like the many-legged insects that lived beneath rocks: you waited for them to scurry back into the darkness, out of sight. And her mother's eager face seemed directly responsible. As she herself might put it, she was one of those people who made their companions sour with their sunniness.

*

On a muggy Sunday in August, Tara phoned to invite Edie to go see a movie with her. Edie hated Sundays; they reminded her of PMS. She felt fat and had acne all over her neck. Stores were closed and the mail didn't come. School was about to start again. Her father had once told her that Wichita sat smack in the middle of the Sun Belt and had three hundred and forty sunny days a year, but Edie didn't believe him — on Sunday it always rained.

"How about *Elephant Man?*" Tara said. "It's only two bucks, over at the Crest. We could walk from your house."

"I'll go but I won't walk. Come get me." It had been a couple of years since Edie had gone to a movie with Tara; then they'd seen *Fantasia,* and Edie had made the mistake of telling Tara she looked exactly like the dancing ostrich.

Claude hadn't come back from Hutchinson. Tara had started going to AA meetings because she'd been picked up on a DUI in Granna's car and AA was the only way to keep her license. Since Claude had gone and she'd stopped drinking, she'd gained about twenty pounds. Edie preferred her fat. She preferred Tara as pathetic and grotesque as possible. At the theater Edie bought a huge box of small Snickers bars and kept offering them to her, feeling pleasantly perverse as Tara tore open the little wrapper and bit into the chocolate. Just sitting here next to Tara was to indulge in a greasy kind of inertia.

"Oh God," Edie said, suddenly bowing her head down.

"What?" Tara asked, looking around quickly, like a bird.

"That guy ahead of us, with the two daughters? He's the guy who gave me this shitty perm." The three of them sidestepped into a row four or five down from Tara and Edie.

Tara watched them for a while, then leaned back. "So what?"

Edie shrugged. "I just don't want to talk to them."

"You know what your hair looks like? Like a sweater

you were supposed to Woolite." Tara laughed at her own joke. "How's your mom?"

"Fine," Edie said. This was an example of what Edie could never quite explain to her mother, the way Tara had asked about her. Her mother refused to understand *tone,* as if she were reading conversations instead of having them. Tara was really saying, "You didn't tell on me, little gutless brat," and, more annoyingly, "I knew you wouldn't."

Edie continued chewing her Snickers.

Tara opened her black purse, which was the size of a small suitcase, and rifled through the contents — scruffed-up compacts and lipsticks, hairy combs, linty Kleenex. "Lend me a couple bucks, will you?"

Edie sighed, lifting her rear to extract from her pocket the five that was left over from the ten-dollar bill her mother had given her for "going to the show," or, as she had put it, "va a película."

"Here," she said, handing the limp bill to Tara. Four rows ahead of her the hairdresser raised his arms like a vulture or vampire and dropped one on each of his daughters' shoulders. Edie couldn't help thinking that this symbolized something depraved about his relationship with them. On the way to the theater, she and Tara had passed Dick Stubbs on Douglas, driving his pokey golf cart, looking quaint and harmless while he had a pistol packed under his belt.

In a minute, Tara returned with her popcorn and Crush, and the theater lights faded to black. There was a timing glitch, so everyone sat uneasily for a few seconds staring at the only source of light, a red EXIT sign. Beside her cousin in the dark, Edie remembered the upstairs bedroom at Granna's, being on top of Tara, every now and then thrilling all over with a forbidden and frightening desire for what she understood to be very bad. She shook her head, shook it hard, imagining, as she did so, shaking her mother. She would begin with the five-dollar bill. She would take her mother by the shirtsleeves and shake the unbearable toothy smile right off her face, enjoying the certainty with which she could declare, "No way in hell you're going to see that money again."

DIRTY WORDS

——— ///// ———

FRUIT

It was a nine-month incarceration. It was solitary confinement. It was dry and stupefying, full of sweets and regression — a hormonal trip to childhood, to cheap candy and bad music and copious tears. It was pregnancy, and Bette saw she might not be reformed by the end of it; she might not turn out to be a good mother.

Already she'd gone slack with gravity, sad and self-indulgent. Her pets, a cat and a dog, sexual neuters themselves, were as fat as she. "Here," she told them again and again, presenting the open refrigerator for their perusal, "help yourselves." There was no kick to be had anywhere but in the kitchen.

She'd called her own mother after six months. "I'm pregnant," she said into the spitting reception. From far away, two time zones and a chasmal continental divide, her mother answered, "Who is this?" Between them was the white noise of futile hope, misunderstanding, and exhaustion. Bette's mother used to claim she hated pregnancy but felt it, in the end, worthwhile. Now she left off the last part. She gave thirty-year-old conventional wisdom as advice, which Bette, newly fluent in the rules of the game, would eagerly, incoherently, defy. She would gain forty pounds instead of twenty, quit her brown-stain habits of coffee and cigarettes, possibly take up jogging. She would not drink. In La Jolla her mother sniffed. "I drank like a fish the whole time, and you and your sister turned out just fine." Bette wasn't sure.

In her family children drank early on, in the civilized tradition of Europeans yet with the exuberance of Americans, glib and intemperate. They drank early on, and, when they grew up, later on — after dinner, post dessert, into the A.M. hours. Where she came from you suckled every flavor of fun and found it good. She took the "Could *You* Be an Addict?" test whenever she came across it, always failing — or was it passing? — within three humorless questions. She'd attended a single AA meeting, staying long enough to feel satisfactorily removed from its ranks. They were hiding vodka in Evian bottles, slipping away to bars far from home, counting hours between drunks and limiting themselves to one a week — in short, they weren't having a nice time. Bette's problem was that she merely missed drinking, like a hilarious friend who had moved away, like a party that had ended.

She'd told the AA circle, a gritty group of ecru-eyed chain smokers, that she'd grown up next to groves of orange trees. But her stories were nostalgic instead of repentant. It was in the groves that Bette learned to drink, fresh orange juice with vodka. Or with rum. Tequila from across the border. In Chicago, where citrus arrived green and hard and undersized, shiny with wax, she longed for the orange trees, driving alongside them, the rhythmic pattern with which they fractured rays of sun.

At night she might dream of parking in the groves. A boy was beside her, the heat of the desert and the car bringing out from his freshly laundered shirt his own heat and the scent of soap flakes. They drank in the groves, playing with the headlights, switched on, then off, trees surrounding them as in a holdup, then fleeing in the sudden dark like spirits. Meanwhile irrigation fog came and stayed, rank water that did not evaporate, a dense pesticidal haze among the orange trees.

Her puberty came back to her. Or she went to it, eating citrus, dreaming of old friends, of the groves. Her dream landscape always had as its backdrop the branches of trees, oranges like bright baubles. When she couldn't sleep, she lay, resentful, beside the baby's father, kicking his ankle whenever she was kicked from within. He would rouse enough to lay a heavy forgiving arm across her chest. He was older, willing to delay gratification. Bette liked grownups. They were generous. They had patience. In their eyes, she was, and always would be, young.

It would have been sweet to have a teenage adventure, a giddy car ride into city lights, laughing with boys she didn't know who handed her cigarettes and beers. Only when she rolled the taste in her mouth, allowed it to unfurl in her limbs, might she remember she was pregnant and wake, stricken, heart banging with the baby.

She cried, buckets of progesterone, wrenching hysterical hiccoughs. Inside her grew a brutish boy, a leaper, a diver, an insomniac, his angular feet and knees and skull stirring restlessly through the night like ice cubes, his image on the ultrasound screen one of a fuzzy swimmer, in focus this moment, fast forward the next, scrotum bigger than his brain.

Down on the floor Bette's loyal dog wheezed with asthma but was happy to be loved, suddenly, so well, so weepily. Bette put her face to his and cried and cried, doomed, hugely and miserably unintoxicated.

HUSBAND

Her husband had been born in 1936 to Polish immigrants who never really learned English. They did not want to be absorbed into America, they had simply wished to leave Poland. He was Sergio Petroski, Serge to his friends. He owned a coffeehouse, which had a Marxist slant: for your latte you paid only what you could. He was a widower. His first wife had been a political poet in exile named Ferosa Rosario, who'd been slain — the word itself was enough to unnerve Bette — for holding opinions. Sergio, by virtue of history (because he had one), intimidated Bette. Would this intimidation pass for love? she sometimes wondered. When compared with his, her California-orange-grove life looked as naive and sunny as a sitcom. Until she'd seen him naked, Sergio had made her feel immorally young and uneducated, which was precisely what she'd come to Chicago to feel. She had not been a victim, she did not grasp oppression. His breadth, his resources, the stacks of books that he could recommend and quote from, the people who called him, late at night, long distance, from prison or deathbed — Bette, alas, had nowhere to link herself in this international chain of passionate intelligentsia.

Then they ended up tangled on a couch together, one Saturday after closing time, after the setting of the alarms and the locking of the doors. It was your basic apolitical clinch. Sergio was stocky and gray, walrus-featured, sadly drooping in the face like Albert Einstein, fifty-three years old, most often found wearing what he called his Greek fisherman sweater, a sewage-colored woolen garment that covered his barrel-like paunch. Bette was twenty-five, two inches taller than he, wearing clogs to exaggerate the difference, to feel some advantage. He held her face in his hands and she could not return the direct gaze he gave her, could only close her eyes and give in to what she knew best, which was the fundamental mechanics of love. She allowed her breathing to deepen, and felt him lick her eyelids. He wore a cologne from France sent to him by a former girlfriend — a pepperminty scent like a cool candy, like sweet schnapps — and Bette on her clogs leaned into it and rubbed her cheek against the crosshatched skin of his neck. Still he stared at her, she could feel his eyes on her arms and elbows, but she imagined herself hiding inside his embrace, trying to believe that this thing between them had nothing, nothing, to do with age. The room around them — the display rack of hand-lettered cards, the walls of framed manifestoes — floated away.

That night, before they eased awkwardly onto the bristly plaid couch Sergio kept in the back office, he brushed his teeth. It was this, and his grandfatherly nakedness, that finally gave Bette a window of confidence. With him she had only one edge, and it had to do with being born in 1964 in California near a grove of orange trees, with taut skin still marked by the three triangles of a long-ago tan, with breath she never bothered to freshen.

They were married in the coffeehouse, attended by employees and neighbors, poets and customers. A woman read a poem after the ceremony, though Bette could discern nothing weddinglike or well-wishing in it. There were dark birds circling carnage in Gdańsk, gutters of blood, scalpels and bombs and bones and clouds that looked like the severed wings of doves. After the woman ended — paused and then dropped her hand, with which she had been conducting her own vibrating voice — the audience, Bette's coworkers and Sergio's friends, gave an artful and depressed appreciative grunt. Bette looked around at them and then laughed, drunk and tall. Sergio tried to smile in her direction, to be a good sport, his face glossy with nervousness and bravura — he'd married such a young girl, so spontaneously, on so little evidence of worth — then applauded vigorously for the reader, who was small and unadorned and whose expression was utterly venomous. Only later did Bette learn the poem was one by Sergio's dead wife.

Ferosa haunted Bette like a guilty conscience. Sergio seemed always involved with a project in Ferosa's memory, the details of which Bette could not keep straight. He raised money and circulated petitions, that was the general gist, but each time the funds went to different people — hostages in prison, booksellers going bankrupt, destitute protesters who picketed the *Tribune* or Oscar Mayer, come snow or heat. Now it was Iraq and Kuwait. Pregnant, Bette had thought she might find her way in. She thought she might appear mysterious and estimable to him, carrying a secret inside her that he could not comprehend, toward which he would have to pay an outsider's homage.

Instead, Bette found Ferosa's book of poems in Sergio's desk. They were, she understood as she read them one long unsleeping and unsettling night, all about the politically correct stance of not having children. *We unmake our country,* Ferosa had written of her skinny shrunk-chile-pepper-shaped home, *gene by gene, cell by cell.*

TOURIST

For the first three months of the pregnancy Bette was hot. For the next three, cold. In Chicago, the weather was either on or off but never what you might call good. She sat on a radiator and watched the parade of service people who kept their building presentable. They all wore uniforms, brown or white or blue, all stopped just below her window to consult their lists, then buzzed a tenant. Her clothes hung like skeletons in the closet and she wore the same frumpy thing every day — her own sort of uniform, once maroon, now weather-washed pink — unwilling to commit to stretch pants, support hose, or underwires. Her libido, she was told by the OB, might run rampant, might drive Dad out the door. She maintained a lookout for such an occasion but remained oddly content reading erotica, never missing the real event. Her husband was a grown-up; he would wait nine months, if need be. He'd done it before, been celibate for two years when he'd grown disenchanted with himself and his relationships with women. Bette thought him wise and profound, like a Buddha, like a turtle.

How could he love her? He simply did. He found in her something she could not find herself. He laughed at her when she did not mean to be funny. One day, nearly crying, he caught her by the wrist and held her when she returned from shopping. She deposited bags of cans and eggs and salty snacks on the table, mystified by his damp eyes, horrified to think she might discover him to be weak, standing above him while he closed her skirt around his face like a handkerchief. Inside her body a boy of their making rolled and punched; outside, the father put his ear to the drama and seemed to despair. Pragmatically, Bette tried to chart a course of action while she stroked his silky thin hair, saw herself en route to California, pregnant behind a steering wheel. But it was an abysmal and unconnected image. Her previous life, filled with forgettable family and forgetful friends, would not tether her. This was her place, yet it depended on Sergio's steady presence. She tilted his face toward her own and squinted into it. "You're all I have," she reprimanded him.

It turned out he'd been reading the newspaper; world events had consumed and grieved him, as they frequently did. Later the two of them shared a pot of licorice tea and watched reruns on the tiny black-and-white TV they kept stashed in a closet, Sergio laughing and laughing at the old-fashioned jokes, hugging Bette and pounding the table with his fist.

She did not believe he meant to make her feel inadequate. "You hide what becomes you," he told her when she insisted on knowing what made her merit his ample affection. "You are sweet when you cross your arms over your big breasts to make them disappear. You are shy with them, as if they might embarrass someone. Don't you see?"

She did — his praise thrilled her; she'd always thought of herself as being a size or so too large — but she made him continue by pretending otherwise. "You love me for my bosoms?"

Though he was smart about her, he mostly played into her hands. "'Bosoms,'" he repeated, laughing. "I was making a metaphor. You don't know those things about yourself that are appealing. That's what I like."

Still, it was tiresome to be mistaken for his daughter, to have people, especially women and especially now, in Bette's seventh month, stare at the two of them with disgust. Sergio's mother, who lived in a nursing home three blocks from their apartment, puffed her mouth when Bette came to visit, as if she might spit a tooth onto Bette's lap. Before moving to the home, before Sergio's father's death, before the oxygen machine they'd attached her to, Matska had been vaguely senile. The apartment always smelled of gas, though Sergio's parents claimed over and over to have had the problem checked by their super. Matska would smile and invite Bette into her seedy kitchen, humbly introducing herself and her husband, never sure who the girl was. Now, purely oxygenated, she knew.

"Child!" she hissed, and Bette did not know whether it was she being addressed or the one in her womb. Matska's English, still a foreign language to her, was full of inconsistencies. She seemed to use child as a term not unlike whore or witch. Sergio was protected from her fury by her evident belief that Bette had tricked him into marriage (via sex or incantation, Bette supposed, which, strictly speaking, might not be so far from the truth) and still held him under a spell.

"Most mothers *want* to be grandparents," Bette whined. "She ought to be *thrilled* with me." Sergio agreed, seeming to think the baby's arrival, this grandson (a linking genealogy Bette didn't like to consider for long), would soften things among them all.

However, Matska was also a drinker. It had been a useful common denominator, because it was a role Bette inhabited the way she did that of a lover — with assurance. Before Matska went into the home, she and Bette used to sit for comfortable hours in front of an open window, wearing coats, drinking cooking sherry, Matska trying to relate the story of her son's life, his tender childhood. Bette continued to visit the nursing home, hoping to discover one day Matska returned to her former hospitality, with a deck of cards — she loved honeymoon bridge — or a friendly bottle of cheap sherry resting on her bedtable.

Sergio did not drink, and he was the only friend Bette had made in Chicago with whom she didn't immediately associate alcohol. Choosing him, she told herself when she worried, showed her willingness to turn her back on frivolity.

At the coffeehouse she had always gotten high with Benjamin. But now that she was pregnant, Benjamin had little to say to her. He was Sergio's oldest friend, a business partner by default, a former this, that, and the other — tired, cynical, gay. What possible use did gay men have for pregnant women? So seeded, so Kansas, so fat. She went to visit one day, dressed not in the artful black clothing she'd learned to wear in her former life but something floral and baggy.

"Yikes, a romper!" Benjamin greeted her, squinting his eyes as if against glare, laughing.

Bette knocked over a pyramid of Melitta filter baskets when she rounded a corner. Squatting among the plastic cones, she tried not to cry.

"How's things?" she sniffed, hungry for the outer world, collusion, jokes.

"Swell," Benjamin said, making the word as ripe as she, holding himself away from her. Embarrassed by association, he picked quickly at the Melittas, as if her condition were transmittable. And then he asked, as everyone always asked, always always in a great solicitous sorry tone, "How are you feeling?"

She smiled thinly and told some version of the truth. "There's only three states of mind to a pregnant woman — suicidal, homicidal, and placid." Like a toppling triangle, these phases followed one another without tangible reason. You woke up and there you were, propped on one pointy corner or another.

Ordinarily they might smoke pot together in the back room. Benjamin kept a stash and pipe in a file drawer for the regulars, for civilized chummy rainy-day intimacies on the plaid couch. How Bette missed her life. Now the back room reeked of underarm sweat and rotted orange peels.

Benjamin turned to face her suddenly, inspired by something, his eyes unaccountably eager. "Let me see you," he said. He was staring at what had once been her waist. "I've never seen a naked pregnant woman. What do you say — gimme a look-see?"

Bette felt herself redden, horrified at exposing herself. "Go get knocked up yourself if you want to see a freak show." Spinning to leave, she crashed into an adding machine, sending it only as far as the seat of a rollaway chair. Benjamin sighed in disappointment, still mesmerized by her midsection.

Other people stared too. A dark and craven man followed her around Dominick's, circling aisles so that he continued to approach her head on, staring intently at her abdomen as if she might be about to burst with prophecy. Something maniacal in his eyes kept her from saying a word. In the presence of all the gaping world, Bette remained mute, ashamed of the large evidence of copulation she carried with her every day. It was worse than a scarlet letter; it forced her to waddle, to buy prunes and healthful cereal that looked and tasted like little haystacks, to require carry-out service. In the checkout line she managed to overturn a display of horoscopes, tiny rolled tubes spilling to the floor like a pack of cigarettes, Bette too ungainly to retrieve them from beneath the magazine stand.

Knocking things over was not confined to public spaces. At home pens jumped from tabletops, papers from shelves. "Could you pick that up?" she would ask the cat. "Oh, never mind. Forget it." From tummy to knee she was a map of bruises, a geography of lumpy flesh and tender veins. Sergio had to kneel at her feet to roll her stockings up her ankles. Counters and the newly tight space of their small bathroom conspired against her. She was a large amoebic belly from which hung incidental appendages, wobbling through the world like an ugly tourist, cloddish, with a loud, guffawing laugh.

BABY

Memory of life before maternity leave had dried up and blown away. She stood on a vast desert like a Russian nesting doll, shiny and round and solitary but for the little clone hidden inside.

Her condition by now was inescapable, the baby a conundrum like a ship in a bottle. In the park, small children, infants, the mere sight of strollers, were terrifying. Parents tried to converse with her. She scurried to dog territory, where others, childless, knelt with plastic bags and paper towels, screeched the names they might otherwise have bestowed on offspring: *Maurice, Chloe, Otis.*

"Help," she sometimes said at the grocery store, hoping someone might hear and understand, as if she were short and old like Matska and unable to reach the desired brand of rye crackers on a top shelf.

Sergio decided Bette was to be spoiled and petted. He fawned, he cooked leafy greens, he brought her grotesque bouquets of blood-red roses. Somewhere he found a bottle of wine containing no alcohol, a promising deeply colored merlot. Bette sipped, then gulped, but it tasted precisely like what it was: twelve-point-eight percent absent. Sergio shrugged sheepishly, then lay behind her and kneaded her spongy skin while she sniffed his sleeve for the adult odors he'd picked up on the el, diesel exhaust and mentholated cigarette smoke.

"Only two more months," he said carelessly, just once.

He was preparing his future nostalgia for these despicable days. She had never felt so isolated — like an astronaut floating through space. *Reel me in!* she might gesture in her bloated white suit, face panicked, but on board the ship her copilot would wave serenely, thinking she was pointing out the idiotic beauty of Pluto.

Denied wine, she substituted chocolate. She'd lost her talent for discrimination; an Oreo was as good as Godiva. The days wore on, not in their usual parade of ups and downs, clowns and cops, but precisely identical to one another. She rolled from bed each morning dreading how many more times she would have to do the same. Sluggish, creating new, deeper-sourced noises on the wood floor, she would sprawl at the kitchen table. She weighed more than Sergio now. Shoes, the one form of clothing that had never betrayed her, had never been outgrown before worn out, no longer fit. She popped from everything, overblown dough, a rhino in her own home.

Sleep was her only recourse, the deeper the better. Each afternoon she prepared a nest. She pulled the phone cord from the wall, shut the blinds, turned the metal radiator up high, stripped naked and then positioned pillows between her knees and under her neck, over her exposed ear. She drifted as if in the ocean, thinking of weightlessness, of sunshine, of being without a body. She put her hand to her hard belly and felt herself as suspended as her child, dreamy and liquid, without consciousness or conscience.

WAR

Meanwhile the Mideast roiled. Sergio organized what was known as an Event at the coffeehouse. Antiwar poetry and music. Bette decided against attending. Wasn't it arrogant, after all, to turn up pregnant at a time like this? Besides, she could not interest herself in the war. It was abominable, but she was busy. (She couldn't even think of the word *abominable* without changing it to *abdominal*.) She signed petitions but had no idea what they signified. Clever peace slogans went over her head. In the evenings, when Sergio flipped on the news (the television now lived on the kitchen counter), Bette retreated to the bedroom and browsed through baby catalogues. She heard the word *scud* and still thought of boys who weren't cool enough.

FELLOWSHIP

The first day of their Lamaze birth class, each couple was asked to reveal the length of their marriage, their occupations, and whether this was a first child. Reminded of AA, Bette stood and confessed to the circle that her name was Bette and she was a pregnant woman.

In the beginning she enjoyed her and Sergio's relative bizarreness. Other moms and coaches spent their days at real estate offices or car dealerships or architectural firms. One coach, obviously unwillingly associated with the whole project, stubbornly announced himself to be unemployed. His wife, an enormous red-faced woman who had fallen into her chair as if ready to put down roots there, socked him on the arm. "He does phone solicitation," she explained. "In between jobs."

The members of the group grew to tolerate one another, and Bette found herself looking forward to their meetings. She began wishing Sergio were as clunky as the other husbands, as young and as easily embarrassed by the instructor's frankness. Instead the lingo rolled right off his tongue: cervix, placenta, lanugo. He read the books, and none of it made him squirm. It occurred to Bette that the rest of her life would be abnormal, that Sergio would train their boy to hug dolls and to cry and to wear without masculine resentment lumpy Ecuadorian sweaters.

"Remind me why I wanted a baby?" she asked Sergio over the telephone. Only over the phone could she concentrate on conversation. In person her body got in the way — the swollen ankles, the popped navel.

"Was it your ticking biological clock?" he teased, squeaking in his boss chair at the café. "Or maybe mine?" He giggled, and Bette was tempted to join him, but she often these days found herself frighteningly close to turning Sergio's jokes into a tragic version of her life, maybe just a scoff away. There was music in the background at the café, loud guitars and drums, manhole covers clashing together. "Benjamin says maybe our marriage was going wrong," Sergio went on, playing. "Actually, I can't remember why we got with child. Can't you?"

The truth was — there was truth — she *did* remember. Every now and then a wash of emotion came over Bette so strongly that she had to sit down and cover her eyes for fear of falling. This was the reason, the scientific principle having to do with the teardrop-shaped female body, inertia or vertigo or something not yet discovered and named. It had to do with her tender breasts, with TV commercials about puppies, with the childhood taste of hot oatmeal and raisins, with Sergio's sleeping face under her wakeful, skeptic's scrutiny, with her part in the dreadful thrilling innocence of new life.

DOG

Three flights of stairs became too many in her eighth month. Plus the dog had never learned to heel, raised as he was in lawn-filled, permissive California. Sergio suggested tentatively that he drop the dog each morning at Matska's nursing home, where they encouraged pets and warm fuzzy feelings, and let the dog make use of the yard the residents themselves hadn't set foot in for the past three months. Sergio spoke out of regard for Bette's precarious physical state, the ice on the back steps, the fact that the dog, eighty pounds, could be considered dangerous in this weather to someone in her condition.

And it was. Bette recalled a day not more than a week before when she'd slid, clinging with one hand to the frozen pipe that served as banister, the other hand resting over her baby, the dog a flight below, sledding comically on his side, legs flailing and catching at nothing.

"O.K.," she agreed tearfully. Pregnancy had made her stupid with commitment to the animal, choked up over his absence. Sergio dropped off and picked up the dog the way one would a child in day care. "It's great, it's so yuppie," Sergio would say, arriving home with the chilled animal. Bette squatted — she did nothing but squat these days — to pull tiny clots of pressed snow from between his paws. These were like hailstones, as round and solid as pebbles from nestling all day in the dog's feet. Meanwhile his tongue would work at her hands, reminding her gently though persistently that he did not like having his paws touched. It was inconceivable to her that she would love anything more than she did the dog.

The nursing home's director, ambassador to the outside world, called one afternoon, three days before the baby was due, to say that the dog was acting . . . well, funny.

"Funny ha-ha?" Bette asked. "Funny strange?"

After a long pause, he chuckled uncertainly. "Your dog is digging our fence up. You must come fetch him."

Bette looked down and discovered herself sitting in a warm puddle. "Yes!" she cried. "Broken water! Yes!"

She set the receiver in its cradle, a lulling voice carrying on patiently from far away, "We wouldn't want to be forced to let him escape. We wouldn't want to have to actually give chase . . ." Before phoning Sergio, Bette stood to survey the damage. Then, while on her feet, decided to have a drink. It seemed the indubitably correct move now that her child was about to be washed from her body.

Grownup Chivas in hand — she'd never drunk Scotch before — she dialed the coffeehouse. Her sweatpants were soaked. Inside her, curious movement began, more articulate, less muffled. All lines were busy at the shop, so she waited, sipping distractedly on her drink, wondering if what she felt was contractions. If so, they weren't as bad as everyone made them out to be. When after five or six minutes all lines were still busy, Bette asked an operator to interrupt the calls.

"I'm the owner's wife," she told the woman, who had no interest in the nature of the emergency. "And I've gone into labor."

"Uh-huh," the operator said nasally. When she returned to Bette, she informed her that no one was on any of the lines; everything was off the hook.

At this, Bette gulped down the remainder of the Scotch and phoned her doctor, whose nurse told her to take a cab to the hospital.

Before leaving, she brushed her teeth.

MOTHERHOOD

Woozily she gave birth. On the way to the hospital, she'd had to lecture her cabdriver. He'd made the mistake of expressing his disappointment at his wife's getting a c-section. His accent annoyed Bette, this and the fact that he'd taken a longer route than necessary to Northwestern. Bette swooned on the stiff plastic back seat, feet straddling the floor hump, forehead propped on the back of the front seat. This, she concluded, was it. Hardly breathing, she could smell her cabby's aftershave, his aging American sedan, the grotesque odors of former fares. "My wife, she did not try hard enough," he said.

"Oh, give me a break!" Bette shouted at the floor when she could take in enough oxygen to say anything. From rib cage to pelvis she was taut as a basketball.

"Is true!" the driver swore. "She only tried one day for the natural birth."

"As in twenty-four hours?" Bette lifted her head long enough to see him nod vigorously. "I feel sorry for her," she said.

"Yes," he said. "It's very bad she couldn't do it the natural way."

"No," Bette said, struggling to speak now. "I feel sorry she's still your wife." But he couldn't possibly understand her. A barge had come pushing through her, a seizure, a pain like amnesia, like a fired missile.

Sergio made it to the hospital in time to cut the baby's cord. The phones had been off the hook at the coffeehouse because the war had ended. Benjamin and Sergio were toasting the possibility of peace and hadn't wanted to be bothered.

"My turn to take care of him," Sergio now shouted happily to the room full of green-clothed adoring women. Bette heard one woman say to another, "It's so unusual to have a grandfather in delivery." The OB dashed out the door, due at another birth party down the hall.

From her room she phoned her mother. For a truce-like time they discussed labor while Bette watched Sergio through the nursery glass, walking up and down with little Ed, named for his real grandfathers, both of them, two men long gone from two worlds equally lost. Bette was teary considering it. From La Jolla her mother told her she had begun writing poetry.

"Oh, please," Bette said in exasperation. "I already have one poet too many in my life."

"Listen, here's a line about all these California grandmas. I'm working with Mother Goose here. You ready? Quote: 'There was an old woman who lived in a shoe. She had so many children she *did* know what to do,' unquote. Whaddaya think? I'm taking a class at the branch library."

Bette said, "I better go lactate."

SEX

Toward her pets she had recalled affection, and this is how she felt toward Sergio as well, a habitual love, her response to his caresses like a segment of a routine: this, then that — not unlike, in a stupor, grinding coffee beans each morning. For his part, Sergio extended his affection to Eddie via Bette; he still loved her best. But between Bette and Eddie, small red-fisted thing, there was something brand-new. He was a high she knew she didn't deserve, his eager face at her breast every few hours, his confused cross-eyed looks and wrinkled forehead that seemed to pose to her a severe and simple question: who are you?

Sergio fetched his mother, who came to the apartment bearing a roast to celebrate the baby's birth and the end of the Gulf War offensive. Sitting in the refrigerator dripping blood onto the milk carton, the clear-wrapped lump of meat looked for all the world like a placenta. Bette gagged down dinner anyway — her mother-in-law was trying to make reparation. At the stove, Matska had mistaken one knob for another: a burner on top glowed red all afternoon while in the cold oven the meat grew gray, remained raw. They sliced it and fried it before eating, but still it was unbearably rare.

"He looks like his father," Matska told them, of Eddie. Bette agreed; but then, all newborns looked like old men to her. Matska held him without supporting his wobbly head, allowing it to loll sideways and back. "You good, you good," she cooed into his slow opaque eyes. Bette drank champagne, one sparkling glass after another, idly subtracting ages until she realized that she was closer in age to her son than she was to her husband, and that her husband was closer in age to his mother than to her.

The baby did many less than pleasant things, but they didn't bother Bette. Sergio, however — his bald head, the hairs in his ears, the saggy paunch of flesh, an odor he couldn't quite disguise — these things began to disgust her, though she spent the day changing diapers full of tar and wiping down the yellow chin of her son. Eddie's skin was remarkably similar to Sergio's, dry as paper and baggy as a pachyderm's. She grew to dread Sergio's touch, to turn her mouth away from his minty kisses. He closed his eyes and groped, like the baby, for the favors of her flesh. She began to wish him dead, to imagine the car accident or heart attack that might take him. In his absence she was ecstatic, autonomous once more, propelling the baby through the neighborhood in his stroller, dragging the dog behind, grinning at strangers and chatting. But at Sergio's arrival home each evening, Bette might dissolve into tears, complain about her sore breasts, the baby's interminable choking cry.

Sergio would hold the boy and walk from room to room,

listening without looking at Bette, who watched him and heard herself as if from a corner of the ceiling. Who was this shrew inside her? Barring his death, she seemed to be set on driving her husband from her life. How much would he take? she wondered. At what point did his adult disposition give way to boyish hurt? Each time, just before she went too far, Bette ran to Sergio and held him tight — she was sorry, so sorry, and he, as ever, forgave.

They could resume relations, her OB informed her. "You really think so?" Bette wanted to ask.

She'd been a prisoner of war; she'd come back metamorphosed, a veteran, politicized. In celebration she drank beer while little Eddie nursed, both of them warm and suckled drunk. Now that he was out and fine — above average in all ways, on all scales, ninety-nine out of a hundred — alcohol became Bette's friend again. Everything appeared through the lens of her successful campaign. Ferosa was a beloved but deposed demagogue, Matska a psychological sissy. And Sergio? An anachronism. His son would be blond. And the baby already preferred his mother: Bette. In the back of her mind sat the dirty words *divorce* and *departure,* like loot in a secret safe deposit box. She was healthy, vigorous, young: a pretty American girl with her own car, her body snapped back prepregnant and firm, virgin. The country stretched to either side of her, festooned with yellow ribbons, offering no resistance. She could drive anywhere, and ever after live happily, happily, happily.

THE OCEAN

—— ⫲⫲⫲ ——

IN MARY ABBOTT'S MORNING NEWSPAPER RUNS A detailed exposé of a Central American dictator. A Sunday edition story, the article takes its time, spreading like blood across several pages and jump leads, full of photographs of grim men with guns and of soft-edged, frightened women shielding babies in the wings of their arms. Small children stand in crumbling doorways and look into the camera with the resolute flat eyes of the long oppressed. If her husband were home, Mary would read the story beginning to end. They would discuss it. Cal would divide the world — there are those who go to bed hungry, he would declare, and those who eat.

Because she is alone, Mary guiltily skims. Poverty, starvation, genocide. It's not that she's unenlightened concerning her own lucky position in an unlucky world; it's just that today she wishes to forget there are two sides. It is Sunday, after all. Tomorrow she will pay the Foster Child bill, donate clothes to Salvadoran refugees, make phone calls for the local, liberal city council. She will atone for today's bourgeois thinking. So she turns instead to the frivolous travel section and reads about apartments for rent in the heart of Venice, Italy, apartments too expensive for the people who actually work and live there to afford, and fantasizes that she and her husband and daughter move into one right over the water.

Around her in the quiet sunny dining room dangle pastel streamers. Balloons cluster at one end of the room, held by the blowing wet air from the swamp cooler, bobbing at odd moments so that Mary keeps looking up, expecting a child or pet or gremlin. The house is still relatively clean and its decorations are mostly intact from yesterday's birthday party. The birthday girl, one year old, sleeps the sleep of the exhausted, having stayed up far past her bedtime investigating her new toys, putting them to her mouth to discover their true colors, integrating them experimentally with all the old favorites, finally nodding off sitting upright in her new rocker, new sand bucket in one hand and tiny new tridentlike rake in the other.

Mary can't concentrate on reading. Every few minutes she goes to check the baby, then returns on tiptoe and sits down contentedly, sips her cream-heavy coffee and eats her fresh raspberries — sultry roasted flavor punctuated by a stinging bite of raw fruit. Her husband, Cal, is playing basketball a few blocks away, and Mary decides that when Lucia wakes they will make an expedition to the court: stroller, bonnet, dog and leash. Their presence will disrupt Cal's playing. He'll nonchalantly show off. The other men might envy Cal his wife and daughter, might watch the muscular turn of Mary's calf. She turns it now, seeing for herself the bladelike swatch of flesh.

And afterward, walking home — Cal smelling of sweat, basketball wedged beneath his arm — she will try to explain the phenomenon that occurred last night, her unexpected and complete happiness, when, for about thirty seconds, her life had been perfect. Twenty-some adults and seven children, gathered in her living room, sitting on the coffee table, feeding one another ice cream, mitigating disputes, watching little Lucia totter madly about — Mary had hurried to get the camera, to catch in parts the whole of it. *Friends,* she had thought, *good* friends, she'd amended, *good* children, and tears had risen to her eyes. To Cal she would say, *This is all we have, these small pockets of bliss. Nothing else. All we can do is help them to happen, as many as possible in a life.* She would say, *This is what my sister can't seem to learn, that life follows a graph, with low points we must come to expect and high points we have to rely on like islands in an ocean. They are what will see us through.*

Mary then tries to imagine what her sister, Gigi, now more than a thousand miles away, is doing at this precise moment. Maybe she is at work in the restaurant, busy and distracted? Maybe she is still sleeping, a hot, humid Chicago day brewing outside her window? But maybe she is alone and crying, unable to find a reason on earth for going on. Mary loves her sister, but it is a love made of constant worry and frustration. In December, two days after Christmas, her sister had taken a boning knife to her own arm, lifting the blade three separate times and reinserting it, cutting a deep broken ribbon from palm to inner elbow. For five months afterward, Gigi had lived with Mary and Cal, caring for the baby, getting better, slipping, getting better, slipping, two steps forward, one step back, until now, May, spring, the season of restitution, and Gigi has gone home to the Midwest. She left only three weeks ago, and Mary has yet to shake from herself the daily attention to Gigi's life. She knows this will happen; it happened for their mother, who at first called Gigi and Mary nearly every day, but soon called only on weekends, and then sometimes forgot.

Daily and endless worry is the part of motherhood that

Mary had no trouble adjusting to; it had been there, barely dormant, all her life. She remembers having insomnia even when so young she couldn't name her anxiety. "I'm worried," she would tell her mother desperately, crawling into her warm bed. "I don't know why, I'm just worried." It darted around in her like a quick school of fish. Now, at last, she has a subject. Two subjects, her daughter and her sister.

Cal tells her, in the night when she can't sleep, "Let go of her. You have to let go of Gigi. You've done all you can." But Mary, despite the number of times everyone says this, persists in her own belief that she *can* make a difference. To Gigi, over and over, she had said, "Try to see yourself in five years. I wish I could give you a picture of your life in five years. You will be so happy not to have ended it now." If only she is able to see Gigi through what must seem like a vast sea of unbearable time in between, she is sure Gigi will arrive at that happier place. So while it's true that no one can prevent another person from taking her life, literally, it's also true that figuratively, it can be done.

Mary hears Lucia — a little bauble of sound, afloat. Simultaneous with her hearing the baby, the dog's head has lifted. The dog is a fine and amazing animal. Mary's maternal compulsions had been showered undiluted upon her for three years before the baby came, and still the dog seems to harbor no resentment at having been supplanted. She and Mary go together to get the baby.

Lucia, dark and curly-haired, stands in her crib preparing to cry. Imprinted on one cheek is a road map of lines from her tangled bedsheets, and she reeks of urine, an odor Mary has come to welcome: she is needed. She hugs her daughter close and murmurs sentences full of reassuring *mama*s into her ear. They walk the floor this way, Lucia slowly coming to terms with the fresh day. She is shown all of her new toys — her bright playhouse with its yellow shutters and plastic thatched roof — her leftover streamers and balloons, fed a small bite of carrot cake and a sip of milk, and taken to the carpeted stairs, her favorite place, and set down to climb. It is on the stairs, midway up, that Mary catches her breath.

From the high, portholelike window that overlooks the back yard, she sees a man. In her yard, his presence is so unthinkable that even the alert and sensitive ears of the dog have not picked it up. The dog is at her feet, and to keep her from barking, Mary tries not to act stunned. She does not want to startle anybody, yet. She watches the man — in jeans and leather vest, thirty or so — come from near the gate, which he carefully shuts, directly to her back door. Approximating prayer, Mary wills the door to be, please, locked. He turns the handle gently, tenderly, so that still the dog does not hear him, still she stands at Mary's feet watching the baby climb. Mary lifts Lucia in her arms. The door appears to be locked and she breathes out, but then the baby reaches in front of her and slaps the glass — the same movement that had made such a lovely photograph, taken against the light of the outdoors, the baby's hands raised on either side of herself in front of the window, as if trying to capture all that light — and yells wildly and happily one of her two words, "Mama mama mama!" and the man looks unerringly up and sees them.

*

Every bolted door of her home requires a key; Mary, caught without one, slips into the bathroom with the dog and baby and throws the lock.

I have nothing you want, Mary rehearses saying to the man in the vest. The VCR is in the shop having a toy removed from it, a little plastic fellow they'd given Lucia for

Christmas, one of the spacemen who roll down a chute, around bends, and onto a Ferris wheel, M. C. Escher style. Does he want the TV? It came from Sears, so many years ago its model is discontinued, the color is lousy, a purple blob is eating its way across the screen, and to change channels you must use pliers. The most valuable thing in the house is the washing machine, and how would you ever get away with it and what would you possibly find to do with it if you did? Surely one did not fence major appliances? No silver, a rotten Instamatic camera, *take what it is you think you could want,* Mary thinks frantically, but of course what he wants, he will take.

He wants her happiness, she sees very clearly, nothing more and nothing less. She divides the world: those who are happy; those who are not. *Her* happiness, her place among this sector, will now be stolen. In the bathroom, thick oak door and ancient bolt lock between them and the rest of the house, Mary feels both hidden and trapped. The dog has of course sensed trouble by now and growls angrily, which frightens the baby.

It had struck Mary during the time that her sister lived with them that Gigi, at some completely unconscious level, also wanted her happiness. (She had stolen other, lesser, material items as well — earrings, socks, a shirt or two. Mary and Cal were still discovering the things Gigi had taken with her when she went.) But Mary's good life sometimes seemed what she wanted the most. Not to have, not even to destroy, but to subvert. Mary's husband and sister had gotten along famously; he was, after all, a counselor, so he could talk with her, knew how to draw from her. He convinced her, when no one else could, to take her pills, to see her therapist. He had stayed up far into many nights talking her out of her depression, only to watch her, the next day, fall back into its dark hole. Still, he did not discourage easily. Mary had less patience, less faith. *Snap out of it,* she would think angrily, then would add anxiously, *Please, please snap out of it.* On these nights, Mary would put Lucia to bed and then lie awake waiting for Cal to come in, waiting to hear Gigi upstairs brushing her teeth, switching off her overhead light, climbing into bed. Gigi had been, in a way, taking her husband. Not his love but his energy. Mary hadn't begrudged her sister this; depression was an illness, they were helping her recover. Only occasionally did Mary blow up — she had learned, if nothing else, that anger must be expressed — and then only in front of Cal. At these times, she believed that Gigi was getting back at her for something, but what?

In the rear of the house glass breaks. Mary flinches, holding wriggling Lucia against her. This would be the window in the back door; she can picture the man's skinny bare wrist reaching for her set of keys beside the dead-bolted door as clearly as if it were happening before her in the medicine cabinet mirror. She imagines him shooting through the bathroom's lock soon, and decides they will be safer in the tub, removed from range. But Lucia does not want to stay in the bathtub. She has spotted her hanging net of bath toys and reaches for them. She wants her new Big Bird. "Bih Bih," she insists. To keep her quiet, Mary raises her own shirt and proffers a breast. The baby looks back and forth, toys to breast to toys to breast, but in the end cannot resist nursing.

Mary has shushed the dog by being so firmly fearful. Yet the dog's hackles stand at attention and she blocks the door with her loyal, solid weight. She is a big white dog, part husky, part Lab, with intimidating facial markings. Her ears lift as footsteps cross the floor, slowly. The man goes into the kitchen, he crosses the dining room, where he must see Mary's cup of cold coffee, her bowl of berries, the sound of him disappearing as he enters the carpeted living room. What does he make of the balloons, the benign clutter of stuffed animals and primary-colored blocks? He is spending a long time in the living room.

Then Mary hears a rhythmic series of clicks and for a moment can't think what this familiar noise is. Oh yes, she knows: he is playing the marble game. They roll down ramps, gaining speed and clacking against one another at the end. Playing marbles. Mary begins to cry. She wills Cal's sudden appearance — he would have some twinge, there at the basketball court, that something was not quite right at home. She wills the sun, burning as always in the Arizona sky, to perform as her personal satellite, to beam to her husband her plea.

Outside the bathroom door a shadow passes. The dog cannot restrain herself and growls menacingly, showing her yellow teeth. Mary, despite all her fear, has to marvel at the dog's fierce love; it has never been quite so thoroughly tested. Then Mary thinks it may be tested further, much further. Lucia, oblivious, sucks contentedly, her hands clutching and releasing Mary's other breast.

*

He has been all through the house; twice he has reentered, going out one door and, using Mary's key, coming back through another. There are many entrances; a southwestern home. Mary's sister had had her own door outside, upstairs. Her bedroom and bath had been directly over Cal and Mary's room; at night, they could have heard her rise to leave or rise to try to kill herself. Mary had imagined finding her sister dead. Their father had found her the first time, on the kitchen floor in their house in Naperville, blood everywhere, telling him that she wanted to die, that she was going to die. And he had called 911 as Gigi ran out the front door, ran down the middle of the early Sunday morning suburban street, trailing blood, finally returning, she told Mary later, because she had seen their father trying to chase her, sliding ridiculously on the ice in his house slippers.

Having heard both of them tell about the morning, Mary felt she had practically lived it herself. She was a parent; she was a daughter. Her sister had lain awake all that Saturday night before and found herself at the bottom of her life. Failing in her classes, short-tempered with her family, weary of her old friends, unworthy of her new ones, a nineteen-year-old woman confused and spinning in her static, little girl's bedroom. In the kitchen, she'd fed the family cat and dog, a saucer each of milk, then chosen the sharpest piece of cutlery from their father's gourmet collection. Mary, in the months Gigi had lived with them, had imagined many potential deaths. The possibility, accidental or intentional, was omnipresent. Death had been a daily issue then and remained one even after Gigi had gone.

It had been passing, though, in recent weeks. Mary had felt its departure last night in a moment of peace and light — a late-setting sun spilling into the colorful birthday party, little Lucia crawling to a plate of melted ice cream and trying to manipulate a spoonful of it into her mouth, a slightly older child helping out, someone telling a story about an absent friend, notoriously forgetful — and death had left her in the face of so much life.

In the bathroom, now, death returns. Lucia's, her own. Cal is forever telling her that they are among the lucky half of the world, whichever way you cut it. But Mary always counters that their life is the result of taking care, being responsible, doing the right things. Luck, she has believed until this very moment, had little to do with it. And perhaps even this is a product less of bad luck than of having dropped her guard? Last night she thought she was safe; today she knows better.

The man again goes by; the dog snarls at the split of space between door and threshold. Mary convinces herself she can smell him, oil and leather.

Is he gathering her jewelry, cheap costume and ethnic? The clock radio? The stereo, so old as to be labeled *record player?* She mouths, in a silent shout, *We have nothing,* beginning to cry again with despair. But he knows they have nothing, by now. Mary tries to think like a thief in a house with nothing to steal.

Yet it's hard to think like someone else. Mary, until the episode with Gigi, had prided herself on her heightened sensitivity; she would have called it clairvoyance if she weren't so bound by rationalism. But when Gigi lived with them, Mary soon realized she didn't know her sister at all. She'd always thought Gigi wanted to be like her. But it became clear during her five months with them that Gigi had no honest interest in such a thing. Gigi was attracted to an entirely different world, a riskier, seamier, darker one. One day she disappeared. For hours Mary and Cal sat around asking each other what to do about it, approaching the telephone but not knowing who to call once they picked up the receiver.

Finally, just after dark, Gigi came home, tired and defensive. In the course of their admonishment of her — their fear and helplessness replaced with rage — she'd begun hitting herself with her palms, giving herself two black eyes. Eventually, Cal took her out. They went to a bar while Mary stayed home with Lucia and the telephone and made calls to the therapist, the psychiatric hospital, her older brother. She took notes and advice and couldn't stop telling everyone about Gigi's black eyes, talking all around it in an attempt to understand.

But when Cal and Gigi returned they were laughing, sweeping into the house the jaded smells of cigarettes and beer. Gigi had insisted on going to strip joints. They'd been to three. She launched into an enthusiastic recounting of the night, gesturing wildly with her hands. There'd been a woman who could isolate different muscles in her buttocks. "It was so sick," Gigi said happily of their evening out. Her eyes were purple and swollen, but she didn't seem bothered by them. Swinging her hips, she took her pills without protest, then thanked Cal for the good time and went upstairs.

Later, in bed, Cal told Mary that Gigi very genuinely associated herself with the meaner, harsher half of life. He broke this news gently to Mary. Gigi could imagine herself being a stripper, he said, or a prostitute. In the dim bedroom Mary felt once more, as she'd felt sporadically since the day Gigi had cut her arm, everything she'd ever believed solid go liquid, rush away from her. A small part of her wondered if Cal too felt an affinity for the coarse landscape Gigi wished to embrace. She could no longer claim shock concerning Gigi, since that threshold had long been passed, but she did not grasp completely the idiosyncrasies of this dark country, could not discern the ruling logic.

A few days later, Gigi phoned an escort service number in the newspaper and gave the man who answered her hair color, eye color, and measurements. He told her she could make $150 an hour, take home $90 of it. She could start right then, he said, but she told him she'd have to think it over. She laughed, telling Mary about it, while Mary looked at Gigi as a woman with long blond hair and brown eyes, weighing 125 pounds. They were in the bathroom, this same bathroom, and Gigi was shaving her legs in this tub while they talked, the razor slightly shaky in her hand. *Careful,* Mary wanted to say, but how foolish, really. There was nothing she could warn Gigi about anymore. It seemed they'd switched roles, that Gigi would now warn Mary. Not long after the call, a week or less, Gigi decided she was well enough to leave her sister and brother-in-law's care, and returned to Chicago.

*

He knocks on the bathroom door as if he were a guest in her home, as if he were politely waiting for her to come out. A soft *rap rap rap*. Lucia lifts her head from her mother's breast at the sound and blinks her long dark lashes up at Mary. A drop of watery milk slides down the baby's chin. The dog, finally believing herself within indisputable rights, lets loose and barks with gusto. Mary's breathing is like hyperventilation. What does he want? She's struck with random aphorisms and song lyrics and things her husband has said to her. She's so frightened she could laugh out loud, she could wet her pants. She thinks maybe this man wants to strike bargains, those bargains Mary has proposed to herself in the past and believed to be a common human impulse: her life for the baby's, the secret to everything Mary has the answer to — just for this hardship, this threat, to go away.

What will Cal do when he finds them? Some perversion allows Mary to see the blood, the violation he will find. It's been her policy, her habit, to imagine the worst in order to prevent it, a shield held up against disaster, now failing her, now erected too late, as it was with Gigi's near suicide. How will Cal tell her parents? Gigi? How will they all survive this year of bad luck in their lives? Mary is thinking a hundred things at once. She wonders if this is her life passing before her or if she is going crazy with fear and if she could possibly faint from it. Has she ever felt so frightened? So near the edge of the end? Can she compare it with anything?

What she recalls, what strikes her now with nearly physical force, is her sister's fear, her sister backing across a room, hands beating her eyes, reaching the wall, sliding down it, terrified beyond coherence. "I'm crazy," she'd said, and repeated again and again, until the words were like gibberish, a foreign language Mary had no way of deciphering, "Crazy, crazy," Gigi shaking her head passionately, as if to throw away her unrelenting fear. Mary, in the tub, tries hard to swallow, but her throat muscles conspire against her and will not respond. "Gigi," she whispers, choked.

Lucia is sobbing hysterically on her knees — the dog's persistent barking and her mother's lapse have scared her. Mary forces herself to snap to.

But he does not knock again. The dog stands with one ear poised, teeth bared, waiting for a reason to resume barking. There isn't a gunshot or another knock or even the rasp of evil breathing on the other side. There is, instead, silence. The silence of shadows flitting over large bodies of water, Mary thinks, like clouds, vaporous and wholly transient. Mary sits there another half-hour, not moving. Lucia, calmed by her mother's assurances, pliant with warm milk, plays with Mary's features, exploring her mouth with curious fingers, pulling her nose, patting her eyes. He has gone, taking her keys with him. Mary didn't hear him leave but she believes her house, outside the door, is empty, and she finally sobs in relief.

Yet doesn't get out of the tub. Cal will have to find her here, she decides, and he may have to get tools and an axe and break in to do so, because she isn't planning to open the door for anything.

NAKED LADIES

—— ++++ ——

LAURA'S FAMILY WAS GOING TO EASTER BRUNCH AT
the Houses'. They were invited every year by Mr. House,
but this was the first time Laura's mother could accept. Mr.
House called the party his Easter Frolic, and Laura's father
never wanted to go. "Frolic at the House house?" he always
said. "We'll pass." The family was going this year because
he was away showing his paintings at spring arts fairs. He
had got lucky, securing more booth spaces than ever before.
Already he'd been gone for a month, traveling in his old
Land Cruiser among his canvases, phoning home every few
nights to report on his earnings. Of the eight checks he'd
sent to them, only one had proved rubber. Laura's mother
mailed a letter to the woman who'd written it, chastising
her for behaving badly. The letter came back from Las Vegas
marked NO LONGER AT THIS ADDRESS, and Laura inter-
cepted it and burned it in the back yard before her mother
got home.

Laura's mother raised other people's children — that
was her job. She departed each weekday morning in order
to arrive at the Houses' before the three school-age children left, which meant that her own family had to fend for

itself. The youngest House child, four-year-old Mikey, had Down syndrome and was her main responsibility. Mrs. House, who blamed herself for his condition, could not be counted upon; she sometimes spent the whole day lying in bed circling catalogue merchandise and punching 800 numbers.

There were four House children, two boys and two girls, just like Laura's family. Except not like them at all. The House children were neatly spaced, like elections, every two years — ten, eight, six, four — while Laura's family was helter-skelter, seventeen, thirteen, eight, and seven, testimony to their parents' ambivalent feelings about kids. In fact, the two youngest — her brothers — were the same age from October until December each year, which made Laura acutely embarrassed about the obvious recklessness of her parents' lovemaking. When she was younger, when her mother first began working for the Houses, Laura longed for the same tidy procession of children, longed to recite the healthy even numbers of their ages. If she could have, she would have arranged for a new sibling to arrive every two years, until there were eight or ten of them, because she loved quantity as well as orderliness. It proved stability, something aggressively substantial.

The Houses did not call Laura's mother Mrs. Laughlin but Nana, a name Laura found irritatingly intimate. Laura's father said that it made her sound like the family sheepdog. More than the name, he hated the almost-uniform she wore, a large green smock with four square pockets. "Cover those breasts, Broom Hilda," he would say when she brought it home to launder. "Hide that butt."

"This gruesome thing pays the rent," she would say to him, wadding it into a ball and throwing it among the dirty clothes. Her husband would turn out his lower lip like a child. Though his paintings sold only sporadically, when they did sell the family was rich for a week or two. This seemed to him to make up for the other, anxious times.

Always as part of Laura's consciousness was the worry that her parents would divorce. They weren't volatile and didn't fight, not the way married people fought in books or movies, but instead picked at each other in a sly, monkey-like manner, each baiting the other until one might be forced to slam a door or yell at the dog. Laura both looked forward to and dreaded what her parents called *scenes.* They didn't like to make them, but after one had played itself out, Laura felt a kind of humming glee, as if she had seen a vision of the future, a moment of her womanly life briefly revealed to her. From her parents Laura had learned to attach weight to the most subtle vocal inflection, the most fleeting glance. She often lay awake at night replaying the day, hearing again and again words that might have been meant, or taken, unkindly, biting her nails until she could go no farther down.

To the Easter Frolic the five Laughlins wore their good clothes. Their mother debated about a hat — hats, at Easter, seemed somehow necessary to her — and decided on a turquoise beret, which sat tilted like a dinner plate on her head. She wore a simple silk dress, a lighter shade of turquoise, belted at her hips with a Guatemalan scarf Mrs. House had given her after their trip over Christmas.

"You look pretty," said Laura's younger sister, Pammy, who was thirteen. "The Houses probably never saw you in anything but your ugly green shirt. Won't they be surprised?"

"Won't they?" Laura agreed, proud that her forty-year-old mother still had a figure to show off.

Admiring herself in the mirror, lifting her chin to draw her throat taut, their mother said, "And at the front door, no less."

*

They were the first to arrive. The day was a perfect midwestern spring day, sunny and still. The Houses' neighborhood was incorporated, a city unto itself in the middle of Wichita. Traffic had to slow to parade speed in order to pass through; Eastborough had its own police department, whose officers drove sky-blue foreign compacts instead of the typical American black-and-white sedans, and whose only responsibility was to issue speeding tickets. Laura's father complained because residents here did not have to pay Wichita city taxes; Laura's friends, crawling through at twenty miles per hour, bemoaned the fact that of course the best mall *would* be built on the other side of Eastborough. Laura tried to pinpoint what exactly distinguished it from her neighborhood, Riverside, because the houses there were older and statelier. But the difference seemed to have to do with the small details — the antique park benches and clusters of pansies along the street, the absence of loud city buses and delivery trucks, the long path of black mushroom lights that led to the House door. Nothing stirred this Sunday morning but the songbirds.

The Laughlins stood on the flagstone front porch while Laura's mother rang the bell. Inside the House home a long elegant bonging sounded — the Big Ben tune, their mother told them — and then Mr. House opened the door wearing a tuxedo jacket over a sweatsuit. Laura understood that this was his outfit. His running shoes were brand-new, the kind into which you could pump air.

"Nana!" he exclaimed. "Well, well, Nana, aren't you a

piece of work!" He was a large-featured, sinister-looking man. His nose was long and wide, his dark hair oiled back from a vampirish widow's peak. His face, greeting them, had the sleek eagerness of a wet dog's. "For Godsakes, come in!" he roared.

Their mother had big breasts, which neither Laura nor her sister had inherited. Mr. House stared at them now, revealed as they were beneath the thin silk. Under his gaze, she lifted her hand to her throat, covering her chest with her forearm. Her face was flushed, her hair — neither blond nor silver — shiny and topped by her rakish hat as she led her children through the foyer of her employer's house.

Mr. House offered them drinks. Laura's mother allowed the three youngest children Cokes and accepted a cocktail of champagne and orange juice for herself, turning her wrist to check her delicate dress watch for the hour. "So early," she said, laughing. When Mr. House tried to give Laura the same kind of drink, her mother shook her head, so that Laura was left with nothing, too embarrassed to take a Coke in consolation.

They were gathered awkwardly in what appeared to be a modern ballroom, done in uncompromising black and white and red. An ebony grand piano shone in the corner like an advertisement for furniture polish. Beside it stood a brilliant white statue, a life-size naked woman whose head was coyly ducked; a marble drape fell lazily from her fingertips to pool at her ankles. The expanse of bright red tiled floor was broken only by white fur throw rugs, which floated on it like clouds. Mr. House seemed to recall that he too had a family and turned his head to shout out their names.

Pammy nudged Laura, pointing above their heads to

the walls. They were lined with ink drawings, also of naked women, but for one astonishing exception: a painting of their father's, a piece from his "Over the Shoulder" series. Though there could be no mistake, Laura looked for his signature in the corner just to be sure. There it was, *Luke Laughlin,* in his typically impatient penmanship. The painting stood out among the women like a beggar. She wondered how it had gotten here. It was of a winter field, silos and shredded haystacks, wind through bare trees, all of it seen over the large foreground shoulder of a scruffy jacket. During this series her father had been using dental tools to scrape paint onto the canvas. He'd come up with a polished steel tone by mixing molten aluminum foil with his oils. It gave the effect of frozen metal, of a surface your warm finger might stick to.

Laura's arms broke out in goose bumps. Around her father's painting and its sober subject, the naked women seemed to preen, silly and moneyed. To them, his painting took itself too seriously, like a street character preaching doom on a sunny day. *Loosen up,* the naked figures implored, their curves and arches like a languorous cat in the sun. Laura's stomach turned with tension, and she began marking time until it would be permissible for her to suggest they go home.

*

The House children trooped in wearing jeans and T-shirts, high-tops and spandex. Mrs. House wore peacock colors — a fashion trick Laura recognized from the discarded French magazines her mother brought home from here. The plumage was supposed to distract from her bulk, but still she looked as if she were filled with sand. Like Mr. House, she entered in high spirits, grinning in surprise at Mrs. Laughlin, eyeing the four children in such a way that the two boys stepped behind their older sisters. Laura felt ridiculous in her dress and hose. Her brothers wore neckties and dark suits from a grandfather's funeral last fall; of course their wrists stuck out, their pants were too short, their shoes were unbearably squeaky. Only Mikey House, unkempt as the retarded often seem, kept Laura from burning up in shame. He had loped over to her mother and thrown his arms around her knees. Mrs. Laughlin ran her fingers through his stiff hair, and Laura saw she loved him at least as much as she did her own children. In what was obviously a ritual, he reached for her wedding band, wrestled it from her finger, and slid it on his own thumb.

"He misses his Nana — don't you, Mikey?" said Mrs. House, unjealous. "And here she is, come to see you on a Sunday. What do you think?"

Mikey snuggled into Mrs. Laughlin's dress once more, this time leaving a large wet spot at her crotch. No one else seemed to notice, though Laura saw her mother's lips crimp as she brushed her palm over her lap. This, Laura understood, was the reason for the smock. Gently, Mrs. Laughlin directed Mikey's mouth away from her. Now that he had attached himself to her, she seemed more at home, asking the other House boy, Frank, Jr., to show her family around.

"Kitchen," he said as he led Laura and the others rapidly through the house. "Dining room." "Pantry." The doorbell began bonging again, and shrill greetings could be heard, women's voices rising in exclamation, then falling into confidences, Mr. House booming out, "Well, come on in, you old son of a such-and-such!" The tour terminated at the back of the house, in a plushly carpeted bedroom that had no windows. They had gone too quickly for

Laura's taste, ten-year-old Frank gliding through each room in a bored, mature manner, reciting square footage, flipping on lights for a moment, then extinguishing them. He'd gestured toward paintings and statues, mentioning the names of artists, until he realized his guests had never heard of them and were not impressed. This bedroom with no natural light was his, and it was with true enthusiasm that he now showed Laura's brothers his *Playboys*, stacked beside his small television.

"I have my own subscription," he said, pointing out his name on the mailing label. "Dad got it for me."

"He did?" the boys asked in unison.

Frank nodded. "He was tired of me stealing his."

Laura's brothers settled happily on the rug, each with a magazine. Pammy, who often didn't know whether she ought to stay with her brothers or go with her sister, finally gave in to curiosity and shyly hefted December's issue, folding herself into a cross-legged position on the floor.

Left alone, Laura returned on the route Frank had just taken, moving slowly this time through the rooms. The house was full of things, each wall hidden by furniture or art, beautiful and unbeautiful clutter like department store displays, pillows and decorative knickknacks, large vases sporting wheat stalks, needlepoint footrests, porcelain dolls, exotic foreign masks and figurines. Laura wondered if her mother was tempted, as Laura was, to pretend she lived in this modern palace. It was cavelike, and there were many rooms that seemed without function, merely pretty, rooms one retreated to for contemplation. They appealed to Laura for that reason — that, and their cleanliness. Each had a peaceful view of the vast lawn — the *grounds,* she imagined it was called — where guests now clustered like floral arrangements.

In one of the rooms rested an immaculate easel, and Laura pictured Mrs. House sitting here, looking out over her estate, using a pristine set of watercolors to render a sunset. The stool before the easel was padded and spun smoothly around; in the corner stretched an old-fashioned chaise longue, rosewood and velvet. Laura could not help comparing this with her father's studio, which was the back porch, and which stank of mineral spirits, oil paints, and kitty litter. His easels, all of them, were chaotic with splattered color and were mended with duct tape. Plastic weatherproofing covered the windows, obscuring the outdoors. From the ceiling hung bare two-hundred-watt bulbs; beside his feet he kept an electric space heater burning — a fire hazard, her mother always claimed.

When her father was home, Laura often sat in his studio with him, listening to him talk about his unsavory and impoverished Oklahoman family, his dismal yet serendipitous life's journey. She was the only one of his children he allowed to stay while he painted; the others always wanted him to paint a particular thing, or if not that, then to explain what he *was* painting, and then felt free to disagree. But Laura was too nervous to do anything more than simply watch him. She brought him his Earl Grey tea with a squirt of honey in it, and sat on a small metal stepladder until her back ached. With the heater on, the porch provided a cozy and heady atmosphere. She'd cried when the gallery in Chicago that showed him had gone under, leaving him and his work to the mercy of arts-and-crafts fairs.

Out of Mrs. House's painting room led two closed doors. The first Laura tried opened into a bathroom.

"Hey!" shouted Mrs. House, who sat inside with her jumpsuit around her knees. Laura slammed the door and stood squinting, willing the thing to unhappen. From the lawn she heard a group of men laugh together, as if at a punch line. A beach ball thwapped the window, then rolled away. Mrs. House's bare flesh, in the glimpse Laura had, was astonishing, plentiful, melting over her like vanilla ice cream.

The second door — she opened it tentatively — revealed the kitchen, where the caterers were heating food. They looked at Laura with disdain, as if she lived in this house, or one like it.

*

Laura moved briskly through the ballroom, through vaporous clouds of different strong perfumes. A glass fell from a woman's slim fingers and popped neatly into shards. "My word," the woman said to Laura, and then walked off, leaving the sparkling mess. Laura found her mother outside, away from the party, and stood in her shadow, safe haven. She and Mr. House were beneath a pink magnolia tree, peering up. Laura had the strange sensation that they had been touching, though they weren't at the moment. Little Mikey sat on the ground at Mrs. Laughlin's feet, playing with a basket of toys. He had tiny Guatemalan trouble dolls — the Houses had brought back sets for Laura and Pammy, too — a Lego doorway, a small plastic reindeer whose legs had been gnawed off, the connector from a Hot Wheels track, a white barrette, and two metal keys, along with Mrs. Laughlin's wedding ring. He had created a game for himself, walking the keys through the doorway, slipping the connector into his mouth to make a tongue, babbling around it to the trouble dolls.

"See him?" Mr. House was saying as he pointed to the tree's branches. "Get out of there, you sneaky shit." Laura looked up. A squirrel stared placidly down at the humans below, his head protruding from a small wooden house. The fur at his neck ruffled like a mane; the hole was not large enough to accommodate him, and Laura wondered aloud if he was stuck. "He chewed his way in," Mr. House said, swinging his arm as if opening a door. "Right into a wren house. Impertinent little shit." He continued smiling.

To Laura, Mrs. Laughlin said, "Mr. House loves birds. He builds them houses in his spare time." To him, she said, "You'll have to cultivate a taste for squirrels." She took a last sip from her glass, spinning the ice as she finished off the drink.

Mr. House went, "Ah ha ha ha," his face distorted with cracks and crevices. He seemed to laugh frequently, whether a thing was funny or not. Laura did not like him, but for some reason her mother did. At home she poked fun at him, imitating his monstrous guffaw, his incessant cursing. But here she smiled serenely at him as he sighted along his pointed finger, which he aimed at the squirrel like a gun. Mikey had looked up when he heard his father laugh and now followed the motion attentively, as if real bullets might emerge from the big hand.

Mr. House said, "This the one who wants to be a model?"

"That's Pammy," her mother told him. "Pammy's been prancing around in her underwear since she was two or three. No" — she paused, rolling her hip toward Laura, reciting the familiar line — "this one is the thinker."

Mr. House instantly fell into a pose, bent at the waist, resting his elbow on his raised knee, fist under his chin. He grimaced as if in pain. His tux tail touched the pale spring grass. "Get it?" he asked. "Row Dan? *The Thinker?*"

Her mother laughed again. Laura couldn't tell if it was with him or at him. She was sly, in her own way — unpredictable and sometimes unkind. At home she had said,

"He's no Einstein, but at least he's jolly. At least he knows how to have fun."

"'Jolly,'" Laura's father had repeated, tasting the word.

"Of course you two know Rodin," Mr. House said, rising and unselfconsciously reaching inside his sweatpants to make an adjustment. "What with an artist in the house." This time it was *his* tone she couldn't read. "Maybe Laura will be an artist herself. You paint, Laura?"

She shook her head.

"Draw?" he persisted. "Play an instrument? Compose song lyrics?"

"She debates," Mrs. Laughlin told him. "She has trophies, don't you, sweetheart?"

He made a sour face. "Careful, you might end up a lawyer, like yours truly." He emptied his glass of ice by throwing it out over the lawn. "But probably in public defense, am I right?"

Laura shrugged. Mrs. Laughlin squatted to put Mikey's toys back in their basket, her thighs pressed together in the tight silk dress, the fabric between them tense. Mikey snuffled disconsolately until Mrs. Laughlin gave him a kiss on the nose. Mr. House turned his fat gleaming face to Laura again and winked. "Quit this debating baloney," he advised as they approached the house and other guests. "You're pretty — nothing wrong with that — so be pretty! Wear nice clothes, be a model. You could make a wonderful model, you just have to smile."

*

It was a tradition of the Easter Frolic to have an egg hunt, Mr. House told them in the ballroom. He had been playing requests at the piano, his long, wide fingers gliding over the keys while people hummed along. The sun shone without remorse through large clean windows, reflecting blindingly off the red floor, off the crystal glasses and ice cubes. Every song had an identical choppy rhythm meant to sound jazzy and light, like one-liners. Beside Laura a woman snapped her fingers a little too slowly. A small man with a strange lump on his forehead danced with whoever would consent. He liked to spin his partners with his fingertips so their dresses flared. Mr. House tinkled a few high keys like a bird trill and then abruptly stopped playing.

"The hunt!" he announced. Weakly, the woman next to Laura snapped once more. Mr. House patted her rump when he stood up, as if in consolation.

"He's crude," Laura told her sister as they wandered around the swimming pool, looking halfheartedly for eggs. The first they'd found was plastic and contained a cheap necklace and pendant: turned one way, Betty Boop smiled under her long lashes; turned the other way, her mouth became an O and her dotted dress disappeared. Pammy put it on. They found hard-boiled eggs with the beginnings of riddles on them ("How many Catholics does it take to change a light bulb?") or with the answers ("Because it was a *hung jury*"), and they found chocolates in the shape of naked women, buxom foil-wrapped little candies nestled in the tender crocuses.

"He sure likes naked ladies," Pammy observed. She, like Laura's brothers, was enjoying the morning. To them it did not spell disaster but adventure — something they would tell all their friends about.

"I think he's having an affair with Mom," Laura told Pammy by the pool. She said it in order to feel her heart race, not entirely concerned with whether she believed it.

"Bullshit," Pammy said. After she'd thought for a moment, she added, "Dad is a lot better-looking, and younger and skinnier and everything. Mr. House is kind of . . ." She searched for the right word. "Gross."

"Like that matters," Laura told her. The prospect of her mother's affair would give Laura a headache — it was her nature to keep peace — but a small, evolving, renegade emotion made her want something contrary to happen. She and Pammy sat by the pool, took their shoes and stockings off, and dangled their feet in the icy water. On the other side of the lawn, guests crawled along the shrubbery, still seeking eggs, absurd in their good clothes. Laura's brothers and Frank held grocery sacks for easy collection. Her mother helped Mikey while Mr. House stood on the porch yelling, "You're getting hot, very hot, hotter!" and laughing loudly.

"I bet anything she tells us not to tell Dad we were here," Pammy said suddenly, as if the whole party had come clear to her.

"No," Laura said, "she'll let us tell him. This is her way of getting back at him for being gone so much. While he's away we're all out here with Mr House, like he's our other Dad, the pervert one." But his compliment — telling her she could be a model — kept lightening Laura's opinion of him. Unlike most people, he seemed to have faith in something besides her intelligence, and she was not above feeling flattered by it.

"Isn't this place funny?" Pammy said. "So funny and weird. I never thought there'd be a place like this. And Mom comes here every day — that's the weirdest part of all." She pulled her pale legs from the water and brushed off the drops that clung to them. "Do you think Dad knows one of his paintings is here?"

"No. If he knew, he'd come steal it off the wall." Laura was positive he had not given it to the Houses. Perhaps her mother had made a gift of it, but that was unlikely. For all their curious bickering, she would not have betrayed him this way, through his work. So Laura deduced that Mr. House had bought the painting, without her father knowing, possibly as a way of pleasing her mother, though Laura understood that it would not please her, and she understood that Mr. House knew it too.

"It looks so funny with those other pictures," Pammy went on. "So depressing and . . . brown."

"It's not depressing," Laura said. "It's just more realistic."

"Naked ladies are real," Pammy said. "They're just as real as a blizzard on a farm, only prettier."

Laura didn't want to argue with Pammy, so she repeated what they agreed upon: "His painting is all wrong here."

Pammy lifted her plastic pendant from between her new, small breasts and fingered it in the sunlight. "If I was Mom," she said, "I think I'd like to work here. It's cool."

"Girls!" Mr. House shouted out at them, waving his arms toward himself like a coach. The lawn was so wide that his voice seemed out of synch. "Come on, you bathing beauties! Come eat, drink, be merry, and limbo!"

*

They joined the party on the deck, passing through a croquet game. The people playing made the game seem glamorous, their disproportionate size to their mallets not at all silly. Bright wooden balls rolled quietly through the grass and went *clok* against one another. Mrs. House sat watching the game, feeding a fat black dog on her lap. Laura avoided looking at her, hoping she had been too stunned to recognize her when she opened the bathroom door. "Here you go," Mrs. House told the dog, handing him a Jordan almond.

Everyone was eating. Plates decorated every surface; a

melting ice swan swam in a sea of ripe fruit. In a budding tree whose two largest branches reached like arms toward the sky, a young man sat with his shirt off, feet above his head, popping stuffed mushrooms into his mouth. Mr. House stood below him, tossing up more. "Handle a beer?" he asked the boy, who nodded agreeably in answer. At one barbecue a side of beef spun, while at another a whole pig revolved, as big and pink as a fat child. The caterers circulated with champagne and miniature quiches, studiously ignoring the goings-on.

Laura found her mother again. She had grown dreamy with drink and lay on a padded lounge chair at the far end of the deck, her beret tilted over her eyes to block the sun. Her bare legs were as white as eggshell, pale blue veins beneath the mildly translucent skin like splintering cracks. Mikey lay asleep beside her, his feet tucked beneath her knees for warmth. His ordinarily strange features appeared normal in sleep, freckled and pug, and this made Laura briefly sad.

From inside, she heard the doorbell ring. Until it sounded, Laura had thought she might want something to happen; now she knew otherwise. No one else seemed to have heard the long chime, and she waited for it to begin again before she went to answer it herself.

Her father stood on the flagstone porch, investigating the House mailbox, to which an enormous black screaming eagle was attached at the claws.

"Dad."

"Hi, honey. How's the frolic?"

"Awful, really."

"Got you answering the door?" He stepped gently past her, moving quietly, as he always did, as if someone might jump out and surprise him.

"I was the only one who heard the bell," she told

him. "We didn't think you'd be home until tonight," she added.

"You don't say?" he said.

"How was Oregon?"

"Wet," he said. "Earthy and impoverished, though happy. They have happy industries out there, Christmas trees and vineyards, happy, happy. I preferred Nevada — you ought to see the neon."

"That's too bad," Laura said, just to say something.

He gave his shoulders and head a slight shake, as if to wake up. "I've been driving since yesterday afternoon." He looked at his paint-dirtied plastic watch. "Twenty-four hours. I was ready to be home." He ran a thumbnail behind his earlobe. "And then nobody was there."

"Want to wait here while I get Mom and everybody?"

"No." He looked around the dark foyer for the first time. He was unshaven and smelled of his vehicle and the road. "No, I certainly don't want to wait here."

Laura took his hand, which was callused and warm, like a work glove, and led him along the circuitous route she'd discovered earlier instead of through the ballroom where his painting hung. He followed, grunting in amusement every now and then, dropping her hand to study an abstract painting in one room.

"Some of it's nice," Laura said about the clutter, "but most of it's junk." She waited for him to agree.

"That's your opinion?" He spoke without looking at her, tipping his face so close to the painting he seemed to be smelling it. "This is a marvelous piece," he said, sighing. "Absolutely marvelous." Art he admired made him melancholy, Laura had noticed. Her father had once spent nine thousand dollars on a painting. That was before the children were born. It now hung in his and Mrs. Laughlin's bedroom at home, where no one but the family ever saw it.

"I interrupted Mrs. House on the toilet," Laura told him as they left the room, trying to cheer him up.

He smiled distractedly.

"Have you been here before?" she asked when they came to a patio door outside.

"Never," he said, stepping onto the porch.

"But not," Mr. House boomed beside them, "for lack of an invitation."

*

Her mother was where Laura had last seen her, asleep on the lounge chair next to Mikey. Her turquoise dress was hiked halfway up her bare thigh and her arms were crossed, as if she were carrying on an angry conversation in her dream. She was deeply asleep and cold, Mikey curled against her so trustingly that Laura forgave her — whatever the infraction, whether it was preferring this child and home to her own or loving peculiar Mr. House or something else, something private between her parents which Laura might and might not wish to understand.

"You must be the mister," Mr. House had gone on when he had so suddenly materialized beside her and her father.

Mr. Laughlin showed his teeth like a hyena, the expression he reserved for people to whom he felt superior.

"Lemme buy you a drink," Mr. House said, waving in the direction of a passing caterer.

"O.K.," Mr. Laughlin agreed. "Get your brothers and sister," he said to Laura, nodding toward the pool, where all the party's children sat eating chocolate and comparing parents.

As she hurried, fearing a fight, she felt the headache she had expected descend like a hat over her skull. "Dad's here," she hissed to Pammy.

Pammy's eyebrows jumped. "Oh, man."

They each grabbed a brother and headed back. Mr. House and their father were standing over their mother's chair looking at her as she slept.

"Hey, Dad!" the youngest Laughlin greeted his father.

"Son."

"Guess what? I won third prize in the — what's his name?"

"Bacchus," Mr. House supplied.

"Bacchus Look-Alike Contest." He held up a Polaroid photo of himself wearing a crown of rubber purple grapes and holding a plastic set of pipes. "I got a prize," he added, pulling a fluorescent orange feather boa from his suit jacket pocket.

Mr. Laughlin accepted the boa, studying it as it slid like water through his fingers and onto the ground.

"First prize was Royals tickets," Laura's brother went on, bending to retrieve the wrap. "But we couldn't go all the way to Kansas City, anyway. Could we?" He looked up at his father, who shook his head.

On the chair Mikey jolted awake, his face becoming the familiar flattened, pink-eyed one of Down syndrome once more.

"Nana," he snuffled, to warn her, and Mrs. Laughlin turned toward him without opening her eyes, nuzzling, attempting to close him in her arms. When he would not comply, she pushed aside her beret and squinted up.

Her husband waved his fingers down at her.

"Surprise, surprise!" said Mr. House.

*

When Mr. and Mrs. Laughlin agreed the family had to be going ("Oh, it's a school day tomorrow, and he's been driving all night." "I've been driving all night." "All night, honey, really?" "Really, all night."), Mr. House said he would walk them to the door. He led them toward the ballroom, and Pammy and Laura gave each other agonized looks. Now the crisis would come, the painting would be discovered.

Curiously, Laura's mother seemed unfazed by what was happening. She yawned and then shivered, crossing her arms and allowing Mr. House to put his jacket around her shoulders as they moved toward the house, Mr. Laughlin in front walking with his nose tilted toward the ground, a pained grin lifting one side of his mouth.

"Goodbye, goodbye!" the boys shouted to Frank, Jr., who stood with his legs spread on the other end of the lawn, waving and laughing, a perfect, reduced replica of his father.

"Thank you, Mrs. House," Pammy told the hostess, whom they met at the ballroom door. The group stopped to give her space to pass.

"You're surely welcome, baby," she said to Pammy. "See you Monday," she said over her shoulder to Laura's mother as she joined her other guests outside.

They could have moved quickly through the room; Mr. Laughlin could have kept staring at the floor, walking on the lipstick-red tile, thinking, smirking. But from the yard came a terrible wail; Mikey House had discovered that his Nana had left, and as he barreled toward her, running lopsidedly, Mr. Laughlin raised his eyes to take in the pictures on the walls.

Without breathing, Laura watched him see them, the naked women, one drawing after another, their rolling seductive ease and then his own painting among them like a slammed door. What surprised her was that his eyes jumped over his painting — no alarm, no anger, not even, it seemed, recognition — and concentrated on the nudes. She looked up again. They were not very well rendered, obviously done by a hobbyist — or, as her father would say, "a draw-er, as in chest of." Laura tried to see what he saw — the round bottoms, the heavy breasts, the faces half hidden in ink smudge. Then her father turned toward his wife, who had bent over Mikey once more, calming him. Her hat fell to the floor and her white-blond hair covered her eyes.

Laura blinked. It could be her, she thought. The woman in the pictures could be her mother — which would make Mr. House the artist. She saw them in a flash, together in the House studio, her mother on the chaise, Mr. House staring at her ardently, scratching away with his pens. She wanted to meet her father's eyes for confirmation, but he would not look at Laura. He waited for his wife, patiently.

In the foyer, Mr. Laughlin removed Mr. House's enormous tuxedo jacket from Mrs. Laughlin's shoulders.

"She can wear it home," Mr. House said magnanimously.

"She *can*," Mr. Laughlin agreed, handing over the dark garment. "But she won't."

*

Mrs. Laughlin never went back. She began working for the phone company a few days later. They didn't divorce, and after Laura left home — first for college, then for law school — she found herself alternately proud of and annoyed by her parents' enduring marriage. As to the significance of what had happened at the Houses', Laura could only look to the fact that soon her father acquired a partner to share booth space with and represent him — a single man, a photographer who lived on the road anyway and didn't mind the traveling — and to her mother's fierce tears one dinnertime when Laura's youngest brother carelessly asked what in the world would happen to Mikey House.

On the drive across town that Easter, Mr. Laughlin told them the story of his trip west, of how he'd had to spend the nights in his Land Cruiser — he illustrated by curling himself spasmodically as he steered — because he'd run out of motel money, of his stiff back and stinky clothes, the way he'd eaten at restaurants that offered two-for-one meals. He kept turning to check Mrs. Laughlin's expression, but she was still sleepy, sluggish, looking blankly out the window, shivering. Even without Mr. House's jacket, every now and then Laura caught a whiff of his cologne, so powerful it was as if he were among them for a moment. Mr. Laughlin's stories weren't pathetic tales; he managed to have Laura and Pammy and their brothers laughing at his bad luck by the time they reached their driveway on the other side of the city.

Later, he and Laura drove back to the Houses' to pick up Mrs. Laughlin's car; her old Maverick had been hopelessly trapped in the overcrowded driveway, Mercedes and Cadillacs and BMWs packed four-deep behind and beside it. "We'll get it tonight," Laura's father had said, guiding Mrs. Laughlin to his boxy vehicle parked across the street. When he and Laura returned for the car, they didn't speak, as if they were in agreement, as if he too had recognized his pretty wife in the mediocre art. It would be easy to say something, and Laura nearly did: a little evidence would go a long way, would twist tight whatever was already tense.

Her father pulled up in front of the Houses' once more. The driveway was empty except for Mrs. Laughlin's car. The windows of the house were dark, as if the family had all gone to bed early. Or as if they didn't want to be seen.

"Your mother's left headlight is out," Mr. Laughlin said to Laura.

It was the first thing he'd said in thirty minutes, and Laura tried to make some symbolic sense of his words but couldn't. "What do you mean?" she asked tentatively.

"Her Mav, the left headlight. You ought to just follow me home." He stretched his arms and tapped the ceiling of the Land Cruiser with his fingers. The smell of his sweat filled the front seat. Then he laughed. "Man, have I driven enough today or what?" And Laura saw nothing was going to happen. They were going to go home and watch television with the rest of the family. The Easter Frolic was over. "Hoppity-hop," her father said, which was his way of prodding her into action.

Laura continued to intercept the mail, which one day led her to think about the woman who'd taken her mother's place at the Houses'. Because the envelope with the Eastborough return address was so light, Laura had thought it might be empty; instead, a slim gold ring slid out. Nothing more. Had her father even noticed its absence? Laura slipped the ring on her pinky and imagined another woman, interviewing for the position of Nana, marveling at her odd employer and, after taking the job, playing with Mikey, loving him, wondering at his eclectic basket of toys — at the barrette and the black tongue, the swinging red door and the legless reindeer, the two keys and the trouble dolls, someone's mysterious, modest wedding band.

CRYBABY

———— +++++ ————

THIS MORNING, IN CHICAGO, WHILE RACHEL HAD
been waiting for the red-eye flight to LAX, the wall of glass
she was looking through crystalized before her eyes. She was
an hour early for her flight, and as a result the only person
to witness the breaking window. As a 747 bound for Paris
had roared down the runway, its wake had somehow shat-
tered the wall of glass immediately in front of Rachel. The
only passenger; the only broken window. She'd felt it shake,
then watched it split itself into fissures, yet hold in place.
She rapped with her knuckles, ran her fingers over the
cracks and felt nothing, no textural indication of distress.
The broken view through it was wobbly and infracted at
once, very pointillist.

It was a young man she reported the window to, a
young man in a uniform who would take care of it while
she caught her flight west. Young men, Rachel thought:
they were steadfast and single-minded, and if somebody
had to rush to arms to defend the country, she was satisfied
that they were the ones.

Later, airborne on another 747, Rachel stared obses-
sively, cross-eyed with concentration, not through her lit-

tle porthole but at it. When the airport window had broken she had been staring into the fuzzy middle distance, thoughts circling in her mind like placid fish in a tank. The sudden break had had the effect of a hard slap on the face: she came out of herself, jarred, embarrassed, alert. Now that alertness would not subside.

She was on her way to Santa Barbara to take care of her former sister-in-law, who had been in a car accident. A truck loaded with fresh seafood had overturned on the highway outside Santa Barbara, leaving a slick living trail of its contents. Wouldn't such a disaster be comical, in other situations? Melody had slid helplessly through the crab and squid and lobster, her little Honda thrown into the oncoming lane of traffic where it was then broadsided by two solid sedans. Her legs and ribs and collarbone and nose were all broken, a piece of an ear sheared off as if she had skidded across the blacktop on her own face. Yet if Melody hadn't been there, if the truck driver had popped from his cab and stood scratching his head or beating his knee with his cap, wouldn't the accident have been a joke? Or the silly premise of a children's picture book, the driver scampering about gathering his load before it crawled back toward the sea?

When they'd heard the news, Rachel and her husband and two sons had reminded themselves of other peculiar truck mishaps: thousands of gallons of house paint spilled like an abstract mural over a cliff in Colorado; cases and cases of beer left like a raided party on the plains of Nebraska; live pigs let loose when their truck died on a railroad crossing just before the train came; and a load of new Cadillacs driven without glamour into the Mississippi River. They had found these stories funny, funnier perhaps because Melody, though alive, would wear a body cast. She would look like a mummy, like the Invisible Man, like all the cartoon creatures who fell from the sky into a puff of dust on the earth below.

Rachel had kissed her family's warm sleeping foreheads before leaving the apartment for the airport. She had launched her sons safely into the world, and now she would extend her services to someone needier. As soon as she'd heard about the accident, Rachel had been drawn to California, to help. Rachel and Melody's husbands were brothers, but Rachel had never felt as close to her brother-in-law as she did to Melody, who, since the divorce several months earlier, was no longer officially related. Melody had been in traction for a few weeks, since February, then sent home in casts to her bungalow in March, husbandless.

Also living with her was her stepson, Tony, Rachel's miscreant nephew, twenty-four, who had decided not to go live with his father after the divorce. The product of a young first marriage Dennis had made just out of high school, Tony seemed incapable of independence. He'd not left home for school or job, had hung around unhappily, complaining of his bad childhood. Melody and Dennis had no children of their own, and Rachel had thought it very odd — racy, gossipy — that Melody would allow Tony to stay once his father was gone. Self-centered and rude, he was not an easy boy to get along with. But now it seemed lucky; he could look after her until Rachel arrived.

At the airport in Los Angeles, safely landed, she bought sunglasses and rented a car. It was early and the city hadn't wakened yet; there was a sense of calm on the freeway, of expanse. Driving along the sunny coast, Rachel thought: California is a young woman, her hopeful vigilant mind up in San Francisco, her complicated spawning organs down in Los Angeles. Here was Santa Barbara, ample and un-blemished coastal hip.

It was still early to knock on Melody's door, so Rachel stopped at the beach and watched sea gulls. She sat in the sand and tried to remember whether sand was broken glass or glass was molten sand. Science had always escaped her — she counted on her brainy elder son to set her straight these days — but she sifted the fine rock through her fingers and felt particularly relieved to be sitting on it rather than looking through it.

*

Melody's bungalow was old, its interior cool and dark, the windows obscured by a thick curtain of growth, green vines and tree leaves. Sunlight pierced through in sharp beams, dust motes floated like glitter. Everything was in bloom in California. Perhaps everything was always in bloom there. Rachel recalled the gray city she'd left behind, the dirty pocked snow that seemed perpetually in its street gutters, the hungry verminish squirrels. Here the air smelled of flowers just about to die, of the thick scent of that cheap junior high school perfume, Jungle Gardenia. Every available surface held a potted plant or dried bouquet, and maroon-colored rose petals fell as Rachel watched. In every room ceiling fans turned so slowly that houseflies rode around on the blades.

Carl from Budget car rental, wearing his red polo shirt and bright white slacks, had agreed reluctantly to deliver her to Melody's house, squealing off before she'd reached the porch, unwilling to do more than pop the trunk so that she could retrieve her heavy suitcase. Her nephew Tony had opened the front door of the house in his underwear, angry at having been wakened, unashamed of his near-nudity; his briefs were so brief, so black, worn so tight. He'd left the door open, Rachel standing with her suitcase on the porch, and staggered back to his bedroom, where he slammed the door hard enough to shake the house, to rattle the two front windows. Young men, Rachel thought crankily. She had a moment of despising her own sons, who were only nine and thirteen but who would of course arrive at impudence and bad manners. It would not be her fault. She pulled her suitcase in by its leash and let it thud sideways on the floor.

In the far bedroom, Melody lay on a huge waterbed, which consumed the space from wall to wall. Replacing the body cast were two leg casts, not white but green, an extraordinary fluorescent color Rachel associated with posterboard and teenagers. Graffiti covered the thighs and calves.

Melody smiled beneath her bulky bandaged nose. "Waichel," she said. "Listen to be — cad talk. Good to see you, Waichel. Sank you for cubbing."

Rachel kicked off her shoes and sort of crawled across the bed to her former sister-in-law, who smiled painfully, patting the rippling surface beside her. They attempted an embrace. Then Rachel propped herself up next to Melody and crossed her legs. "Vivid," she said of the cast. *You should see my husband!* said Melody's right leg. *Surf's up!* said the left.

Melody shrugged. She lifted her arms, her only undamaged parts, and said, "I feel like a berbaid, stradded on da land."

Rachel laughed. "This is fairly oceanic," she said, pressing into the bed to create a wave. "What's Dennis sleeping on these days?"

"On a guildee conscience, I hope."

They sat for a moment, vaguely rocking, smiling pleasantly at each other.

"What should I do for you, Mel?"

"I donno. Maybe brig me my pot?" She pointed at a Corningware casserole dish beside the TV. Rachel crawled across the bed, stood, and handed it to her. Melody said, "Cub back in a cubble minutes."

In the kitchen all the cabinet doors were open, dirty dishes and pans were scattered around unrinsed, cereal and cracker boxes and chip sacks and cookie bags were gaping and spilled. Water dripped patiently in the sink. Rachel recognized this kitchen as a boy's kitchen; her own boys did this to her own kitchen. But she knew its remedy, so she set to work. Half an hour later, as she stood at the sink scrubbing the last of the dirty dishes, she realized the window she was staring dumbly out had a hole in it. She put her finger to the prismic chip and felt a thin steady stream of cool air flowing through it.

"BB," said Tony, behind her. He had a clean glass in his hand that he'd taken from the rack. He nudged it toward her, and Rachel was confused until she realized he simply wanted a drink. "BB shot by that little asshole next door," Tony went on, filling his glass. He was meatier than Rachel remembered, thicker than any man she'd ever seen up close. Because he was wearing a tank top, she could see his tanned neck and shoulders and upper arms, all of them as round and tight as balloons with muscle. Freckles like pennies floated here and there on his skin. He also wore cutoffs and, curiously, snow boots, which were fur-lined and looked as if raccoons had been stuffed into them before Tony's feet.

"Going to work," he muttered. His anger did not threaten Rachel because she understood it had nothing to do with her. To him, she was inconsequential, a visiting neuter. She let the water drain from the sink while he stomped into Melody's room for a moment — their two voices took turns — then stomped out the front door, slamming it and rattling the windows.

"He cleads a whale boat," Melody told Rachel. "A whale *watcheen* boat." Rachel had returned to the bedroom. The *bed* room, she thought, since besides the bed, there was room for nothing but the TV and the stand where the Corningware pot had been. Now the pot sat on the bed, a blanket of Kleenex discreetly covering its contents. After Rachel had emptied and washed it, she found Melody leveling the television remote control at the set, browsing through channels as if turning pages.

Rachel said of Tony, "So he's a scabby on a boat?"

Melody laughed. "*Swabby,*" she corrected. "He's had lods of jobs, bud he likes this wud."

What Rachel now recalled about Melody was her tolerance. Actually, this was the thing she both liked and disliked most about Melody, her good-naturedness. She was an unambitious, uncompetitive, pleasant, slightly boring person. She had made a good partner for Dennis because men in his family, including Rachel's husband, were especially zealous in collecting achievements. Rachel knew those men well enough to know that Dennis had another woman already, that he had left Melody to trade upward. She would be a young woman whose tanned skin had not yet turned on her, whose body had not yet fallen victim to the gourd-shaped tendency of gravity.

Melody said, "I take Deberol sood, so I'll be asleeb for a while. Go on the whale cruise, it's fud. Take by car. I'b certedly not goan to use it."

Rachel had not planned to leave the house — she was here to do nothing but look after Melody, like a nun with a calling — but true to her word, Melody fell into a deep sleep after breakfast. Rachel had changed Melody's shirt and panties for her, wondering how Tony performed the same delicate chores — emptying the pot, unbuttoning his step-mother's shirt to powder her chest and retape her ribs, stretching her nylon underwear carefully over her two leg casts. She felt close to Melody — not quite like a sister, but like a good friend — and yet had held off from inquiring into the house arrangements before her arrival.

Rachel drove down State Street and, on impulse, parked at an outlet leather store. The new Honda, identical to the wrecked one, was so easy to park, quick and clever as a cockroach. In the store windows, on fluorescent green posterboard, a clearance sale was advertised. Most of the items were sleazy — fringed vests, miniskirts, yellow suede hot pants — but she managed to find plain black jackets and decided to buy them for her husband and two sons, three identical ones — a large, a medium, a small, as if for the bear family. She imagined them standing in the apartment living room, arms akimbo as they stared down at themselves and each other, newly attired. Was it ever inclement enough to wear leather coats in Santa Barbara? She had the salesgirl, who wore a short red leather dress with a large keyhole cut into the back, package the jackets and send them to Chicago. Doing so made her feel carefree: she had dispensed with her home duty. She then drove Melody's brand-new car toward the water.

*

Tony never actually got to go see whales, he explained to her in his clipped way. His hair, she thought, matched his voice, shaved bristly. Instead, he mucked out after the cruise, after people'd thrown trash or grown seasick. For being his aunt, she got a discount on her ticket, but only fifteen percent. These tours were guaranteed — guaranteed you would see whales. In California, Rachel supposed, such claims could be made. The sky had grown dark as the morning progressed; the whales, heading north up the spring coast, were uncooperative. Rachel enjoyed the cruise anyway, and the bunch of high school kids lying on the deck in their shorts and goosebumps, cold and nauseated, sharing among them a jawbreaker the size of a tennis ball, which was simultaneously chalky and sparkly, like something inedible. Their teachers and chaperons stared glassy-eyed at the choppy water, waiting for a spout or fluke they could eagerly instruct upon. Rachel chastised herself for feeling the same desire to teach, for pining for her sons just to gab gab gab at them.

Beside her sat a dying man and his two grownup children, two thirtyish siblings sad and resigned, smoking cigarettes, the woman as beautiful as a model in her jodhpurs and felt hat. She and Rachel were the only people who'd thought to bring sunglasses. For Rachel this meant she could stare unimpeded; for the model, it meant haughty anonymity. Or maybe the haughtiness was supposed to be grief over the dying father. But *he* didn't seemed grieved, merely tired, watching the metal-colored water dully. Ten years ago, Rachel realized, she would not have hesitated in naming the man's daughter the most interesting person aboard. Now she knew that exotic-looking people always disappointed you; the truly interesting appeared absolutely ordinary — frumpy, in fact.

Hers was the first cruise of the season unable to make good on its guarantee of seeing whales. They bumped along for two and a half hours, Captain Joe talking and talking over his microphone, all about whales and their habits of conceiving and delivering and protecting their young, but without any hard evidence. Back on shore, he dashed off a raincheck for Rachel, redeemable anytime before the season ended. Tony the scabby had leapt onto the boat as it had puttered backward into its space, wielding his bucket and

garden hose. The teenagers, who'd stampeded aboard earlier, lolled their way off, listless and moody. Their bus was
waiting in the parking lot. Behind it was supposed to be
Rachel's borrowed car, Melody's new Honda, but it had
disappeared.

"Towed away," Captain Joe told her. "You shouldn't
never have parked it there." It was Tony who grudgingly
saved her, taking her to the towing company in his big
bouncing red truck, shifting carefully beside her, concen-
trating hard on providing a smooth ride, as if this ability
proved who he was. They rode a good two feet above anyone else in traffic and Rachel felt absurd.

"Your truck looks as if it's wearing braces," she said to
him conversationally. The grillwork was brutish, the music
on the tape player hostile.

At a red light, he calmly drove over the curb and green
parkway and sidewalk, so easily and gently, around the car
in front of him, and back down onto the cross street.
"That's what these tires are all about," he said with satisfac-
tion, as if Rachel had commented on their size. Perhaps he
understood that he was going to have to defend himself
with her, erect a few barriers in advance of her skepticism.
She looked behind them to see if anyone was outraged, if
the police were coming. Nothing. The clouds on the lush
mountain east of the city had continued to slide toward the
water. All these cheery negative ions, Rachel thought. Nobody blinked an eye when an upstart cheated and drove on
the grass.

She thanked him at the towing company parking lot,
reclaimed Melody's car, then spent half an hour rambling,
lost, through Santa Barbara. It should have been a simple
city to navigate, with its natural landmarks of mountain
and sea, but Rachel managed to require help, which came,

once more, in the form of a young man, one who worked at the Shell station not four blocks from her destination. It seemed to her she would be indebted to young men from now on. This was what it was to be almost forty years old.

*

Was it the drugs that made Melody so suddenly silly? The blow to the head? Was it only a matter of the speech impediment? Rachel had known her for fifteen years — they'd been married to brothers; their wedding anniversaries were only a few months apart — but now Melody seemed disturbingly adolescent and unfamiliar.

Tony was telling the two women a long anecdote from his day at work, and Melody was limp with laughter. Rachel smiled, though she felt her expression was a utilitarian one, signaling perplexity or indulgence as easily as it did appreciation of a good story.

"This old guy, I call him the bane of my existence, he's such a bastard, had like a hundred strokes or something, all hunched over" — here, Tony hooked forward like a vulture — "and he's eating these American cheese slices, you know, the kind you have to peel the wrapper off?" He peeled an imaginary wrapper from a slice of imaginary cheese, painstakingly slowly, his face pursed and squeezed like the mouth of a rubber balloon, his hands trembling in imaginary palsy. "Oh, this bastard loves his cheese. He comes every day to sit outside Captain Joe's and like make my life hell, cheese in every pocket. He pisses on the pier if I don't keep an eye on him, just like unzips and lets it fly, right in front of God and everybody. And he's always throwing cigarette butts at the seals and cussing at me. Shit. I give him hell too, though, I'll tell you. And he likes it, he keeps coming back, crazy fucking guy. Peels that cheese so slowly, today the gulls got hold of it before he was finished. He unwraps it and unwraps it, and before he can like get it to his mouth — I swear, you want to just scream, his tongue is out, he's salivating, the cheese is just flapping in his fingers, moving to his mouth, getting there like in slow motion, you can't believe how long it takes to get there — before he can pop it in, a sea gull snatches it away!" Tony clapped his hands. "Oh, you should have heard him wail on that bird: 'Goddamn you! Goddamn you!' I nearly bust a gut!"

Melody fell sideways on the bed laughing, snorting through her bandages. Rachel had somehow gotten herself involved in the story at two different, wrong places. First, she'd studied Tony as he told it, the way he could so admirably animate for Melody's enjoyment, and second, she'd identified with the old man trying to eat his cheese, thwarted by birds, not exactly missing the humor but coming upon it after the fact. Tony now scowled at her and she excused herself, leaving the two of them on the bed.

When the sun shone on her second Friday in Santa Barbara, Rachel returned to Captain Joe's and presented her raincheck. Tony, in his snow boots and shorts, shook a mop in her direction as she boarded the boat. She knew he was beginning to dislike her. Out into the Pacific they went, a load of senior citizens and Rachel and Captain Joe, who today had brought an infant in a backpack. Nothing can befall us, Rachel thought, if Captain Joe has his baby along. And indeed nothing befell them, not even a view of whales. They stayed out two and a half hours — the old people were wilted and burned — and saw nothing but a few sea lions and gulls. "Folks," Captain Joe said forlornly as they returned to the harbor, "this is only the second time this year Captain Joe's come up short concerning whales."

Rachel wanted to let him know it was her fault — she'd begun to feel connected to his business — but his baby was crying into his ear as he issued rainchecks, and he handed her one without appearing to recall that she'd been there before.

Tony remembered, of course. He followed her to the parking lot, his snow boots flapping along on the sidewalk. Since she'd been at Melody's, Tony had hardly spoken to her. When he was home, he stayed in his own room or sat on the waterbed with Melody. He slept late every morning, stumbling into and out of the kitchen and bathroom just minutes before he was due at the dock, leaving his boy's residue, soaked cornflakes and blond razor stubble, the lifted toilet lid. On his days off he disappeared in his boatlike truck, off with his friends, whom he had introduced to Rachel by what they drove ("This is Dave, he made himself a Land Cruiser through the mail, and this is J.B., just bought a 300zx, lucky fuck").

Looking at him now, fresh from having seen a few, Rachel thought he resembled a sea lion, with his wide-set small eyes, his bristly hair and fatty ridges above his ears, his thick upper body that showed no striking distinction between chest and skull, as if his head were a mere swelling of his thick neck.

He asked her how long she was planning on staying in town. "I might go live with Dad, if you're going to be here a while."

Melody's car had not been towed today. Rachel opened the door and wondered why his muscles offended her. Why must she always look at them and hate them? "I thought I'd stay till Melody's mobile." She spoke to his pectorals.

He performed a gesture she knew well from her own boys, an exasperated sigh that sent his weight to one foot, his face to the heavens. "But there's no *room* at Dad's," he said.

"I'm not asking you to leave. Stay. I just think Melody

could use the help, the company. This is a hard time for her." Rachel wondered if he would strike her if she suggested that he find a place of his own.

"I've been doing fine," he said. "*We've* been doing fine. You can go back to Chicago whenever you want." He put his hands on his hips, which would have seemed prissy had he not been so menacingly built. Rachel wanted him to reveal the source of his irritation. She was curious how things had been going before she arrived.

"Let's let Melody decide," Rachel said as she swung into the warm Honda.

At home, she could smell the presence of another person, the swath of medicinal air that cut the odor of bouquet like a scalpel.

"Tony?" Melody called out eagerly from the bedroom.

"Me," Rachel answered, trying not to be annoyed that Melody seemed to prefer seeing Tony. As far as Rachel could tell, he hadn't been as attentive as she was being, hadn't made soup or meals but had ordered pizza or brought home tacos, hadn't fetched books and magazines, hadn't spent hours discussing Dennis's childish insensitivity. And perhaps he had not changed Melody's underwear and shirts. Perhaps she had had to struggle into and out of clothing he merely left within reach. How could he possibly have been any use to her whatsoever?

It was Melody's nurse who had left the strange odor; she had come and removed the facial bandages. Melody sat in bed like a princess holding a hand mirror, studying herself. She did not look the way Rachel remembered — not from this morning, not from eighteen months ago, when she'd visited Chicago with Dennis. Melody seemed to have lost years with her accident, more than a few. The dewlap Rachel recalled was virtually gone, the face clean as if erased. But did a polite person say, "You look a hundred times better than you used to?"

"My new nose," Melody said clearly. "Te gusta?" She turned a profile unselfconsciously.

Rachel sat on the bed's edge and steadied herself in its rocking aftermath. She said, "You look wonderful."

"New nose. I had to have a plastic surgeon for my ear anyway so I figured, what the hell? Take a tuck, burn off a few moles, get myself another nose. All shined up like a new car. Bodywork." She reached behind her and twisted open the shades. "Still a little green around the gills, though." A mild turquoise shading colored the skin beneath her eyes and on her cheeks, along the lines of her brow, deep purple at the tear glands.

"Frankly, I can't remember your old nose."

"Well, it was bigger, with lumps." She touched her face tenderly. "I wish I could show Dennis, but I guess Tony will have to do."

"I'm here." Rachel hoped not to sound peevish, but Melody only laughed. Rachel added, "You don't see Dennis at all?"

"Not since the hospital. He came there because he thought it was his fault I'd been in an accident."

"Men are so self-centered, aren't they?" Rachel said. "The whole damn world revolves around them. Can you imagine *you* going to *his* hospital room and claiming responsibility for the car wreck that had left *him* in traction?"

"I thought it was sweet." Melody set down the mirror beside her and turned her attention from her own face to Rachel's. "You got a sunburn."

"No whales. Again."

"You see Tony?"

Rachel struggled off the bed without answering. Now

that Melody mentioned it, her face *did* feel hot, the back of her neck tight. At the bathroom mirror she pulled the soft loose skin behind her ears taut and studied the effect. After that, she broke off a piece of aloe vera, cracked its thick shell, and smeared the sticky cool pulp on her cheeks and throat.

*

If California was a woman, Rachel thought, then Illinois was a man, an old man with bad habits, Chicago his damaged yet still beating heart. She missed her city, its sour flabbiness. Here in Santa Barbara people drove clean new cars and knew the names of a thousand varieties of flowers, whereas Rachel was familiar with little more than the kindergarten prototypes, daisy and tulip. At Melody's house none of the books were literature, not even mysteries or cookbooks, but were field guides to the wilderness: birds, trees, rocks, mountains, hiking trails, boat tours. Even Tony, the boy who drove the hundred feet to the convenience store around the corner, the boy whose every third word was *like,* could identify every bush out back, every squawking bird.

At night they rented movies, Rachel and Tony prowling opposite ends of the bright and busy VideoLand. His choices had heroes who looked like him, their hairless flesh bulging with muscle, clips of ammo around their necks, righteous chins jutting toward nearly nude women clad invariably in red, white, and blue. Rachel supposed her video choices resembled her too — wistfully British with not much plot, everything colored khaki. Tony noisily wandered around the house during Rachel's movies, making phone calls, playing his music. If he watched, he complained of not being able to hear the dialogue. It was true; Rachel's actors often swallowed their lines. And they were frequently in, or near, tears, a tendency Tony wasted no time in pointing out. "Here's the crybaby scene," he would say. "Cry, baby, cry."

Melody would laugh with him, then lean around to apologize parenthetically to Rachel. Tony always leapt onto the bed beside Melody, plopping a big aluminum bowl of popcorn between them. He had randomly healthy impulses and doused the popcorn with brewer's yeast instead of salt. Rachel sat on the bed's edge, her feet on the floor. She came and went during Tony's movies, which were always the second feature, doing motherly things like putting away dishes, locking doors, turning off lights. Melody, the bedridden arbiter and judge, seemed more taken with Arnold Schwarzenegger than she did with dear earnest Jeremy Irons. Lying idly indoors probably gave her more time than she wanted to have her own psychological dramas.

On TV tonight the hero held a villain by the foot over a cliff, then dropped him. Back at the overturned red sportscar, his woman asked what had happened to the other fellow. "'I let him go,'" Tony said with the literal-minded hero, clapping his hands happily. To Melody he said, "Arnode, yoo're so cool."

To be honest, to be perfectly honest, Rachel herself was coming to prefer the high-action, low-credibility movies. The sunshine was doing this to her, that and living out of a suitcase, sleeping on a couch in her summer nightgown — the West Coast was rubbing off on her, like pollen. She stretched her legs out on Melody's covers. It was easy to surrender, to recline on the amniotic bed. Beside her, Tony brushed Melody's hair with a spiky tool. "I would never let my sons watch this," Rachel said, as she suspended disbelief as well as disdain, letting them go like balloons on a string, like a stern frown, and instead riding the swell of a stirring soundtrack. There was an appealing clarity to Tony's mov-

ies, their bright, primary-colored themes, their unfathom-
able budgets: all those exploded automobiles, the army of
expendable dead, the exhilarating breakage of pane after
pane of glass.

*

Her job in Chicago was housewife, and it did not bother
her the way it was supposed to. She'd had other jobs —
a short career as a social worker, another as a substitute
teacher, once as the leader of discussions of Great Books.
Basically, she had been hired to keep people "on task." It
had finally occurred to her that she could be doing that in
the comfort of her own home, and she quit. Now she took
classes, read magazines and novels, shopped, gave and went
to parties, transported and tended and took care of her
boys, kept them on task. Her husband was a pediatric
dentist, busy these days grooming a young partner so that
he could have more time off to spend with Rachel. He
wanted to take the boys over the summer to visit American
League baseball parks. Rachel was willing.

Her flexibility had made her seem the ideal companion
to nurse Melody back to health, but she saw, in her third
week in the bungalow, that this was not so. She depressed
Melody. She, Rachel, was not the family connection Melody wished to uphold.

On crutches, balanced on two little rubber stubs under
her long fluorescent green legs, Melody emerged at last
from bed and stood erect, saying apologetically, "I don't
want to keep you from your children . . ." And Rachel was
relieved that Tony was not home to smile smugly as tears
formed in her eyes. *Crybaby,* she scolded herself as she
phoned the airline. She considered saying things to hurt
Melody, using the ammunition of what she knew about
Dennis that Melody did not. She'd not seen him in Santa

Barbara, but she had expected to run into him and his new girlfriend, whose existence Rachel never doubted, despite there being no mention of it. There had been other affairs. Dennis called his brother, Rachel's husband, often, to discuss them, to express his remorse. Her husband always prescribed fidelity and therapy, and though Dennis liked receiving this advice, he never followed it.

"I'm really, really glad you came," Melody pleaded from the door. "I don't know what I would have done without you."

*

On her last night in California, Rachel, swallowing and gasping, wakened from a dream of drowning. She looked to her neatly packed suitcase for comfort, her folded blouses and satin slip. Someone had closed his legs around her as she'd swum between them, trapping her, killing her. She'd thought they were playing a game. Open-mouthed, anxious, she breathed in the humid air of the living room, which seemed to threaten also to close around her.

Besides her own heart, which throbbed in her ears, she heard the rhythmic bump of something else in the house, something she identified immediately as Melody's enormous headboard, moving against the wall under the weight of sex, with the accrued power of waves. Proof was what Rachel had wanted all along, she now understood, proof of a darkness she had sought, had known.

She waited, unable not to imagine Tony's large naked boy's body hurling itself against his stepmother in the unnatural blue light and static of the television. Rachel literally had to swallow in order not to exclaim; she was drowning once more. His force, she feared, would shatter Melody, break apart the bones so recently repaired, so carefully tended by Rachel, patted and coddled. What they were doing was dangerous, absolutely forbidden. She squeezed her eyes shut, rolled her face into the rough nap of the couch, braced herself against the more amazing possibility that it was this, dispensed so violently, that might heal Melody.

*

Hadn't California promised Rachel a whale? On her last day in Santa Barbara, she fled Melody's house to redeem her raincheck. At the pier, she saw the old man Tony had told them about, perched like a buzzard on a bench, dragging a cigarette slowly from his mouth. Tony, a few feet away beside Captain Joe's shack, lifted his head for a moment to look in her direction, unforthcoming, indecipherable. She watched his shoulders as he worked, stocking sodas in a mottled metal cooler, the wet bottles dwarfed by his hands as they slid into the slush. His presence sent a chill through her; she figured she could manage never to see him again, discard her aunthood just like that. Same for Melody, good-bye, goodbye. She would share no kinship with them anymore. She would have the length of her airplane trip today to decide whether or not to tell her husband what she had learned. She was entitled, was she not, to her secrets?

The boat puttered away from the dock, Rachel sitting this time in the front (aft? she wondered, bowsprit?), her face to the damp air, reassured by the now familiar routine. Over the public address system, Captain Joe told the story of the gray whale, dispelling any hope on the part of the teenagers aboard that they would see anything hazardous, hammerhead sharks or killer whales. Strictly browns and grays, the legion of the ordinary.

The water was choppy, its glassy surface fractured in many small parts, like panes in a wide, undulant window. The wind blew, clouding the million mirrors the way breath will always do. When the breeze died, the water shone and the boat drifted, its ride nearly equestrian. Rachel had adjusted herself to its cant, bumping along distractedly. She wondered if it was really disgust she felt toward Melody, if that was the pesky emotion swimming around in her. Or was it envy, the self-pitying variety?

When the whale finally emerged beside them — first the dappled back and then, like an exclamation mark, the erect fluke — Rachel gasped at its proximity, clutching her arms as if threatened. Captain Jack yelped into his microphone, "Here's us a honey! This one's a gray, a young male, probably with his pals, maybe another male and a young cow. Oh he's playing with us, folks, watch how he'll come up nearby and then circle back to surprise us!"

Rachel stared hard, everywhere. She'd not brought her sunglasses today so had to squint at the white-tipped water. The whale's hide had been speckled with the parasitic barnacles Captain Joe had talked about, which were white and scaly like bird guano, and which would increasingly cover the animal as it matured. Nature was ugly, she thought, and nothing like what you saw of it on PBS.

Farther out, the whale appeared again, rolling its back toward the boat as if enticing them to follow, then was gone, leaving what Captain Joe called footprints, valentine-shaped smooth places in the water. She wasn't going to see a whole whale. She would have to content herself with patchy little glimpses, with the fact of the beast beneath her in his thick wobbling sea. "He's toying with us!" Captain Joe crooned gaily.

"Ahhh!" said the crowd. Fingers shot out, a video camera panned back and forth.

Off the coast of her known country, bobbing around in an ocean that was itself a vast habitat, Rachel watched without moving. She had no choice but to defer: a young boy-creature would break this world open before her.

THE WRITTEN WORD

———— /////// ————

THIS MORNING DAVID AND BEN'S STEPFATHER SHAVED his face and put on his uniform. It was his annual late August ritual, performed the first day of classes at the college where he was employed as head of the department of criminal justice. His uniform, the boys had just grasped this year, was a generic one, unaffiliated with a branch either civilian or military. "A rent-a-cop," David, the eldest, deduced. Still, that did not make his stepfather's presence this morning less governmental, his scoured yellow face atop the stiff blue starched corners of his costume less brutal, or the heavy college badge with its Latin words — an obscure message of threat — less menacing. He was what he appeared to be: officially hardhearted.

It was the Texas custom, and despite the fact that they'd been raised in permissive California, the boys complied: they called him Sir, though his name was Marshall. Anyway, David thought, there was hardly a difference between Sir and Marshall, was there? At the breakfast table Marshall breathed loudly through his nose as he ate, shoveling in cold cereal along with the boys while their mother sat on the edge of her chair feeding the baby, who was eight months old. "Reading matter," Marshall had declared when David and Ben and their mother moved in two years before, "will not come to the eating table." The boys were accustomed to comic or coloring books, to the clattery spread of a big newspaper. But here the four of them sat, waiting for the baby to make noise. She was the only one allowed to say precisely what she felt like saying. Even their mother, after a cheerful honeymoon and a whirlwind of redecorating, after her long pregnancy and stoic delivery of the unusually large girl (twelve pounds, six ounces), seemed to have given up trying to strike compromises between what her boys wanted and what Marshall would accept. "I was married to your father long enough to realize that security can be its own reward," she told David and Ben. This new home was nothing if not secure.

Marshall at last pushed his chair away and stood, fist to his mouth to cover a burp. His cheeks, beginning to show the vague tracks of razor burn, puffed to contain the air. "Adios and good day," he told the room, laying his hand on the baby's big bald head before he went out the door.

*

The baby's soft spot was a large indented diamond that pulsed beneath a thin layer of scabbed skin like the steadfast heart of an alligator. David wondered what would happen if the spot were punctured. Would she die? Would air from her brain escape? He put his finger lightly to her skull to feel her tangible heart, the throb that meant she lived. She herself — huge and shrill and strong, her face a rubber mask of anger and delight — seemed daunted by nothing. She was so fat she could not find balance on her own and frequently listed sideways, never completely falling because the folds of her heavy flesh prevented it. Upright, she resembled a stack of plastic ring toys, designed to be immovable. Monster, David and Ben called her when Marshall was not at home.

Their mother they had learned to circumnavigate, her presence becoming less and less of this world. The baby's head already eclipsed hers — it was as if the child were feeding off her like something parasitic, flourishing while she, the host, dwindled. Nowadays she had difficulty lifting Rosalie and wandered around the house always with a slight limp, palm pressed to her lower back.

When Marshall's car could be heard — roaring unnecessarily, then gliding away — and then not, their mother also rose from the table and stood before the open refrigerator, contemplating its contents. "Why is it," she said without turning, "that no matter how much food I buy, there's never anything to eat?" Her bathrobe was a man's, too long for her and torn at the hem. David stared at the bits of hair and dust and Cheerios that clung to the fringe, wondering if his father, in California, had given her his robe or if she'd stolen it. Suddenly she slammed the refrigerator door and began crying, scurrying from the kitchen and down the hall to her bedroom, whose door she also slammed.

The boys looked at each other. David, who was twelve, wondered if this was reason enough for him and Ben to stay home from school. Who would watch the baby if their mother was crying in her room? Ought they to call Marshall's office and leave a message?

Ben, as if reading his brother's thoughts, spoke up. "I have a cursive writing test today. I can't miss it or he'll kill me." *He* was Marshall, whose fixation on the boys' grades was such that even they had become removed from their initial fear and cast into a state of mind more objective and curious: what made a simple A, when applied to their efforts at school, so superior to the other letters, B, C, D, and F?

"It's cool," David said. "I can handle her."

"I'll be home for lunch," Ben answered, standing to leave. "I can stay after lunch." They both now watched the baby, who had been steadily picking individual Kix from her tray and dropping them over the side. She did not ordinarily settle on small chores like this; she had, usually, a taste for the more chaotic. Ben's standing had caused her to lose her train of thought. Startled, her hands flew out and she made a contorted face at him, half smile, half shriek. Her legs came up and banged the chrome table rim. Ben edged around her chair as if afraid she would reach out to try to stop him. First he went to their mother's bedroom door and listened, shrugging his shoulders at David, and then he exited through the front door.

*

David listened at her bedroom door too, hearing absolutely nothing. The house, low on a flat plot of ground, did not disguise the lives of others in it. Words could be heard through walls, movement felt across floors. Sometimes their mother would call to Ben and David to make noise so that she would know they were alive. On a normal day she played the radio, listening for the emergency broadcast signal. How else, she had asked David, would she know of a disaster?

David wondered if she might be dead in her room, or in her small pink bathroom. He quietly tried the door handle, hoping it was locked, relieved to find it so. "Mom," he said, "I'm still here. I'll watch Rosalie, but you have to write me a note for school."

He wasn't sure, but he thought he heard a noise of acquiescence, a sniffle or squeaking spring, a drawer sneaking shut, something that meant she was breathing and grateful. A few minutes later he had diapered and dressed his half-sister, coated her thick arms and face and head with sunscreen until she gleamed like a white waxed fruit, stinking of essence of orange. Then he stood outside his mother's bedroom door once more, hesitant to investigate. "We're going for a walk," he finally said.

*

His mother had pictures in her night table drawer, naked photographs that David recognized from their old home in California, pictures that he'd never bothered to study until they were hidden away here in Texas. In order to get to them you had to pull out a piece of plywood beneath his mother's scarves, a false bottom to the drawer. There they were, a thick manila envelope full, with two buttons and a string to secure it. Inside, there appeared to be one of everything, all in black-and-white: a man on top of a woman, a man on top of another man. Two women with their legs clamped scissorlike around each other, two men and one woman like a sandwich, a man holding his penis like a big firehose. A closeup of fat breasts with no head or legs. A pile of nude people all with their mouths open, waiting for somebody to stick something in.

The photos were arranged in an order whose logic David could not discern, ending, unaccountably and always disarmingly, with the picture of a scowling rat, nothing titillating about it. He borrowed them as often as he could, replacing them with such precision he was afraid they would be noticeably too perfect. Their power frightened him — not only what the pictures could make happen inside him, but what their constant presence in the house did to him. He wanted to stare at them every minute; he felt sometimes he could actually press one against his body and achieve release. Or maybe eat one of them. He could not tire of them, they were new every time. It was with real reluctance that he would realize, now and then, that his mother must also look at them, must also somehow make use of them. He tried to believe they were Marshall's, but he knew — he could see them in his mind's eye tossed casually on his father's desk in San Francisco — they were hers. Unbidden, he would sometimes think of her, hand busy beneath the blanket, and a thing more powerful would overtake him, a thing so dark and sinful and inhuman he would later cry in fear for his nasty soul. He would have thrown them out, but to do so would be to let his mother know he looked at them.

He could not believe he would amount to anything redeemable, though it was a fact hidden from everyone else. Everyone, it seemed, except Marshall.

But Rosalie liked him, and she consented to being taken out in her stroller. The air was clotted with heat and moisture; the noise of lingering summer insects made thinking impossible. David was beginning to forget the short weeks he had spent that summer with his father at the Pacific Ocean, he was beginning to forget that he had been laughing then, laughing so hard and so desperately his ribs hurt and he was blind. His time there had flown by effortlessly, as if he'd napped through his visit. And then at the airport he'd dared to ask if he could stay, if he could stay in his old home, in his room where you could still see rectangles of missing plaster from when he'd yanked posters from the wall, and his father had flinched — just a minor jerk, as if a tiny bug had flown up his nose — and told

David his home was in Texas. This scene was one David would have liked to forget; it made his palms wet to think of it.

He pushed Rosalie quickly down the street, cutting through the dense terrarium-like atmosphere as if he might break out of it, as if he were in a plastic bag. Dogs did not bark this morning. People stayed inside breathing air conditioner air. David felt alien to the neighborhood on a school day; he felt under suspicion by the drivers of cars, who cruised along with their windows tightly sealed. He was a kidnapper, stealing an ugly fat child for ransom. He was a pervert, taking a baby to perform the unspeakable upon her. No one would assume the truth, David thought, that he was a good boy, walking the baby so his mother could rest, so that she could be entirely alone.

And then he thought, *Ransom.* It was a word like any other, but when played long enough in his mind it lost meaning and jangled there like a discordant and foreign sound, a sound like a monkey or hyena might make in a jungle. *Ransom, ransom, ransom.* You could *say* words, and they might be nonsense. But if you wrote them down . . .

He had a plan before he knew he was constructing one, excited now, speeding down El Paseo Boulevard without watching for turning cars, fording the puddled driveways and soaking Rosalie's feet. She rotated her fat arms like propellers. She was a robust, hearty child who loved action; her favorite toy was an old jack-in-the-box of David's which sprang on exposed rusty wires, its painted leering face chipped and grotesque. As a child, the family legend went, David had cried when it was sprung on him. But Rosalie, when distraught, annoyed, or bored, could be brought to life with the jack-in-the-box. Just grinding the lever, producing the wobbly menacing tune of "Pop Goes the Weasel," made her clap in anticipation. Then out would slam the devilish clown with his smile made of fangs: she'd laugh and laugh.

He would kidnap his sister and send Marshall a note. While he and Rosalie dashed pell-mell along the road, headed nowhere in particular, David saw himself typing up his demands: five hundred dollars left in a paper bag, or else. Or else what? he wondered. Obviously he could not hurt her, but there was a distinct pleasure in pondering what he might threaten. He would tape a knot of her hair to the note, just to make it real. He would type it at school, after three, when the janitors left the annex doors open. His homeroom teacher, Mr. Torres, never stayed after three; he watched the clock with the rest of the class, leaping when the buzzer sounded, as eager as they to flee. It was Mr. Torres David thought he would miss most, after Ben and, he supposed, Rosalie. Mr. Torres encouraged his students to write poems about their sadness, and though David never got further than "I feel sad because," he still thought Mr. Torres understood him better than most grownups.

David would take his five hundred dollars in ransom money and buy an airline ticket to San Francisco, to his old life, one way.

*

All morning as they wandered through the San Antonio suburbs David skirted the problem of how to deliver the note. He knew what would happen before, he had some hope for what might happen after, but the carrying-out, the part in between, he still had to consider fully.

Rosalie was tired of dashing around the streets. They met Ben at his grade school and accompanied him home for lunch.

"How's Mom?" he asked.

David had forgotten his mother's odd behavior until Ben brought it up. "I don't know. Stop chewing until we get home."

Ben was gnawing his left hand, something he'd started doing just a couple of weeks before, when school began. He claimed it itched and only his teeth helped. There was a rash, a shiny purple bruise like a plum in the webbing. He saved his right hand, though, for writing. His classmates called him Mandible. Already he was weird, and he had so many years of school left to go.

"You don't have to stay home this afternoon," David told him as they entered the quiet house. It still smelled of morning, coffee and wet towels. Nothing had been disturbed. There was no idle radio chatter. They whispered as they made bologna sandwiches, though Rosalie crowed loudly, balanced in the middle of the kitchen floor, surrounded by green peas and bright julienne beets, small edibles she would not choke on.

"That guy Ray called me a homo again at tornado drill," Ben reported to David. David sighed. He would have to go after school sometime in the next few days and throw Ray on the ground. He'd done it last week, but it didn't seem to have made a big enough impression. In San Francisco David had taken judo lessons in the center down the block from their old home. He could dance around as if he knew how to destroy someone, though his parents had divorced before he graduated from yellow belt.

Without their mother there to tell them to sit, they stood to eat their food. Only after they'd finished — glugging milk from the carton, spitting into Marshall's jar of olives, feeding Rosalie a lime slice just to watch her pucker — did David see the folded card on the kitchen table.

It was a small pink card reading, in his mother's handwriting, *Please excuse David's absence yesterday, he was ill,* followed by her signature. He didn't need this note until tomorrow, but David understood that he was to watch Rosalie for the remainder of the day. "Lucky," Ben said, exhaling. David poked the paper into his jeans pocket.

Before Ben returned to school, both boys tiptoed down the dark hallway once more to listen at their mother's door. All they could hear was their own breathing, the scratch of their hair against the thin plywood, and Rosalie complaining at having been left by herself on the kitchen floor.

*

The last bell found David and Rosalie behind the 7-Eleven across the street from David's middle school. She chewed a packaged oatmeal cookie David had bought to silence her. The school building emptied; kids began lining up outside the 7-Eleven doors, because only three of them at a time were allowed inside. When his homeroom annex appeared vacant, its door propped open, David quickly wheeled Rosalie across the street and over the sandy yard. Given a choice, he would rather his friends did not see him with the baby, though once he'd run into a few of the girls from his class at the mall while he was sitting with Rosalie, waiting for his mother to come out of a bathroom. The girls had thought Rosalie was sweet. They each took a turn holding her. He was more popular with them afterward, as if they had discovered he had a cute hidden weakness for babies.

Mr. Torres had left the door open for the janitors. David pulled Rosalie up the five steps in her stroller and parked her in front of the aquarium while he uncovered the typewriter on Mr. Torres's desk. On notebook paper he typed *We have your baby.* He looked over at her. She was falling asleep, her fleshy face slumped against the metal stroller frame so that her mouth pooched open like a change purse, her half-closed eyes rolling. On her lap she still held the oatmeal cookie, still wrapped, a sack of crumbs and loose raisins. Assuming he managed to deliver the note, what was he going to do with her while he went home to wait for the ransom money? He needed an assistant, and as if in answer to this need, ZoBell Bussey suddenly appeared.

She clutched her throat when she saw him. "You scared me," she said angrily, crossing the room to her desk. ZoBell probably weighed more than Mr. Torres, but she was not the typical placid fat girl. She had a terrible temper and everyone was afraid of her. David had decided that his sister Rosalie might turn out to be a fat girl, and if she did he would prefer her to be like ZoBell rather than a docile cow.

"What are you staring at, cretin?" ZoBell demanded. She'd begun rampaging through her desk, slamming books onto the seat from the messy cavern. "You stealing something?"

David pointed to his sister, as if Rosalie might defend him.

ZoBell found what she was looking for — a five-dollar bill — and banged her desk lid down. She now rounded the row of seats to the fish tank, where Rosalie still slept in her stroller, as slack as a bag of potatoes.

"What's wrong with her head?"

David didn't know whether ZoBell meant the shape, which was slightly rhomboid with a caboose, or the texture, which on top was reptilian. This was a condition that his mother called cradle cap but that David and Ben referred to as "crib rot."

ZoBell said, "Looks like major eczema. Heartbreak of psoriasis."

"Babies get it," David told her.

"No duh." ZoBell rolled her freckled eyes at him. Watching her fold the five-dollar bill into a tiny square in her fat palm gave David an idea.

"I'll pay you fifty dollars to do me a favor," he said.

ZoBell, victim of many cold-blooded pranks, frowned at him. She moved her lower lip while she listened, curling it back and forth over her upper lip. David quickly explained his plan, ending with his justification. "My stepfather's horrible. I hate him."

ZoBell settled on the top of the last desk in the row and propped her feet on the seat. Her toes, through the plastic strap of her sandal, were as big as thumbs, and under each toenail was a sliver of black gunk. She said, "I hated my stepfather too."

"'Hated'?"

"My mom divorced him. Your mom might divorce yours."

"She might." But he doubted it. She'd already divorced somebody, somebody nothing at all like Marshall.

ZoBell said, "Nobody's going to have five hundred dollars just laying around the house."

David sat on the desk across from her, Rosalie, asleep, between them. "He has a cash machine card."

"There's two hundred."

"He keeps money in his wallet."

"O.K. Three hundred."

Suddenly David did not have the energy for his plan. In a second he had become as sleepy as Rosalie. Just talking to ZoBell had begun depressing him. He'd never talked to her before. Everyone was afraid of her, even Mr. Torres, who, though goodhearted and seemingly intelligent, nevertheless spoke English with a faint accent that ZoBell had made clear she found fault with.

But kidnapping the baby appealed to ZoBell, and it was she who finished typing the ransom note David had begun. In it, she explained how four hundred dollars could be extracted from the bank if both David's mother and step-father went to separate cash machines and took out two hundred each at the precise same moment.

David had to admire her genius. And her typing, which was without error. But he hesitated in leaving Rosalie in her care.

"I babysit all the time," she told him, pushing the stroller out the door. Watching her, he didn't doubt it. He'd never before today identified what, besides her largeness, was so peculiar about her looks, but now he understood: she wore grown-up clothes — shiny blouses and stretchy pants, dirty silver plastic sandals.

Mr. John, the janitor, was approaching when they left the annex. He was retarded and knew everybody's name. Upon seeing them, he began singing, "David and ZoBell sitting in a tree, K-I-S-S-I —"

"Shut up!" ZoBell commanded him, but David was busy wondering whether Mr. John would qualify as a witness.

*

Rosalie was still sleeping when ZoBell wheeled her south while David headed north, toward home. There were only a handful of people in the world who were ever happy to see David, really happy, and he was letting one of them ride off with a virtual stranger. David couldn't figure what had gotten into him.

He ran in order to lose his wind, stopping at the front porch only long enough to tuck the folded ransom note beneath a rock. Marshall would find it when he went to retrieve the evening paper. Otherwise, no one ever used the front door.

David then dashed around back and burst into the kitchen. "Mom, Mom, Mom!" he yelled as he flew down the hall. He pounded on her bedroom door. "Rosalie's gone! Someone took Rosalie!"

The door sailed open, his mother on the other side of it looking frightful. "What are you saying?" she asked him.

"Rosalie was stolen!"

His mother was on the phone before David could finish telling his story. Soon Marshall appeared, then the police. David sat at the kitchen table among them, shaking, crying, repeating his tale over and over, launched into a kind of hysteria that made him believe himself. He could see himself falling asleep at the park, Rosalie sleeping in her stroller beside him, himself waking up an hour later to find her gone.

The two officers talking to David were former students of Marshall's and kept looking nervously at him as they took down what David said. After they'd finished with his account, they requested a photograph from his mother, who still wore her bathrobe. The picture she gave them was on a coffee cup. They'd had it taken at the mall: Rosalie in a bright pink dress with a bow taped to her bald head. It looked nothing like she had looked today.

"Well," the white cop said, holding the cup out in front of him, "why don't we make a tour of that park?"

The black cop nodded. "Shall we all go, sir?" he asked Marshall. "You and your son?"

David's head cleared for a moment when he heard the word *son* and he almost corrected the cop, then was glad he hadn't. Marshall would not stop staring at him, his left eye twitching closed the way it did when he was thinking hard. He alone would expect David to have orchestrated a kidnapping.

Only after he'd climbed into the squad car and fastened his belt did David remember there was a ransom note on the front walk. Marshall, of course, had foregone retrieving the newspaper this evening. Before he'd left, he told David's mother to keep off the telephone, that someone might call.

David turned and looked over his shoulder at the receding yard of Marshall's house. Marshall was sitting in the front with the black cop while David shared the back with the white one, who reached over and shook David's knee, smiling at him. "We'll find her," he said.

"Anybody you know of might want to get at you?" the black cop asked Marshall, then added, "Sir."

Marshall said, "As you are aware, my students have strong feelings concerning me, both bad and good. But this was not a premeditated abduction; the child is not typically at the park under the care of her brother. This was an impulse, and I expect our finding her will be a matter of expediency and luck."

David's heart picked up speed again. Marshall, in his usual way, had complicated things considerably.

*

At the park David selected a large shade tree as his napping spot. Beneath it was a brown and white wrapper from a Snickers bar, which he cited as his lunch. Already a new plan had begun to take shape in his mind. He would call ZoBell and tell her everything was off; the ransom note still waited under the rock, safely undiscovered. ZoBell would return Rosalie, claiming she'd found the baby unattended at the park. Her stroller could have rolled away from David while he was sleeping under the tree.

"No baby carriage tread here," the black cop reported. The white cop made David lift his shoe sole for a check.

"Are you sure this is your tree?" he asked kindly.

"Where is she?" Marshall suddenly demanded. He took hold of David's shoulders and stared him deep in the eyes. "Come on, enough of this. Where's your sister?" Marshall's face had tiny pits and pores. He was ugly and harsh. He loved Rosalie and he might, someday, love Ben. But he would never love David, no matter what David promised, no matter how upstanding his grades. These things became evident to David in the length of time his stepfather glared at him.

"I want to go to San Francisco," David told him, blinking hard as tears began streaming down his face. "I can't stand it here!" he shouted suddenly. "I hate it! I hate it! And I hate you! I want my dad, my real dad!"

Marshall blinked wildly, his eyes like flashing sparklers. "Am I to understand this as *blackmail?* You mean to tell me you'll give me Rosalie, your *sister,* if I send you to San Francisco?" He turned to the two cops, seeming to remember their presence. "Take us home, please," he said to them, then marched to the car, tilted forward as if biting through the air in front of him.

*

"It's my fault," David's mother said as they sat at the kitchen table waiting for Marshall to return with Rosalie. Ben, who'd bought the kidnapping story as quickly as the adults had, was furious with David for not letting him in on it. He'd cried when he thought Rosalie had been stolen; now it embarrassed him. His mother had handed him the phone receiver so he could hear his sister screeching at ZoBell Bussey's house, alive and well.

David's mother had gotten dressed in green jeans and a T-shirt with an enormous tomato on the front of it. She'd put on makeup and wound her hair into a bun. The two policemen had offered to stay with her while Marshall went to pick up the baby, but Marshall had sent them on their way. The black cop had tried to say something to David — what? he wondered now — but Marshall had more or less pushed them out the door. They still had the coffee cup with Rosalie's picture on it in their car.

David's mother said, "I should have made it clear to you a long time ago, David. Your father doesn't want you to live with him. He's having a different life now. Sometime he'll tell you about it, but it just doesn't include you. Except for a week now and then."

"I hate Marshall," David said. Saying it once had made it easy to say it again and again.

"But so what?" his mother said. "I mean, I'm sorry you do, but what can we do about it?"

"Divorce him?" Ben said softly, as if guessing at answers.

"And then we have nothing," their mother said. She motioned for them to join her, to scoot their chairs closer to hers. When they had done so, she put an arm around each. "This is your life," she told them confidentially.

*

But Marshall sent David away. Four days later David was flying over Texas admiring the patchwork below him, on his way to San Francisco. He'd got what he wanted, but of course this wasn't at all the way it should have been. The woman sitting beside him was returning home to Chihuahua, Mexico, from Chicago, where she had entered the $15 million lottery for her whole neighborhood. She hadn't won. In front of David sat a gray-haired man holding up sheets of color slides. David stared at the pictures until they came clear to him. They were of a human hand cut open, the skin held splayed by pins, the internal workings exposed as cleanly as the inside circuitry of a telephone receiver. The gray-haired man pressed the sheet to the small plane window, studying the slides without any sign of emotion, pausing to take a drink from his grapefruit juice. David leaned forward to see better. It was a small hand, a child's hand, belonging to someone Ben's age or younger, still chubby at the wrist. David looked at his own hand. The woman beside him reached over and patted his leg. "No look at that," she said, smiling with lips like a camel's as she wagged a finger at him. "No very nice." For a second David thought of the pictures he'd stolen from his mother's bed table drawer, the ones hidden away deep in the airplane's baggage compartment with the rest of David's things. He'd found himself unable to leave San Antonio without them.

At the airport Ben had made jokes about bombs despite the written warnings everywhere, and David's mother had had to give him a swat just before David's plane was boarding. Rosalie had stayed at home with Marshall. "We could all go to San Francisco," David had proposed softly at his gate. His mother smiled, teary and sad, and shook her head.

"Call me," she told him. Ben got to go on board to receive plastic wings, to check out David's seat, and to leave a folded piece of notebook paper in the pocket in front of David.

Over Phoenix, David opened the paper. BOMB ON BOARD, it read, in Ben's perfect penmanship. He'd been getting nothing but A's. The passenger beside David, not the woman who'd lost the lottery but the tall woman in the suit who'd boarded in El Paso, gave a gasp. Before he could say anything, she'd poked the button, and the flight attendant had taken the note from David without listening to his explanation. When the captain's voice came over the public address system, David's stomach turned. They were already circling back toward Phoenix.

He anticipated, somehow, a hundred variations of uniform, a session in a closed windowless room, phone calls across the country. There were going to be papers to sign. He had had in mind something so simple — his old family sitting around a table full of food and happy bottles, or down at Moon Bay dashing about on the sand — but the rules of the world conspired against him thoroughly. It was the confusion that would thwart him, the distance between what he could imagine and what he could execute. That, and just plain old bad luck. Once upon a time his luck had been good, back when he too was good.

HER SECRET LIFE

//////

—— //////// ——

ZITA HAS BEEN STALKED BY CANDY REEVES EVER SINCE Volkswagen introduced the Vanagon, since the New Age, since Boy George came and went, since the public debut of AIDS. It has been ten years, eight of them married ones for Zita, married to Tom, whose romance with Candy lasted only six months. Zita has been stalked by Tom's former girlfriend for longer than the marriage and the six-month mistaken relationship combined.

Now the dreaded Candy has finally moved to Los Angeles, far enough away from Chicago for Zita to believe the siege is over. "The reign of terror ends," Tom has said, but neither of them ever felt terror. There was impatience, exasperation, pity, sheer awe, perverse flattery, and flat bewilderment, but never terror. Finally Candy is gone, has driven off in her red Vanagon like Zita and Tom's red Vanagon, taking her rottweiler like their rottweiler, wearing the clothes Zita once sold to the Twice Around resale shop on West Howard, undoubtedly chattering gibberish to the two-year-old daughter who was born the same year Tom and Zita's son was born, moving to a city neither Tom nor Zita has ever spent more than the length of an airplane layover in.

*

Zita and Tom fell in love during an election year in a graduate seminar on political campaigns. For their first project, the two of them followed a charismatic, irascible Republican state senate candidate named Buzz for a month as he stumped through Kansas. His platform made them cringe: he objected to a number of things that had recently been fundamental in one or the other of their lives, such as abortion, food stamps, and recreational drugs, but they both came to like the man himself enormously.

Wearing a green John Deere cap, Buzz flew a tiny airplane from town to town, using the campaign as an opportunity to practice his flying skills and hunt quail. Zita's classmate Tom was of a generation unsure how to approach women, but Buzz exerted his good-old-boy manners without apology or abashment. He also knew that both Tom and Zita were unsympathetic to his campaign, yet held no hard feelings, picking up the tab whenever the three of them happened to eat together, opting against political discussions, choosing to tell war or hunting stories instead. Buzz always pressed palms around whatever greasy spoon he inevitably chose, politicking in a down-home style that made Tom crazy but that Zita considered kind of endearing. Buzz's conservatism reminded her of her father, who could no longer speak as a result of a number of strokes. His debilitation had undermined Zita's leftist tendencies, as if her latest rebellion were somehow responsible for her father's illness.

It was Zita's car that she and Tom drove all over Kansas that fall, her little orange VW Karmann Ghia, already a rusting relic in 1982. She and Tom had met a few weeks earlier, when the semester at the University of Kansas had begun. They were matched when they both volunteered to pursue right-wing candidates, Tom because he liked to argue, Zita because of her father. Plus the professor wanted some gender-specific responses to each campaign.

Zita was involved with three different men at the time: one she lived with, one she corresponded with, who was on sabbatical in Portugal, and one a married man she'd slept with only a single night but who wouldn't leave her alone. She spent a good deal of the driving time between towns considering what to do about her love life, preoccupied so thoroughly that Tom periodically had to warn her of tailgating or speeding.

She loved to talk about her dilemma, and since Tom never spoke unless she asked him a direct question, she told him everything. She was twenty-two, only marginally interested in the graduate program she'd opted for at the last possible moment, and fretted endlessly about the scenario should all three of her lovers somehow meet. She kept looking at her face in the Volkswagen's vibrating rearview mirror: did she look love-torn and haggard yet?

"The one in Portugal is the one I really like best," she told Tom, "but he's thirty years older than I am, and that's a problem, I can't deny it. The married one I used to like, but I think he was a forbidden-fruit kind of thing, and the guy I live with, I live with just to help me get over the one I really like, in Portugal. You know?"

Tom frowned. He was thirty, divorced, returning to graduate school after working for NASA and finding the space program without ethics. He'd taken a cut in pay and prestige, and he intended to get as much from the university as possible. In all pursuits, he was serious. He had already played around in career and in love; his expression worried Zita, as it seemed to her that he was more upset by her entanglements than she was, and that made her wonder if she shouldn't be more tormented.

At night they slept in separate motel rooms, Zita placing intrastate and transatlantic phone calls into the wee hours. Her lover in Portugal, thirty years older and wiser than she, enjoyed long Zen-like silences on the telephone, the maddening white noise crackling between them as Zita tried not to track the minute hand on her watch while it made its costly little sweep. The one in Lawrence, with whom she shared a house, would recite gas and water bills, relate to her the antics of their cat, Freud. And the married man insisted she phone him at his office, only on Tuesday or Thursday, when he stayed late. He would masturbate as she spoke, a practice Zita couldn't identify her feelings about.

She didn't know that at the same time, Tom was talking to his girlfriend, Candy, every night. The difference was that instead of Tom phoning her, Candy had to ferret out his whereabouts and place the call. She sometimes threatened to kill herself if he didn't promise not to fall in love with Zita.

"I was already in love with you," he told Zita three weeks later, on the election night when Buzz won the right to retain his seat in the senate by a narrow margin, the same night Zita and Tom celebrated as if they'd voted for the man, toasting him earnestly as they guzzled sweet champagne, as if they'd been converted, the same night they decided to share a motel room and queen-size bed in Topeka, the state capital, rather than drive the twenty-nine miles home.

*

In the spring after Candy's departure for L.A., Zita is responsible for a car accident she and her two-year-old son, Leo, have on Lake Shore Drive. Their Vanagon hits a piece of ice no larger than a carpet runner; they are sent spinning through two lanes of traffic, their boxy vehicle swept off its wheels by centrifugal force, skidding on its left side into the median. During the accident, the great whirling sickness of it, Zita believes she and Leo will die, then understands that only she will die and that Leo and Tom will have to go on without her, and finally comes to think — all this within the few seconds of her horrifying revolution — that Candy will return to Chicago and take up with Tom once more. Oh, she can so vividly see the scene, the two little toddlers clinging to Tom's and Candy's knees.

Then there's silence, and then Leo's shriek, finally catching up, like a bad dub job, with his open mouth and red face and lusty lungs. They are fine, Zita and Leo, wobbly but fine, and what sticks with Zita, after everything is swept up, hauled away, signed for, and hammered out, is the image she had of her husband and Candy during what she had no reason not to believe were her final moments on this earth.

She is in the habit of telling Tom everything — he knows, for example, that she occasionally has fantasies about other men, that she now and then shoplifts — but she does not tell him this.

*

Zita and Tom had come off the campaign trail ecstatic and chagrined: so many others to pacify — the professor due home soon from Portugal, the problematic roommate, the married man, and the pathological Candy.

Tom lived in an apartment he'd chosen specifically for its smallness: he didn't want Candy to think there would be room for her to move in. Candy lived in a dorm on the hill as a resident associate, someone the freshmen girls were to take their problems to. Zita lived in an old house downtown divided into four apartments, hers and McFarland's the upstairs rear. The place had mice and roaches, faulty heating and plumbing, but Zita loved it. The rooms were painted bright colors — yellow for the bedroom, orange for the kitchen, a turquoise study, and black-and-white-striped wallpaper in the bath — and all had long thin windows looking down into a yard crisscrossed by brick paths that led through gardens now run to weeds, and a carriage house in the rear where a crank who made animated movies using Play-Doh lived.

For a few weeks after the election nobody knew about Tom and Zita's romance. Later this turned out to be Zita's favorite time of the relationship. Its secrecy excited her, the way they met at clandestine places so that nobody involved would ever see them, especially Candy or any of Candy's charges, the whole fourth floor of Corbin Hall, a gang of girls who all knew everything about Tom. ("She told them about the abortion she had last summer," Tom blurted out in exasperation one night as they walked by the Kaw River, leaning into each other, shoulder to shoulder, and Zita tried not to be hurt by the fact that she hadn't known there'd been an abortion.)

Zita and Tom would arrive in separate cars at the steakhouse in Ottawa (Candy was a vegetarian), Tom morose and guilty, Zita giddy and euphoric, and spend their brief time together holding hands, discussing what they ought to do next.

Tom was trying to extract himself gradually from Candy. He didn't want to hurt her, he didn't want to be responsible for her suicide or even her inclination toward it.

"Are you still sleeping with her?" Zita asked one Thursday in early December. She was supposed to be meeting her study group for American Values; Tom had told Candy he had to drive to Emporia for a prelaw assignment on a hearing.

"Sort of," he said. "We're sleeping together, but not having sex, not since I got back off the campaign trail."

"You mean you slept with her *then?*"

"I said we've *been* sleeping together."

"You had sex then?"

Tom leaned forward over their booth table. "We had sex then."

"But not now?"

"Not now."

"I didn't know you were sleeping with her, though." Zita didn't like this, even though she herself was still sleeping every night with McFarland, the two of them hardly touching, he angry with her in a smoldering way that seemed uncharacteristic of him. He drank his coffee in the morning standing in the bathroom with the window open, allowing in cold air, staring at the bare trees out back. He was suffering in such a way that he seemed to be plotting something; Zita often wondered if he didn't have his own secret life.

Tom sighed. He didn't look well. His brown eyes were tired, cupped in soft half-circles of shadow, parenthesized by wrinkles. The deceit was hurting him, worrying its way into his face. Zita knew *she* looked happy, her new love for Tom, which eclipsed the other love she'd thought she had, making her shining and radiant as an apple. Watching him as he wrestled with his duty toward Candy, Zita had begun to understand that he was an honorable man. It slowly dawned on her that she could lose him if she weren't careful, that his fretfulness over her affairs of the heart had to do with her character, not her relative or comparative affection for him.

It also occurred to her, for the first time in any serious

way, that she was *not* particularly honorable, that she was rather cavalierly hurting people.

And so she spent her first Christmas holiday away from her parents, spent it alone diving honestly into the mess she had created so blithely, confessing and crying until she felt empty, until her eyes hurt from dryness and she had to lick her forefinger every few minutes to dampen them. McFarland moved out on New Year's Eve, his belongings in brown bags from the grocery; the professor wrote her a letter demanding she return all of his correspondence to him immediately; the married man took her hunting in the Flint Hills with his dog and wept when she wouldn't let him kiss her breasts.

Now she was free. Clean. Now she waited alone in her brightly painted yet dimly lighted apartment, snow falling, the students all away, the campus closed, Zita alone at home and alone at restaurants and alone on the street, oddly saddened by the serious way she'd suddenly perceived and then treated her life. Was it always to be approached with so much care? Around her morning, noon, and night — had there ever been so much snowing? — snow descended like an icy emblem of adulthood, and she did nothing but wait all that lonely, noble Christmas break for Tom.

*

Two days after her car accident Zita wakes immobilized with pain. She lies in bed keening, unable to find a position that does not send lightning down her spine into her legs. Tom drops Leo off at Montessori and then takes a personal day from work, alarmed at Zita's pain. The two of them hobble down the back steps of the apartment building and over to the hospital across the way. Zita requires a wheelchair at Admissions. The pain is searing and spastic, unpredictable. In its surprising angles, Zita finds it not unlike labor, yet without the certainty of closure. An intern shoots her full of Demerol; she is guided home by Tom, who carries her up the two flights of stairs to their apartment like a new bride and deposits her, dead weight and misery, on their bed. For three days she does not move from the bed, not even to empty her bowels.

*

In Lawrence, in the early days of 1983, Tom left his little hermit's apartment and moved in with Zita. They painted the yellow and orange and turquoise rooms white, the single condition Tom insisted upon. Without his permission — they weren't married, after all — Zita adopted two kittens, tabbies from a litter that the professor returned from Portugal to find in his garage. McFarland had taken Freud with him when he left.

Tom and Zita argued over the kittens, but Tom began liking them before he could win. This was the birth of the seesawing way the two of them disagreed: Tom would be reasonable and conservative and Zita would be excitable and spontaneous, each in exaggerated increments, depending on what was at stake and who cared most about its outcome.

They were happy together. They spent an inordinate amount of time that semester watching television, lying together on their squeaking couch, and eating chocolate. The kittens also liked chocolate, and hung around on their chests, slapping at the crumbs.

Sometimes the phone rang in the middle of the night and they knew it was Candy, desperate to hear Tom's voice, even if it was only a snarled greeting. Sometimes they saw her on campus, scurrying in the other direction, hiding her face in her scarf, or turning to tell whoever she was with something secret about them. Zita tightened her grip on Tom, or held him in bed after he'd hung up the phone, as if further to solidify her claim to him. Before this relationship, she'd never felt particularly mature. It was usually she who phoned men in the middle of the night, she who reveled in the drama of games. Now she lay awake after Tom had fallen asleep, listening to the cats as they raced from one end of the apartment to the other. She could so easily imagine what Candy was thinking, what tortured passion had brought her to this hopeless phone call. Calmly, Zita understood that she and Tom would marry; this would be her life. The knowledge seemed both to weigh her firmly to the bed and to send her rocketing around the dark atmosphere.

Downstairs lived a guitar player and a hassled older woman working on an MSW. A month into the new semester, when the landlord had to evict the guitar player for not paying rent, there was a chillingly familiar laugh resounding in the shared heat vent. Tom literally sat upright in bed one night, the kittens springing on his feet as he jerked them from beneath the blankets and sheets. "That's Candy," he told Zita. "Candy Reeves is in this house." He stood naked in the cold, his head tilted toward the heat vent, listening. To Zita, it sounded as if Candy wanted them to hear, as if she were leaning into her heater with her hands cupped around her mouth, projecting her phony, flirting laugh.

The next day Candy's name appeared on top of a mailbox, one down from Zita's and Tom's names. Her bicycle, which had been Tom's brother's bicycle, leaned against the newel post, its pathetic combination lock the same one Tom's brother had used in high school.

This turn of events excited Zita; besides the peculiar set of romances she'd just extracted herself from, she'd never had to live in such a knotty emotional tangle.

Candy had been fired at the women's dorm for buying liquor for her underage charges. Now she lived downstairs, and Zita saw her everywhere: at the coffeehouse, in the poly sci hallways, driving in the next lane. Usually Zita was alone when she saw Candy. At home, Candy had always either just come in or just left; there was always the faint sense of her movement, a current of recently vacated smoky air.

One afternoon Zita sat in the student union restaurant to eat lunch and noticed Candy at a table across the room in the smoking section. It was late for lunch, and most tables were empty. When Zita's order came up, the waitress took it to Candy by mistake. Candy sent it back while Zita watched. The waitress next brought it to Zita, explaining that she and Candy looked alike, setting down the sandwich. Zita studied Candy while she ate, wondering if they actually did look alike, wondering if Tom thought so, wondering if such a thing was to be treated lightly.

*

From Kansas, Zita's mother sends Zita an article about Anthony "Buzz" Atwater's death. Outside, snow falls. Inside, Zita drinks brandy, watching its warm trail drizzle down the side of the snifter, an icepack between her tailbone and the chair. Buzz's death saddens Zita more than she would have guessed possible. Sitting gingerly at her round table, beneath a frosty window in her dark kitchen, she finds herself crying, the impulse upon her without warning. She hurts: not just her back, but her suddenly mushy heart. Wedding ceremonies ambush her in precisely the same way: at some point she will burst inexplicably into tears. Inside her live just a few emotional enigmas such as this.

*

Tom and Zita married in the summer, after having known each other ten months. The ceremony was held in Kansas City, at Tom's sister's house. Tom's sister, it turned out, was the one who had introduced Tom to Candy. She invited Candy to the wedding, but only after Candy had phoned to invite herself. Sally, the sister, spent the day apologizing to Zita.

"It's okay," Zita told her. "Really, it'll be kind of funny."

Candy arrived early wearing a tight lacy dress, ivory colored, more beautiful and formal than Zita's dress, which was simple cotton, apricot colored. Candy's eyes had the caved-in, bruised quality of a drug addict's, and she slunk around the perimeter of the party, eventually latching onto Tom's mother, who was too big-hearted to shun her. Candy followed her, making gestures toward helping out. It was Candy who gathered chairs for the elderly guests, scooting backward in her tight dress and heels, pulling folding seats over the lawn; Candy who separated a pile of paper plates with her trembling fingers; Candy who stood behind the serving table and dished up lasagna, her beautiful dress flecked with orange tomato sauce, her wild hair hanging in her face over her sad nocturnal eyes.

"She makes you feel responsible," Tom had said of Candy. She used her potential suicide as a way of constantly re-ensnaring Tom's attention. It did not seem to bother her that his concern was of the nature of a fireman's in response to a blaze.

Zita tried to become indignant over Candy's presence

at her wedding, but in truth she felt utterly flattered. Candy made Zita treasure Tom's affection, made it seem rare and worthy. Candy made Zita feel like the victor, the one to whom the spoils had gone. She could not deny that part of her happiness came from having won.

After the wedding, Tom and Zita rented a small house in Lawrence a few blocks from the house where Candy still lived. That fall, Candy made it a habit to ride her bike — Tom's brother's bike — past their little house on her way to classes. She always acted as if this were necessary, as if Tom and Zita had positioned themselves directly in her path. She rode by staring straight ahead of herself, hurrying. Sometimes Zita sat on the front stoop, waiting for her.

She and Tom still had their two kitties, and now Zita brought home a dog, this time having gotten Tom's approval. He thought of himself as a dog person. Their dog was a rottweiler puppy they named Buzz, for their senator. A sloppy, shy puppy, he became Zita's constant companion. She was spending the semester working part-time in the financial aid office on campus. Graduate school, she believed, was not for her. Living with Tom made her realize that she was not suitably driven.

She was allowed to take Buzz to work with her at Financial Aid. He played with her shoelaces in her tiny cubicle or investigated the other student employees. In the late afternoons, she and Buzz waited outside Flint Hall for Tom's classes to end, Buzz peeing on trees and chasing squirrels. Together they'd walk to a bar or cheap restaurant and leave Buzz tied up out front, where he slathered on other students. People began recognizing Buzz, calling hello to him on campus.

Then one morning in November, when the ground was

slick with frost and Buzz was leaping in delight and confusion across it, Candy came by on her bike with a puppy in the basket. Zita only made out its little muzzle over
the rim, a black and brown face she recognized as a rottweiler's.

Inside, she pulled off her clothes and returned to bed
with Tom, sticking her cold feet into the hot enclosure of
his bent knees.

"You won't believe what I just saw ride by," she said into
his warm ear.

Her friends were more angered by Candy than Zita
was. They couldn't believe Candy had gotten a rottweiler.
Zita wondered what Candy had named the puppy.

She found out from Tom's youngest brother, Jack, who'd
moved to Lawrence from Kansas City to start school. Jack
had been Tom's family's black sheep, dropping out of high
school, getting arrested a few times, working for minimum
wage at a lube pit. Now, at age twenty-five, he wanted to
earn a degree. He told them he was through with the school
of hard knocks.

Zita liked having Jack in town. He was a good audience
for her domestic performance. In front of him, she could
exhibit her and Tom's perfect love, their cute house and
charming pets. He ate dinner with them sometimes, or just
dropped by to watch TV or drink beer.

There was a seductive tension between Jack and Zita:
Jack was a little in love with her, and Zita liked him enough
to lead him on. She dressed up when he came over, yet
clung to Tom. She knew Jack's eyes followed her around the
room, yet he would never act on any of their flirtation. Jack
was ideal because his envy did not equal jealousy.

But somehow Candy got hold of him. They met in the
line at Joe's Donuts, according to Jack, Candy there with-

out any money, her dog tied up outside. It was late, so Jack paid for her sack of goodies and then walked her home, to discover on her front porch his high school bicycle, complete with ancient lock.

Zita didn't believe any of it was a coincidence. She believed Candy had followed Jack until a ripe situation arose. As for the bicycle, it had never been parked anywhere but in the foyer the whole time Zita and Tom had shared that house. Why would it be on the front porch now, in the dead of winter?

Jack began dating Candy, and Zita and Tom saw a lot less of him. When they did see him — sometimes just by accident, on campus — he would glance quizzically at Zita, as if he'd heard something about her that he was trying to verify. Zita felt his idolization of her and Tom's life slip away, and she was lonely for it.

She always meant to inquire into the name of Candy's rottweiler, but never quite could. Then, in the spring, Jack told them the dog had died.

"How?" she asked, shocked.

"He drank something funky, I guess, STP or paint thinner. Candy found him under the sink, with all the poisons and whatnot."

Zita put her arm around Buzz, who'd become a big dog with wide shoulders. When he was happy, he closed his eyes and appeared to be smiling like a drunk. Tears welled in Zita's eyes as she thought about Candy's dog. She blamed Candy, who was too fucked up to care for herself, let alone another living creature.

Jack said, "We buried him at night, in the back yard."

"What was his name?" Zita asked, finally having a graceful entrance.

"Tozi," Jack told her. It was a few beats before Zita

figured out those were first two letters of her and Tom's names, but it didn't seem wise to let Jack know this.

*

Zita is sent to an orthopedic surgeon for her continuing back pain. He sends her to have x-rays and then to have magnetic resonance imaging. At every step of the way, someone — her GP, her orthopedic surgeon, her physical therapist — taps Zita's knee with a little rubber hammer. Her reflexes are so strong that she kicks a clog off at the magnetic imaging office. "Sorry," she says sheepishly to the aide into whose forehead the clog has flown.

At home, Zita walks tilted sideways, in pain and angry about it. Little Leo comes to her side and pleads to be lifted. "Uppa," he says to her, over and over, arms raised. "Uppa, Mama."

Slowly the pain leaves her. Every day for the entire month of May she goes to physical therapy. Zita would never have confessed her troubles to a psychiatrist but feels no inhibition whatsoever in discussing everything with her physical therapist, Berenice. Berenice, she knows, listens in the way bartenders or hairdressers do. Zita gets to ask Berenice questions about her life too. Naked, lying on her stomach beneath an electrical stimulator or ultrasound wand, Zita chats amiably into the rectangular face hole, speaking to the floor. Berenice makes comments and adjusts heat or intensity. Zita tells her about Candy. Berenice recommends a chiropractor for Zita's back and shoulders, and a psychologist. She believes Zita is under stress.

"Stress?" Zita grunts into her face hole as Berenice rubs her thumbs deep into Zita's tender sacroiliac. "Not really. I mean, my daily life is stressful, but I had a car accident. That's why the back trouble." Yet after all the tests and observation, nobody can find a physical reason for her

continuing spasms. Since the accident, Zita has twice found
herself writhing in pain on the floor, having been suddenly
betrayed by her back. For these episodes she is given muscle
relaxants and painkillers. She lies immobile — fuzzy, sleepy,
oblivious — for a few days and moves tenderly through the
apartment after that. As a result of her injury, Leo has been
enrolled full-time in Montessori; Zita is no longer able to
lift or carry him.

She is wary of nearly everything now, watching for the
movement that will send her into pain. She and Tom have
not had sex for more than a month. Tom, in the beginning, joked to her that an orgasm would be good for her,
would relax her. They tried to make love — Zita trepida-
tious, Tom gentle — but failed. Her tension and protec-
tiveness prevent any pleasure. In bed, he sometimes mas-
turbates beside her, reminding her vaguely of the man she
had an affair with long ago, the one who masturbated over
the telephone to the sound of her voice. Sometimes she
takes Tom's penis in her mouth, but even this makes her
uneasy, the way she crouches, the way her spine has to
curl. And it reminds her of the professor she dated, as it
had been his habit to insist she take him in her mouth,
his hand resting firmly on the back of her head until they
were finished.

These memories make Zita uneasy; they have been
resolutely in her past until now. Whatever became of her
roommate McFarland? she wonders. What would any of
those men have done with someone like Candy Reeves?
Is the dissolution of romance always so skewed and crazy?
Lying immobile gives Zita more than enough time to en-
tertain questions like these. Physical debilitation makes her
understand what she has previously taken for granted.

*

In the summer of 1984, Candy purchased another rottweiler puppy. She also broke up with Jack.

The summer was hot; Zita took a job at Dairy Queen just so she could stand in the air conditioning all afternoon. It did not surprise her when Candy applied for a job there too. Zita came by her application form one evening and held it up and shook it at her boss, who had a gratifying crush on her. "I cannot believe this chick," she said, laughing. It was a slow night; she told him all about Candy. Outside the sliding windows through which they served ice cream, thousands of dusty little bugs fluttered in the humming greenish light.

"It's as simple as this," her boss told her, eager to be smart and psychological. "She wants what you have."

"I know," Zita agreed, "I know. And it's like she's casting a spell, gathering all the magic ingredients so she can have my life — the house, the dog, even Tom's brother."

"Do you feel threatened by her?" he asked. "Do you think she's violent? I'd be terrified."

"You would?"

His sober interpretation did not seem solely intended to flatter her; he made Zita wonder if she shouldn't be more upset. She felt the way she had when Tom had fretted about her character — that she'd been too involved in the glamour of the situation to see the serious risk.

Her boss didn't hire Candy. He told Zita she should take precautions.

But the Army-Navy mercantile down the block *did* hire her, and every day Zita had the opportunity to see Candy and the new rottweiler, who apparently was allowed to go to work with her, as they tripped along the sidewalk. Candy was the kind of young woman who believed a certain gawkiness to be sexy; she wore big black shoes that made her legs seem spindly and that gave her gait a loose teeter like her puppy's. From her mouth poked her perpetual cigarette. Watching her, Zita felt frumpy and inhibited.

It wasn't long after Candy took the new job that she broke up with Jack. She'd begun sleeping with her boss, Jack explained flatly one evening at Tom and Zita's. "She's a big pain in the ass," he said. "As you know." He had fallen into the round wicker chair in their living room, the one piece of new furniture they'd purchased. You could sleep in it, it was so welcoming and comfortable. But you also had to struggle out of it, which Jack now tried with a glass of wine in his hand. The wine splashed on the chair, on Jack, on poor Buzz at his feet. Zita sighed. When the phone rang, she leapt up to answer it, to leave her husband and his brother alone to discuss their former mutual nuisance of a girlfriend.

"Hello?" she sang into the receiver.

The silence that greeted her let her know who was there: Candy. Soon there were gasps, the splutter of re-strained tears. Candy wanted to talk to Tom, not Jack; her boss had given her acid and now she couldn't come down, she was having a bad trip, over near the Kaw River, walking in circles, trying to remember where she'd left her dog.

"Where's the dog?" Zita demanded. "What have you done with the dog?"

"I . . . don't . . . *know,*" Candy wailed.

"Don't hang up," Zita ordered her. "Stay right there. *Tom!*" she yelled without leaving the phone.

It was agreed, in hurried exchanges, that Tom would stay on the telephone with Candy while Jack and Zita went to find her. Over and over Candy asked for Tom, the sound of his name in Zita's ear suddenly alien, inviting in a world of references — intimacies — she'd successfully avoided. No longer. On the way to the river, she and Jack were silent, each thinking about Candy and Tom.

Candy had apparently been swimming before she decided she was on a bad trip; she wore a knitted pink bikini, huddled at the pay phone in the PicQuik. Her pasty skin was covered with goosebumps from the air conditioning. She stared wide-eyed at Zita and Jack as they came toward her; she was whispering something furtively into the black receiver, telling Tom some final secret thing.

"Pl-pl-pl-please take me home," she said to Jack. "The drug is making me stutter and shake." Jack took off his garish Hawaiian shirt and draped it over her shoulders.

"Where's your dog?" Zita demanded again.

"At my house," Candy said.

"I thought you lost him. You said you lost him a minute ago."

"When?"

"On the phone."

"No," Candy assured her, her eyes utterly black with dilation. "He's at home. I was partying without him."

"Come on," Jack said, leading her away. Zita purchased a large coffee before joining them, stepping into the back seat of her own car, slamming the VW door closed behind her. Candy's hands shook so violently she spilled coffee all over the seat. Another mess, Zita thought, remembering the wine on her favorite chair at home.

All the way home — to Zita's house, to Tom — Candy kept showing them with her quivering fingers the tiny little size of the windowpane acid she'd let dissolve on her tongue. So small, yet so powerful. "My cheeks hurt," she complained. "I've been smiling since four-thirty. And I'm so cold." Her boss, they discovered, had taken her to a party near the river, which she'd just walked out on. She was tired of him, she let Zita and Jack know; all he wanted to do was trip. "Where are all the good men?" she wailed in Zita's van. "You and Tom are the only good men I ever knew, especially Tom, no offense."

But Jack took offense. At Zita's house he dropped off the two women, then roared away, shirtless, on his motorcycle. Zita tried to avoid touching Candy, who walked in deliberate angled lines from the driveway to the porch. Inside, Tom made Candy sit in the friendly lap of the round wicker chair. He crouched beside her and began saying things, quiet and calm things, nonsense and reassurance. Slowly the neighborhood lights went out, the city slept, Zita wandered around the house with Buzz, whose nails clicked on the wood floors, and Tom — sitting now, his knees having weakened — droned on for Candy's benefit. She had started running her forefinger over the knuckles of her other hand, tracing the veins there, methodically, listening in a trance. Her eyes were still black, her pupils dilated to a frightening degree, but her expression no longer seemed terrified.

At three-thirty, when Tom finally joined Zita in bed, he lay restlessly beside her, flopping from one side to the other like a beached fish.

"What?" she asked. She dreaded the morning, Candy out in the living room, leaving her peculiar smoky odor in Zita's chair.

Tom said, "Promise you won't hold this against her?"

"This what?"

"This that I'm going to tell you?"

"O.K." The room was black; she could imagine that he was going to say he still loved Candy. In an instant Zita manufactured her own hurt and sadness, a not entirely unsatisfying scenario.

He whispered near her ear, "I think she lost her dog in the river. I think that's why she freaked."

"She killed another dog?"

He tried to hold Zita, but she wouldn't allow it. "She killed another dog?" Her rage made her wake fully.

"Accidents happen," Tom said. "She's very unlucky."

"'Unlucky'? She's just plain hazardous, like a toxic waste dump, a big festering blight, waiting to suck others in. I can't believe she killed another dog!" Zita threw herself back against her cool pillows. Below her, sleeping deeply and happily on the floor beside the bed, Buzz groaned. His contented rest seemed to Zita an affirmation of her own virtue.

*

To replace the banged-up Vanagon, Zita and Tom consult *Consumer Reports.* They breeze through car advertisements, attending to safety features, airbags and antilock brakes. They settle on a four-wheel-drive vehicle from an American carmaker. It resembles something a hunter or a Republican might drive. This is the first non-Volkswagen Zita has ever owned. In parking lots she has a tendency to forget what it looks like. The dutiful checkout boy pushing her cart of groceries wanders behind her as she scouts out her new car. Driving around the city, she always swivels her head when she sees a red Vanagon like her old one. Occasionally it occurs to her that Candy, out in L.A., is still, undoubtedly, driving a red Vanagon. Candy cannot know that the icons have shifted here, that now Zita and Tom are in favor of gas-guzzling, metallic gray, militaristic vehicles made in the U.S.A.

Sometimes Zita sits at traffic lights that have already turned green. Sometimes she forgets to pay attention to where she's going. Sometimes she will be headed one place but end up en route to another. Sometimes she purchases cigarettes and smokes them as she drives, listening to loud music, squelching her habit of reflection or hope: she wishes, suddenly, to inhabit only the present.

*

Tom and Zita moved to Chicago after Tom received his Ph.D. and was recruited for a position in the public relations office of a liberal city alderman. Zita taught swimming at the North Side YMCA; soon she became aquatics director. They made a few friends and went to a lot of movies. At the end of their first year in Chicago, Tom ran into Candy at an AIDS rally held on Navy Pier. She'd just moved to town a few weeks earlier; she was living with a new boyfriend and a new dog. She'd dyed her hair a kind of purple but otherwise looked the same, unhealthy from too many cigarettes. She'd made Tom walk her to her car after the rally because she was afraid to walk alone. There in the front seat of a red Vanagon sat a big rottweiler, her third. This one was named Tennessee.

"The name of our street!" Zita exclaimed when Tom told her about it. Tennessee was where they'd lived when Candy lived downstairs. "And our car," she added. "Unbelievable."

A few weeks later Candy began swimming laps during lunch hour at the North Side Y. Zita was taking a group of teachers of handicapped children on a tour of the facilities, kneeling at the pool to demonstrate the salutary temperature of the water. A thrashing body in the far lane drew her eye: gawky pale figure, purple hair clinging to her face as she made the turn at the end of her lap. Candy. Flailing hideously in the water. Her pile of belongings, resting beneath the diving board, had gotten soaked. Later, as Zita hurried across the street to eat a quick lunch at Hot Sammy's, she noted a red Vanagon like her own with Kansas plates in the lot. Inside sat the doomed rottweiler.

At the time, Zita didn't know anybody in Chicago well enough to share the comic idiocy of her stalker. She resorted to the long distance phone, calling her sister-in-law and friends from Kansas. But they were weary of Candy as subject matter. Deflated, her thunder long expired, Zita moved into a stage of simply feeling sorry for Candy. She and Tom saw her at rallies and plays, at films and art galleries, in bookstores and coffeeshops. Time was creating a funny haze over the reason for their knowing her; now they simply accepted her, like any other acquaintance, someone to whom they nodded or waved.

Then Zita became accidentally-on-purpose pregnant. She and Tom had begun discussing babies while they were making love — surely this was considered bad form for prevention of pregnancy. Their birth control, never exactly exemplary, was falling further and further from care. Instead of damp spongy doughnuts or withdrawal, they began relying on rhythm. And when their rhythm got reckless, they seemed to agree, by default or simple indolence, to have a baby.

There had been other incidents of synchronicity with Candy. She was not always following Zita's lead; occasionally she happened upon Zita's predilections at the same moment. There had been that day at lunch in the K.U. union when the waitress had delivered Zita's food incorrectly. Candy hadn't planned that. And there were other odd coincidences. Zita had joined a Great Books discussion group in Chicago and found Candy at the same meeting, for example — almost as if Zita had followed Candy in-

stead of vice versa. But now, as Zita and Tom discovered
themselves about to be parents, Candy showed up pregnant
as well. She notified Tom's sister, who of course told Tom
and Zita.

Who was the father? Zita wondered. The boyfriend
Candy had come to Chicago with had moved on. It would
not have surprised Zita to learn that Candy had found
someone who resembled Tom to mate with. Zita's pregnancy was only six or so weeks ahead of Candy's; there was
no way in the world it could have been modeled on hers.
And this fact scared her — that Candy could sense Zita and
Tom's haphazard inclination toward parenthood so precisely, that she might be on some life track similar to theirs.

The shadow Candy cast then began to intimidate Zita.
Removed from caffeine and liquor, sent spinning by hor-
mones, Zita believed every paranoid reflex to be real.

Zita's son was delivered in late May; Candy's daughter
came on the Fourth of July. The children never met. Zita
forgot everything after returning home from the hospital.
Leo became her life; Candy was a presence like the past,
mere shadow play. When Zita took time to consider her old
nemesis, it was with genuine concern for the baby. What
could Candy have to offer a baby? And how was she doing
it without support? Zita herself was having difficulty imagining anyone could adequately care for a child alone. She
and Tom were exhausted. Leo lay in bed between them,
depleting every substance they had to offer. For months the
three of them operated as a single living unit, insular and
whole.

Then the outside world leaked in again. Tom's alderman
was accused of embezzling $200,000 from a city project to
employ gang members. Tom was beside himself with disil-
lusionment. Then Jack, off in Alaska, phoned to tell them

about Candy's delivery. She had had a c-section, and the baby was undersized. In August, when she materialized at the Brookfield Zoo with her tiny girl strapped to her chest like a monkey, Zita could not believe how thin Candy was, how quickly restored to her prepregnant self.

"Jaundice," Candy said quickly when they peered into the cloth sack her baby occupied. Yes, she was yellow, so unhealthy-looking compared with fat Leo, the pinkest, roundest-headed little fellow imaginable. All Zita's emotions swung around inside her. Had she aided somehow, inadvertently, immaturely, in that yellow baby's new bad life? Moreover, was it really bad? Or did Zita just need to believe it so?

"What's her name?" Zita asked, smiling at Candy.

"Leah," said Candy, immediately blushing and quickly explaining that she hadn't heard what Zita and Tom had named their son until after she'd already chosen. "Really, I wouldn't rip off your name."

Zita didn't care. She could not help herself from touching Leah's scabby scalp. "That cradle cap goes away," she told Candy. "Leo had it too."

*

There are a few things that help Zita manage the pain in her back. One is the hot whirlpool at the Howard Street Women's Fitness Center. Another is the oily massages Tom has learned to give her. The third, secret from everyone, is the careful combination of ibuprofen and wine and Valium, just enough of each. Zita might recline in her own bathtub on a chilly Chicago afternoon, languish with her feet up between the spigots, her neck on the rear rim, sit in the steam with her Chianti and let a sweet shameless relaxation absorb her. That this behavior must be kept from Tom is obvious. But is she not entitled to her secret, reckless life? Oughtn't people to have a private corner in the world? Her old friend Buzz snores on the bathmat, waiting to struggle up when she steps groggy and pain-free from the water, waiting to lick her damp reddened ankles. A mile up the road, Leo plays intelligently and safely at Montessori; Tom follows his new liberal alderman around town, becoming indispensable in his driven, saintly way.

From Tom's sister and brother, Zita has learned that Candy is pursuing physical therapy in Los Angeles. That's only fitting, seeing as Zita visits *her* physical therapist every week. Someday she may rise from her session to discover Candy standing over her in the white smock, her hands moist with lotion, a maddening servile grin on her face.

It's sunny out in southern California today, despite the apocalyptic nature of the place. On the color weather map in the back of the *Trib,* the West Coast is a glowing band of deep orange: a beautiful day for the beach. Zita finds herself fascinated by Los Angeles now, checking on its climate and politics, comparing them with her own city's as the year wears on in Chicago. And as her life passes through its lonely phases, she often wonders what in the world Candy Reeves must be doing.

FAMILY TERRORISTS

——— /////———

THERE WAS ALWAYS A SCOTTIE AND IT WAS ALWAYS a male. Though his head was larger than his body, his brain seemed unquestionably small. At home he cowered in the bathroom, barking from behind the toilet, yet in public he always picked and then lost fights with larger dogs, and never came when he was called, never. How the family had found, over the years, four dogs with precisely the same characteristics no one knew, but there was always a Scottie, and there always would be.

This one was McWard. He was young, bought as a Christmas gift by the four children to replace the Scottie that had died six months earlier. Experience had taught the family that replacing a pet immediately was a danger; there'd been one Scottie they had had to take back to the breeder, a little fellow who'd come too soon on the heels of his predecessor. McWard was the first Scottie to belong exclusively to Lynnie Link's parents, the first to be doted on in an utterly fresh, grandparently way, the first not to have at least one of the children in the house. As a result, or maybe just coincidentally, he didn't like any of the four grown children.

But they all had an inordinate fondness for him. They liked to cuff him behind the ears and make jokes at his expense. He was a new dog, but he played the role in a familiar manner, nipping and bouncing, snarling and yapping in his midget falsetto, eternally underfoot. This constancy was precisely the opposite of what Lynnie had come to expect from her human family members, who were the same people but always different.

Lynnie's parents were marrying each other again. Dorothea and John had been divorced for six years, during which time they had been living together. Preceding that, they'd still been married but living apart, Lynnie's father being involved with another woman. Now it seemed they'd put the pieces together, lined up variables once more, agreeably intersected. Lynnie wondered what they did on their old wedding anniversary, February 8, and how many years they thought of themselves as married. Their new anniversary was going to be August 29, four days from now. Next year, would they consider it their first anniversary or their thirty-sixth, or, nullifying the divorce, their forty-second?

The first time they'd gotten married it was 1951, and in the photographs, Dorothea looked just like her daughters looked now. In fact, the first time she'd gotten married, Dorothea had been twenty-six, Lynnie's current age. This fact made Lynnie afraid: she didn't feel very different about marriage from the way she had as a child, when the idea of pledging eternity to a stranger, someone unrelated, struck her as a version of her worst nightmare. For many years she'd planned to marry her brother, to live with her parents, to wear her mother's party dresses and high heels.

In her parents' first wedding photos, the first Scottie, Maxie, sat on his tail at a distance, watching, his head tilted in that timeless Scottie pose of perky curiosity. Lynnie's grandparents and young aunts and uncles had come. But her grandparents were dead now, and the aunts and uncles were no longer close, not geographically, not emotionally. There'd been feuds over inherited money and property. In the new wedding pictures would be Lynnie's two sisters, her brother, herself, and the novice Scottie, McWard. The setting would not be Kansas, where the family really lived, where the original wedding had taken place, but a small town in Montana, where her parents had recently bought a summer house.

Like tiny faraway countries whose names changed every few years, Lynnie's alliance within her family frequently repositioned itself. This year she loved her brother, John Gamble, though it was a love tinged with pity and impatience. The youngest, Lynnie did not feel comfortable pitying her siblings — weren't they supposed to feel superior to her? — but with John Gamble it was impossible not to.

She left her apartment in Dallas at midnight — the plan had been to rise at dawn, but she was too excited to sleep, too agitated with expectation — and drove west through tornadoes. The wind knocked her worn old VW van from one side of the highway to the other; her Irish setter kept thumping to the floor in back, then scrabbling onto the seat once more. Lynnie preferred little two-lane highways; she was sentimental for a time she'd never inhabited, frightened of the current decade, and wished to travel in the mode of the 1950s, pre-interstate. She enjoyed small towns, especially late at night — their blinking yellow traffic lights, their dark bungalows fronting the main thoroughfare, their weathervanes and loveseat porch swings. They were sweet and easy, safe and welcoming. Even now, with twenty-four-hour convenience stores everywhere you looked (bearing names that were supposed to be so clever and chummy —

Love's, Quicky-Mart, Kum 'n' Go — but that Lynnie found sleazy with innuendo), she avoided the freeway.

Route 180 seemed abandoned. The flimsy wipers rubbed and then screeched at the windshield, a frantic tempo over and over, revealing a clear landscape for only an instant before water washed across the glass. On the inside Lynnie pulled her shirt cuff over her palm to wipe away fog; the defroster, like most of the other rubber dashboard knobs and buttons, had become purely ornamental. She navigated in the moments when she could see, depending on Texas's flatness to keep her safe the rest of the time. For many miles hers were the only headlights in either direction, her van a weaving illuminated toy on the plain. She did not consider stopping.

Her family had survived a tornado before she was born. Their car had been lifted from a Wichita city street and turned neatly over on its back, like a bug. Then, an instant later, the car was rolled right side up again, now in a parking lot. Inside the station wagon, her parents and sisters and brother suffered cuts and bangs and breaks. Lynnie's mother, Dorothea, had been eight months pregnant with Lynnie at the time, yet had somehow managed to fly over the front and back seats to the end of the car, where her littlest child, John Gamble, had been playing with his Matchbox racers. But he was gone, had disappeared into the roar of dark wind and rain.

Across the parking lot a windowful of Baskin-Robbins customers had watched the whole episode. The sky split open with lightning every few seconds; the clouds reflected the brightness in an eerie pink, which John Gamble said he could still remember, twenty-six years later. Everyone in Lynnie's family could contribute memories of the evening: the fat bright bolts of lightning, the telephone wires snap-

ping loose from poles and sparking against the wet pavement, the roof that ripped from a nearby house and landed
beside their mashed car in the parking lot — a picture
Lynnie liked to imagine, flattened house and flattened car
beside each other, like something a disturbed child might
draw.

John Gamble lay under the pink sky calling for his
mother. He'd been four years old, sucked from the exploded
rear window and flung onto the ground, a drinking straw
driven by the wind embedded in his right cheek. He still
had a faint scar, a tiny crescent moon like a dimple. His
mother had finally heard his voice, her name under the
howl of the storm, and had managed to retrieve him, despite high winds and her own ungainly size.

Natty, eight years old at the time, remembered the car
the family had sought shelter in, one parked a few spaces
away from where their station wagon had landed, a rotund
red sedan untouched by the great swirling vortex of the
tornado. They'd made their way to it, then sat in it in the
usual family assemblage — their father behind the wheel;
Dorothea, massively pregnant, beside him; the three children in the back, John Gamble whimpering at having lost
his little Matchbox Thunderbird — the only strangeness
being the fact that they were all drenched, bleeding, sobbing. Their father pounded on the horn of the stranger's
car, swearing, leaving his blood on the steering wheel and
turn signal stick. The children listened as sirens approached
and then subsided, more alarmed now by their father's
uncharacteristic fury than by the accident they'd just en-
dured. Inside the ice cream store the faces of people lit up
— icy green and ghostly — when lightning cracked, then
were gone, like the switched-off image of a television, the
last focused prick of brightness.

Joanne, the oldest daughter, twelve, had been photographed for the *Wichita Eagle and Beacon* by a reporter who arrived with the ambulance. Her picture was picked up by the wire service and appeared in newspapers all over the country, its caption proclaiming her to be "Young Joanne Link with Unidentified Man." The man was her father, sans his eyeglasses, which lay smashed in the wreckage of the car. In the picture he looked alarmed, holding the ambulance door open for Joanne as she climbed in, her dress torn up to her thigh, rivulets of blood on her pretty face. She'd always been beautiful, even then, damaged and afraid.

She didn't recall having her picture taken, though she did remember the ambulance ride and the hospital, where she'd been allowed to stay in a room with her sister and brother, where the television had been suspended from the ceiling. The children had rolled through the halls on gurneys, carrying packs of chewing gum, secretly bestowed on them by the admitting nurse, on their tummies beneath the white sheets. Joanne remembered chewing the soft warm gum, great spearminty wads of forbidden sweetness. She and Natty and John Gamble had sat terrified on their hospital beds, waiting for their grandparents, for word about their parents — their father, whose back had been injured, their mother, whose arms glittered with broken glass and who carried their unknown brother or sister.

Me, Lynnie thought now, wrestling with the large VW steering wheel as water flowed across the road before her like a river of milk. Because her family had already been in a tornado, Lynnie believed it unlikely, statistically speaking, for her to end up in another one. It did occur to her, however, that her death by tornado, in an automobile, would put a definitive shape on her life. It would be ironic if she died out here, it would be somehow poetic and fitting. On the radio she could find no coherent voice, no weather or music. Wouldn't music indicate that she need not worry? That disaster was not imminent? Who would tell her, she wondered as she sailed sideways, that she was in danger? What would her parents advise? What would John Gamble or Natty or even flighty Joanne do in this situation?

On nostalgic Highway 180 there were no lights to be seen, no mile markers or billboards, no truckers, no traveling salesmen or families, nobody to solidify the world. Lynnie tried to recall the weather lore she'd heard her whole life. During thunderstorms the car was one of the safest places to be, grounded by its rubber tires, but tornadoes were another story. There were ditches on both sides of the road for her to duck into, yet if this turned into flash flooding the ditch would be deadly. Like most of Lynnie's dilemmas, this one's solution looked to be in the hands of fate.

She drove on, the rain subsiding then resurging, her old van sliding and then regaining traction, Lynnie needing desperately to fill the gas tank, to empty her bladder. During other trips this was how she kept herself awake, drinking coffee until she could drink no more, staying awake with the need to urinate. But tonight fear kept her alert, fear and philosophy squaring off in her head while she navigated the turmoil. Oh, she was too young to die, she thought, she was too unimportant, too small, too lost in the huge state of Texas, off by herself on an insignificant, afterthought kind of road. But that was precisely why she *could* die — what pity did acts of God hold for skeptical atheists like herself, tiny nothings like bugs, simple to whisk up and let fly? Lynnie only struck bargains with God, with her conscience, when faced with her own demise, in airplanes, on highways, near the edges of cliffs.

Preoccupied horribly, giddily with her own death, with the completion of a circle begun twenty-six years earlier when she'd ridden sloshing and preconscious in the womb through a similar stormy night, Lynnie forged on. She longed for another car on the highway, for company in this disaster, other victims or survivors or at least witnesses. Before her came the vision of a windowful of faces, ghostly dispassionate people watching from a safe distance, licking ice cream. She wished particularly for a car carrying a family, for a station wagon that might hold a passel of children, escorted by their bedraggled responsible father, their mother leaning over the back seat to dispense Life Savers and reassurance, her lap as big and heavy as a medicine ball with the next baby, at her feet the fierce and cowardly Scottie. That was the car that would successfully ford the flood, thwart the lightning, plow some reasonably safe passage through a field full of tornadoes.

*

Lynnie's brother, John Gamble, had no telephone and no television: "Tele-nothing," he always said. So at dawn in Carlsbad, New Mexico, Lynnie phoned his next-door neighbor in El Oro to warn him she was four hours away. "And tell him I'm fine, that I made it through the tornadoes."

This addendum was an example of what John Gamble called family terrorism. Since he had no TV, he would not have known about tornadoes in west Texas; he would not have been concerned about her driving through them until she mentioned it after the fact. This was Lynnie's particular brand of family terrorism, although it was usually her parents she phoned, and it was usually in the middle of the disaster. Since they weren't around to behold her life, she had to notify them of its perils. She wanted them worrying.

John Gamble wouldn't have minded missing his parents' wedding. It was Lynnie who insisted he attend and then was forced to drag him there herself. He did not feel compelled by celebration; he labeled all rites of guilty duty to his parents or sisters family terrorism.

This would be Lynnie's first visit to her brother's little town on the Rio Grande River, practically at the Mexican border. Two months earlier John Gamble had turned thirty and received his inheritance from Gran. Each Link child had one hundred thousand dollars awaiting him or her; Lynnie would be the last. Fifteen years ago, her grandmother had sold the family hotel in Aspen, Colorado, setting aside money for each grandchild, to be used when he or she reached a mature age. After getting his check, John Gamble had immediately moved out of the family house in Wichita; he had bought an old adobe church through the mail, then driven his wreck of a car to its death at the bottom of the country and planted himself in a town where no one knew him. Gran, Lynnie knew, would not have found this the act of a mature person. But she was dead — Lynnie's mother often sighed with relief that Gran had missed the worst of the family acrimony — and John Gamble didn't appear likely to change.

Lynnie found his church by looking for John Gamble's car, a 1972 black and white Maverick also inherited from Gran, now covered with dirt and sticks, as if some animal might be dwelling in it. The car's engine had blown when he arrived and he had yet to fix it.

John Gamble's church was pink and did not lean so much as slump sideways. He was proud of its adobe construction and had enumerated several times for Lynnie his muddy plans for renovation. The building was shaped like a meat loaf, with a stucco cone at each corner, a pair of battered green doors for an entrance. Cyclone fencing surrounded it as if it had been condemned.

John Gamble sat on his front stoop smoking a joint. Lynnie's VW dieseled behind the Maverick, a phlegmatic sputtering that sounded almost human. She habitually anthropomorphized belongings, and she thought of the van as asthmatic and finicky, a sort of cough-racked bookworm on wheels — Nester, she might have named it. Her dog, Rebel, a ten-year-old Irish setter gone to gray, had spotted John Gamble and was waving his tail maniacally, whimpering. Her brother was one of only a few people in the world who did more than tolerate Rebel, a crotch-snuffling, smelly, hyperactive, horny dog, and Rebel seemed capable of knowing such a thing.

Lynnie let him clamber over her and jump out the front door. She hopped down and looked around, stretching her fists to the sky. It was late morning, already in the nineties, the sky huge and as bright as aluminum. John Gamble's village was poor and undone, as if a load of bricks and boards had exploded here half a century before and been only haphazardly arranged in the time since. Off in the distance gray hills marked the plain like beached whales. Rebel ran circles around John Gamble, his tail spinning. John Gamble made his way to Lynnie's vehicle, propping open a metal Texaco sign that served as a gate. "Howdy," he said, putting an arm around her shoulders.

John Gamble was her height, weighed less than she did, and stank. As always, he seemed smaller than she recalled, more frail. In her memory he was handsome enough, but in person she had to acknowledge his curious looks, his complete disregard for personal toiletry. His hair receded from a deep widow's peak, and his forehead was a shining tomato red. Though the whites of his eyes were bloodshot from marijuana, the blue was bright and luminous. *Your brother's so intense,* Lynnie's friends had always exclaimed. "I gotta water my plants," he told her, turning back to the yard. She followed the seat of his baggy corduroys.

His front yard was a hodgepodge of recent cheap plantings, piñon and cane and ocotillo and agave, cuttings from his neighbors, with a dribbling gray garden hose lying in between. Picking up the hose, he offered Lynnie a hit from his cigarette as they toured, John Gamble flinging an arc of water at each plant, which was perhaps sufficient here in the desert — who knew? Though they had not seen each other for eight months, since last Christmas, he acted as if she lived around the corner, as if her presence couldn't have surprised him less.

She loved him more than anyone on earth. To be near him was to put her heart in real jeopardy.

"Hold on to Rebel," he told her as they neared the farthest side of the church. "I have some so-called critters back here in the bushes."

"Critters?"

"Birds and bunnies. They adopted me." Lynnie was alarmed when he smiled: three of his front teeth were gray. He quickly turned his face away, though usually he liked to broadcast his physical problems, turn them into topics for general discussion. As a teenager, he'd had a fungus on his hands that had been endlessly fascinating for him, and each night at dinner he would let the family know its progress as it ate the skin down his wrist.

To Rebel he said, "You stay indoors, you old fathead

sad sack," and he nudged the dog through a small door in the back of the church.

"What's with your teeth?" Lynnie asked, giving him an opening.

John Gamble began to whistle, inhaling instead of exhaling, ignoring entirely her question. She felt herself beginning to adjust to being with him; in her family you did not communicate directly or consistently. To discover where you stood, you had to work covertly, by circumnavigation. And there was little room for error: you said either exactly the right thing or exactly the wrong one. It was tiring to consider, and Lynnie sighed.

In response to John Gamble's whistle, a pair of peacocks strutted out from the thick weedy foliage. "Romulus and Remus," he said. "I'm waiting for one to kill the other." The two birds promenaded with their tails dragging the ground, pecking apathetically. Then abruptly one of them turned his butt to Lynnie and fanned open the burnished turquoise eyes of his species, shaking the feathers as if bored by the requisite spectacle.

"They shriek at night," John Gamble said. He squawked to illustrate and the bird's plumage quickly retracted, settling in the dirt behind him like a bridal train. "That Romulus has a bullet hole in his head. Shot skimmed right over and left a trough." John Gamble cut a part in Lynnie's hair with the side of his small dirty hand.

"Pretty boys," Lynnie commented.

"The females are louder *and* uglier," John Gamble said. "You'd think it'd be one or the other, not both."

"What's that supposed to mean?"

He shrugged, grinning, lips sealed. "Come inside," he said. "You sure you want to go north? Maybe we ought to just hang out here. You could help me skin chiles." He led her around front again and through his green doors, into the cool, stale church.

"You said you'd go," Lynnie told him. "I wouldn't have almost killed myself in a tornado if I'd known you weren't going to go. And I hate chiles."

"How can you hate chiles?"

"Are you going or not?"

"I'll go."

"They give me diarrhea," she said, of the chiles.

His church was one long, high-ceilinged room, dim because the windowpanes — plastic instead of glass — were colored with saints and their lives: the one with the animals, the one with the swords, the one with the big spiked wheel. John Gamble had studied saints and written his master's thesis at Brown — a blue, bound book sitting on Lynnie's parents' mantel at home, dusty and unread — all about them. John Gamble's church was dark and damp-smelling, like a prison cell, its floor an undulating black wooden surface obviously well worn, perhaps by the knees of the devout.

"This is great," Lynnie said in the merry way her mother would have — and for the same reason. She walked through in awe of the place's enormous ugliness. The dingy walls sagged inward, and all of John Gamble's furniture — stove, refrigerator, table, sink, bed, desk, chair, stereo, coffinlike speakers — was stowed against them, the center of the room cleared as if for dancing. On the refrigerator was a Post-It note that read "Remember the Austerity Plan."

"The austerity plan?" Lynnie asked.

"If I'm frugal," her brother told her, "I won't have to work for ten years." His hundred-thousand-dollar inheritance was not apparent in the room. The church itself had cost him twenty-five; its furnishings, appliances and furniture Lynnie remembered from childhood, had been taken from their parents' basement and garage in Wichita. The only things John Gamble had ever spent money on, had ever required to be first-rate, were music and drugs, and this, it seemed, was still the case. His black stereo equipment was beautifully streamlined, perfectly high-tech. And Lynnie could smell bong water, its dense, dusty stench just under the odor of old building.

Her brother had not changed dramatically since he was fifteen years old. In his bedroom in Wichita he'd kept mice and played them music, his windows open to draw smoke away. Lynnie used to walk down the hall to his closed door — the towel rolled against the crack, wadded beneath the door when opened inward — to ask him questions. He'd convinced her he knew everything, that she could ask him anything, *anything,* and he would know the answer. And if he didn't he could — and would — find it for her. For many years Lynnie had depended on his unchangeability, his patient response to anything she was willing to ask him. At the end of high school she had turned into a snob, shunning her brother, flouncing off to college to be in a sorority and buy clothes. But a few years later she'd come back, repentant, humiliated by her shallowness and appreciating him anew.

Now she worked hard, in his church, among his stark array of used things — "pre-owned," he would say of them — not to feel sorry for him. He was heat-seeking when it came to deception, and her pity would enrage him. Besides, did she know for a fact it was pitiful, his life?

"Come see my projects," he said. "But leave Rebel in here. Stay here, you old nag." Rebel fell panting and smiling in front of the stove as if he might choose to stay there forever. He lay on a braided rug Lynnie could clearly see before their stove in Kansas, one her mother had used for many years, one Lynnie had lain on herself as a child to stare at the kitchen ceiling, pulling the pale blue threads from it and running them under her fingernails. She wondered how John Gamble could endure facing these things every day.

In the back yard stood a tangle of metal and tumbleweeds and litter. "My Re-bar art," John Gamble said, picking the weeds and trash away and throwing them over the fence into the alley. He'd made crosses from the rusty metal, a whole fleet of grave markers. "One of my neighbors sells them for me. Cheap."

Beside the crosses sat an upended spool table with a pile of broken toys on it, Barbies and sand buckets and plastic soldiers and cars and fat baby dolls with ratty hair and no arms. "My toy art," John Gamble explained. "I've been taking their pictures. Dad gave me his old Roloflex, which works great, really, and I've been having some fun. You hungry?" High, as John Gamble usually was, he could never be far from hunger.

"I'll watch."

They ate at a restaurant on the highway called Tio's, just a few blocks from the church. The cook and waitress were husband and wife; they knew John Gamble, they brought him beans and tortilla and rice and salsa without his having to say a word. He rolled everything into a tube and ate happily while Lynnie still made her way down the menu, finally settling on a hamburger.

"If we *didn't* go to Montana," John Gamble said, "we could go to Mexico and —"

"You said you'd go!"

"Just hypothetically, if we didn't —"

"John Gamble!"

"I'll go."

Their plan was to leave at dawn, but in the late afternoon, sitting listening to ecstatic Van Morrison, taking hits from the bong, they both decided they might as well get on the road — John Gamble with resignation to his fate. Rebel staggered to his feet, John Gamble threw a few shirts and socks into a duffel, and they piled into the car. Just as Lynnie turned the key, her brother snapped his fingers. "Wait," he told her, looking at her eyes, revealing his three gray teeth for a second. "I've got to get the Visine and my shovel."

Lynnie nodded. "Your shovel," she repeated as he hopped down from the puttering VW. She never got high until she was around John Gamble. Then she remembered how much she enjoyed it, how contented she was just to sit and think. Was she hot? she wondered, lifting her elbow to see if her underarm was damp. Somehow placing her sunglasses over her eyes had the effect of cooling her down. She observed John Gamble's little village from an entirely different perspective, admiring the way the wind blew up dust devils, the fast-food wrappers whirling so gracefully, the tumbleweeds rolling casually through. Now she sort of wished they were staying longer in El Oro; in fact, what was to prevent her from moving here herself? She could call the Horse and Hound Feed Store, where she clerked, in Dallas and have them forward her last paycheck; someone in El Oro might hire her to weigh bags of animal chow. She had a real desire to sit on John Gamble's stoop and look at things, bake in the sun and forsake spongelike Texas. Wasn't it interesting that El Oro was not built on a grid plan? And could mistletoe, thriving in all the old trees, be such a terrible thing, really, if it was green and living?

John Gamble popped open the passenger door and pulled himself in — she had no idea how much time had passed, one minute or fifteen — and threw a small shovel in the back with Rebel.

"Groovus shades," he said of her glasses, tapping a plastic lens with his fingernail. "Let's roll."

*

It was John Gamble's peculiar craziness to worry over animals on the roadway. And not only animals, but the discarded boxes or sacks that might contain hidden kittens or possums, chipmunks or prairie dogs. He felt responsible for rescuing them. If he was too late, if there was a body beside the road, he would have to stop and throw a shovelful of dirt on it, saying his highway prayer ("God help those creatures who must cross the road").

He was unselfconscious about his sentimentality concerning animals, and did not hesitate, just outside Truth or Consequences, to command Lynnie to pull over. A days-old coyote lay like a stiff throw rug on the shoulder. John Gamble retrieved his shovel and pushed the carcass off the pavement, then dropped a few scoopsful of sand on it. High, watching him mumble his prayer, Lynnie realized that her brother probably believed in God now. John Gamble had gotten religion since childhood. Growing up, they were atheists, taught by their father to find funny the Catholic school down the block, the neighbor children trudging, uniformed, to Blessed Sacrament to be slapped on the knuckles by the nuns. As an adult, Lynnie had felt annoyed with her parents that they hadn't let her know how seriously most of the rest of the world took its faith. John Gamble's thesis on saints might have seemed somehow literary or intellectual, but his unscholarly devotion would give their father another reason to think his son an idiot, so Lynnie decided she would work to keep it secret.

For a long while after the dead coyote, they rode north without talking, listening to space music, warbling zithers and electric synthesizers, on John Gamble's portable disk player. When Lynnie finally came out of her high, she was irritated to find her brother staring at her, grinning his jack-o'-lantern grin.

"What?"

"Check out your speedometer," he said. Lynnie discovered they were traveling at thirty-eight miles per hour.

"We're never going to get to Montana if you let me drive this slow!"

"You hungry?" he asked.

"I can't eat this way, constantly, or I'll get fat," Lynnie told him peevishly, accelerating to sixty.

"I'm hungry," he said. "Starving. Plus I want to drive."

Lynnie always forgot how much she hated coming down from pot. Her throat felt full of straw, her head throbbed, and her eyesockets seemed too small for her eyeballs. She too was hungry — empty, ravenous — and conceded to stop in Albuquerque. It was ten-thirty and she realized she hadn't slept for a day and a half.

After buying a dozen guacamole tacos and a six-pack of Jolt, they were back on the road, John Gamble behind the wheel. "I haven't driven for ages!" he said happily, dialing the big steering wheel side to side. "And a stick shift, no less!"

"Careful," Lynnie said without confidence. After eating her tacos, she fell into a nightmarish sleep that was interrupted only by faint recollections of brief stops, either for gas or burials, bright lights from passing semis cutting sharply across the VW's ceiling, bits of gravel flicking against the van's underside as it rocked in each drafty wake. She dreamed of storms and accidents, severed heads falling through the pocked ceiling, panic dreams that would not quite let her either fully relax or fully wake until daylight, when she heard John Gamble urinating behind the car. Why would the quiet splash of urine wake her?

Her brother was standing beside a stranger, the two of them arced forward as if distending their navels, peeing with their backs to Lynnie. She sat up, discovering an unfamiliar backpack at her feet, a large sheathed knife strapped to its flap. John Gamble had picked up a hitchhiker.

They were parked at a rest stop; the bathrooms across the sandy lot were out of order. A sign dangling in the wind cautioned of rattlesnakes thereabouts. After having bad dreams, she would ordinarily have found consciousness sane and peaceful. Now Lynnie had to deal with an armed stranger in an abandoned rest stop. She pulled open the sliding window next to her.

"Hungry?" John Gamble said to her in greeting as he zipped his corduroys. His buddy, a short fellow in military fatigues with a lumpy shaved head, was still launching urine into the scrub. Lynnie looked hopefully around the parking lot, trying to see how they might leave the guy.

"Where's he going?" she asked John Gamble.

"Don't know. He was standing on the other side of the road when I picked him up."

The guy shouted over his shoulder, "I'm going to Nebraska."

"Nebraska?" Lynnie said. "What state are we in?"

John Gamble climbed back in the driver's seat. "Utah. We've been in Utah since one or two this morning. We might be about to leave Utah, in fact." He turned the rearview mirror to check his face, rubbing his dirty thumbs alongside his nostrils.

"Did we go through Salt Lake?"

"Not that I noticed. Hungry?" he repeated.

The hitchhiker climbed in the passenger side and turned to tell Lynnie his name: "Dante." Perhaps it was because he was bald, but his head looked distinctly too small, his eyes swollen shut and seemingly jammed together, the pupils hardly visible as they moved quickly over Lynnie's body. She hated his presence, hated the thought of him sitting in her car while she slept, hated the uneasiness that would accompany her until they'd dropped him off or he'd decided to use his sword on them — hated mostly that her brother had welcomed him into their trip.

"I'm starved," said Dante. "How about you?"

At breakfast he and John Gamble ate two bowls of oatmeal each and a basket of salty biscuits the texture of sand. Dante kept the waitress busy filling his cup with coffee, which he then loaded with multiple packs of sugar and powdered creamer.

To Lynnie he said, "Man, I woulda stood out there all night going the wrong way if it weren't for your bro."

"He got disoriented," John Gamble said.

"Fuck yes, disoriented. Slept in a horse trailer all the way from Las Vegas, got left in the dark, just staggered to my feet and hefted the old digit." He poked his thumb out and swung his fist through the air. "I could be back in Las Vegas by now if not for you guys." He smiled at them, showing his own bad teeth, the gold frames around the front ones.

John Gamble, beside Lynnie in the booth, shrugged. Beneath the table Lynnie could feel Dante's army boots shifting around, crushing her toes, shifting again. She did not want him in her car.

Now he frowned, tilting forward to stare at John Gamble's mouth. "Man, you gotta get those teeth checked out."

John Gamble said, "I'm not going to spend money on my teeth. They don't hurt, they're just discolored."

"Oh no, they're dying," said Dante.

"They look rotten," Lynnie added. She felt sour. Her own teeth were furry, her blue jeans dotted with food stains. Next to her, her brother ate a handful of linty pills from his shirt pocket and abruptly stood up.

"What are those?" she asked.

"Good for what ails me," John Gamble said, turning away.

Dante paid for their breakfast, which further endeared him to John Gamble. As part of his austerity plan, her brother could not afford to be generous. He didn't even leave tips. Lynnie, who had been a waitress, overcompensated by leaving an extra dollar. Her delight in seeing her brother was being eaten away by both his miserliness and his generosity: she could not believe he'd picked up a knife-bearing stranger. Dante headed off for the restaurant bathroom before they left, giving Lynnie an opportunity to tell John Gamble how stupid he'd been.

"I knew you'd bag on me about this," he said. "If you don't watch out, you'll turn into another Natty." This, for John Gamble, was the ultimate risk in life, becoming like their sister.

"If you knew I'd be mad, why'd you pick him up?"

"It was raining. He was wet. Aren't I on this trip? Don't I get to make some decisions?"

"It's my car."

"Great. I'm a hostage."

"You're not either. He's in the *army*, he's a trained killer. He's packing a goddamned sword."

John Gamble laughed. They stood in the early morning

sunshine outside the restaurant. Lynnie now noticed that her neck was stiff from sleeping in a peculiar position.

"Tell Dante we can't take him any farther," she demanded.

"You tell him. You're the one who's paranoid." John Gamble opened the sliding back door and joined Rebel on the seat, stretching out with his arms crossed, shutting his eyes.

Lynnie was setting Dante's backpack scabbard side down on the pavement when he came out of the restaurant. He blinked his tiny puffed eyes in the light. She felt momentarily sorry for him when he looked hurt, but she decided she could not spend the rest of the trip wondering when he would slice open her throat and steal her car.

"I'm sorry," she said lamely.

"Oh."

"I'm sorry, I just don't feel comfortable . . ."

"It's cool," he said, hitching his fatigues with his thumbs. "You can't trust anybody."

"Amen," said John Gamble from the van, not looking at Lynnie.

To John Gamble, Dante said, "One more toke for the road?"

John Gamble agreed. The two of them took big bong hits in the back seat, the smoke leaking from their mouths as they smiled benignly at Lynnie. Then Dante shook her hand and ambled to the edge of the parking lot, his thumb in the air.

"Other side!" John Gamble shouted from the back window as Lynnie pulled out. "You want to go *north!*"

Dante waved, crossing the road in Lynnie's wobbling rearview mirror.

"I'm not paranoid," she told her brother, but he didn't answer.

A few minutes later Lynnie heard him slapping his shirt pockets, looking for his Baggie of pot and lighter. "I don't suppose you want to have a conversation with Mr. Long?" he called out as he made his way into the rear of the car. John Gamble named his bongs and this current one was Mr. Long. Mr. Long rode behind the farthest back seat because bong water nauseated Lynnie. They were only twenty miles from Salt Lake; they would make the little Montana town where her parents had bought their summer house by that evening.

She agreed so that he would forgive her for kicking out his friend. But once she was high she began to remember that she had a right to be upset. Her recurring problem with her brother was that she could never keep in mind her valid complaints. Perhaps that was her problem with her whole family: she too desperately needed them to like her.

"You want to hear some tunes?" John Gamble asked. He still sat behind her.

"O.K."

Instead of putting a disk in his player, he began to sing. Lynnie stiffened; as far as she knew, she'd never heard her brother sing before in her life. "According to the *Kinsey* Report," he began, working his way toward the refrain. "It's too darn hot," he sang, not happily but with remorse. Maybe it was just from having to yell over the VW's noise, but his rendition of an old song Lynnie had always believed cheery struck her as remarkably melancholy. In the rearview, his face was sweet, his eyes mere slits, his shining red forehead swaying from side to side. He had Rebel's head in his lap and was massaging the dog's flabby neck. Rebel groaned and rolled onto his back, his leg twitching, his long toenails clicking at the window. Lynnie watched as John Gamble ran his fingers down Rebel's ribs, scratched his tummy, circled his little lump of a penis, and ended in the dog's feathered haunches. Her brother was not afraid to touch an animal, dead or alive, at the mouth or the privates; Lynnie tried but could not remain angry with him.

*

Where does metal come from? Lynnie wondered. Did other people arrive at adulthood knowing such things, or was ignorance of the most profound nature the way of the world? She and John Gamble were having dinner in Butte, just three hours from their destination, sitting in a restaurant window watching a man unload new cars at a lot across the street. Lynnie was sliding down from another high, wondering where aluminum and steel came from, tire rubber, paint and vinyl. She had dim images of lavalike molten matter being hammered by muscular men as they sang grim slave songs. John Gamble had been telling her about a new sort of train he envisioned, one that moved automobiles from coast to coast, letting people off to finish their journeys by road. "From New York to Wyoming, you sit in the club car guzzling gin," he said, "then pop in your car and head off to the hills. I'd do it, wouldn't you?"

Because she was an impressionable person and latched onto other people's habits as her own, Lynnie began thinking about ways to save gasoline, unlikely inventions for easing travel, inexpensive means of acquiring food. She'd forgotten this about her brother, his preoccupation with things impersonal and pragmatic. He and Dante had probably spent the night chatting about a more perfect military. Her own tendency to inhabit her companion's world was what made her and John Gamble mostly get along. As far back as Lynnie could remember, John Gamble had devised the games and she had played the supporting parts.

She did this with other people, too. For instance, last

year she'd had a roommate who was a lesbian, and after a few months they were having sex. Lynnie had liked Kit's breasts, which were big and soft — lovely to lay one's head against — but found Kit herself a little overwhelming. Even now, after Lynnie had moved to her own apartment in Dallas and quit answering Kit's calls, she felt Kit's angry pursuit of her. Lynnie had enjoyed being with a woman, but it wasn't her real inclination, she had discovered. Her whole life she'd been like a chameleon, dutifully fading from one characteristic to another. Now, consorting with her brother on the road, she was becoming a happy-go-lucky pothead, thinking about pleasanter traveling modes, fretting over dead woodchucks. She had decided not to eat meat anymore ("flesh," as John Gamble so vigilantly put it), since her brother didn't.

His eating habits fit with his austerity plan — beans and rice and whole loaves of mushy wheat bread. At the restaurant in Butte they consumed scrambled eggs and Tabasco, John Gamble having convinced the waitress to throw in some onions and green peppers and cheese as well. John Gamble was the fastest eater Lynnie had ever known, not sloppy about it but certainly speedy, like an efficient beaver.

"John Gamble!" Lynnie nearly choked when she realized something. "I didn't bring a wedding gift."

"So? Were we supposed to?"

"They're getting married, aren't they? Oh, I can't believe I was so stupid as to forget a present."

"I really hate this obligation to buy gifts all the time. Every time I look up I've missed somebody's birthday. Are you going to drink that water?"

She shoved her glass his way. "Mom and Dad have everything, anyway."

"Not in Dukeyville. New house, new stuff." He drank her water and continued. "I could have brought them a salad spinner I got at a garage sale. I have two."

"'Dukeyville'?" Lynnie giggled. When she was high, ordinarily unfunny things made her giggle. The town's real name was Lewisburg, but she knew she would never call it anything but Dukeyville now. She swung her eyes around the restaurant to see if she was laughing too loudly. "How much would it cost to stay high all the time?" she asked John Gamble in a whisper.

He snorted, swiping in the last of his eggs with his finger. "I'm working on that very problem right as we speak, you drug fiend, you."

She felt she could curl up on the upholstered booth seat and sleep till morning, her stomach full, her head cluttered with images that had nothing to do with her personally, but John Gamble had finished eating and was ready to go, running a toothpick around his checkered teeth.

"Why bother?" Lynnie asked him, giggling again.

"Why bother what?" he said, then repeated, "Fiend. Pothead."

"Bad influence," Lynnie said as they crossed the parking lot to her van. "Attractive nuisance. *Un*attractive nuisance."

When they left Butte, Lynnie was driving again. Her brother was her ally, so she did not now, as she often did at the threshold of reunion with her parents, dread what was coming. It occurred to her to concentrate on her contentedness, her physical happiness at driving an unfamiliar road, full of food, her brother beside her, music playing on his machine. It reminded her of trips she and John Gamble had made in high school, before Lynnie snubbed him, back when she couldn't drive but could navigate. They would travel to little fishing lakes around Wichita, park, fry steaks, drink beer, sleep on the rocky ground. This had been their idea of camping. Lynnie thought John Gamble had made his life an extended version of those trips, and to be with him was to feel as if she were on a vacation, and the vacation was to her own childhood.

She had always been welcome with John Gamble.

From the restaurant he had brought a white "to go" sack containing a hamburger for Rebel. The dog ate the meal in two bites, lettuce and pickles and onions and all, snuffling at the foil wrap until Lynnie reached blindly behind her to pull it away from him.

"Rebel's the only person I know who eats faster than you," she told John Gamble.

But he was watching the trees pass, his hands folded on his lap. He looked like a child, studying the landscape, and Lynnie had an urgent desire to know what he was thinking, which people occupied his musings. She wondered whether he was in love. His girlfriends from Wichita had always disappointed Lynnie. They were too average — pretty rather than exotic, tittering rather than witty, with names like Mary Jo or Christy. But while his eccentricities had excited girls in high school and college, Lynnie doubted they still would. He smelled terrible; his clothes were permanently dirty. Really, if Lynnie saw a stranger who looked like John Gamble she would be convinced he was homeless, an unemployed drug addict — which was pretty much what her brother was. And yet, of course, he wasn't anything that simple.

"Stop!" he suddenly shouted. Lynnie braked, alert for road kill, and thereby missed the road sign. "Perfect!" he exclaimed. "I got a photo op."

Lynnie's dim vibrating headlights illuminated the green

sign. Two cities were listed, arrows pointing in opposite directions, one to Wisdom, the other to Opportunity.

"And just think," John Gamble said after he'd taken his shot and they were zooming along again, "we're not going to either one of them."

*

Their parents' Montana house was a big green place their father delighted in photographing, an old clapboard house square and symmetrical like the one in Kansas, door like a mouth, upstairs windows like eyes, the roof a pointed hat. Lynnie'd received a packet of pictures in Dallas, showing the place from all sides, approaching and retreating, featuring not her mother but McWard, whose big mustachioed head dwarfed his ottoman-like body. From the looks of it, the house was on a hill in the middle of town, right beside the sheriff's office and jail. Retired, her parents had decided they deserved a respite from the sultry midwestern summers of Kansas. Lewisburg, Montana, population 800 and falling, had seemed perfect.

Lynnie found the house by locating the police cars parked next door to it. The darkened street was wide, and she executed a fat U-turn to pull behind her sister Natty's Volvo wagon, purchased four years ago, when Natty had reached thirty and inherited her hundred thou.

Ahead of the Volvo was her parents' Toyota sedan, a modest, reliable car, white for visibility, equipped with a flashlight, candle, blanket, fold-up cardboard SEND HELP! sign, Fix-a-Flat, and small flare in the trunk, and fitted with ultrasonic sensors on the hood to warn away animals. Parents.

Lynnie and John Gamble hesitated after the VW's engine sputtered silent, both looking timidly at the unfamiliar house — yet somehow familiar, rising up before them like a major appliance, avocado colored instead of white. It was as if a hard rain were falling and they were trying to gauge the correct moment to plunge through the storm.

"I feel a certain reluctance," John Gamble said. His foul breath decided Lynnie. She popped the driver's door open and jumped to the pavement. Lewisburg was absolutely still. From the highway came the sound of a lone upshifting truck. The sky overhead was clear and thick with stars. "We should be able to make out the aurora," John Gamble said, staring into space.

A single light was on at her parents' house, and as Lynnie looked, her sister Natty's face appeared in the window. Of course it would be Natty waiting up for them.

Natty was the family scorekeeper. She knew birthdays, she sent cards, she phoned long distance to interrogate. She analyzed, she attacked, she competed. Younger, she had been an athlete. Nobody else had any inclination whatsoever, avoiding physical activity, shunning competitive sports. Natty was trim and tanned always, her hair in little bobbing ponytails, her freckled shapely legs ending in anklets and white Nikes. She always resembled a gymnast, someone who could fling herself effortlessly at a parallel bar and spin around in perfect form, even after her three pregnancies.

Eleven years earlier, just before meeting and marrying her cloddy husband, Natty had had her breasts enlarged. Lynnie, fifteen at the time, had been thrilled to see the results. She'd also been sworn to secrecy; as the family baby, she held no power to reprimand or punish, not even particularly to judge. Natty had invited her into her bedroom for a showing of the new breasts, which were round and large, perfecting an already near-perfect body. Natty had held them like fruit in her own hands, her shirt opened like stage curtains framing the display. She stared down with unabashed pleasure, encouraging Lynnie to touch them too. It was the only time in her life Lynnie could remember touching Natty's skin, feeling the heavy heat of her new Playboy breasts, Natty's delight provoking in her something like warmth.

But she did not often smile, Natty Weiner. It was not one of her routine expressions. When she opened the door for her younger brother and sister on this chilly late August Montana evening, she instantly put a finger to her lips to shush them. "Everyone's in bed," she said in greeting. "I had to trap the dogs in the shed so they wouldn't bark at what's-his-face."

"Rebel," Lynnie supplied. She'd left him in the car. He had a tendency to pee on rugs where other animals lived.

In the moment when they might have embraced, they stood eyeing each other until Natty said, "What took you so long?"

John Gamble didn't bother answering, sliding around her and into the living room. He had quit liking Natty as a teenager, when her bossiness finally surpassed his toler-ance of it. Lynnie could think of nothing that proved John Gamble's fallibility more than his treatment of Natty, which was simply mean. Just before Christmas every year he asked Natty to "go cheap," which meant not purchasing him a gift. He would go cheap in return, he always told her. This infuriated Natty. "I already got you a gift," she would say to him. "I don't care whether or not you get something for me. I *like* to give gifts. I'm going to give you one." It was true that Natty liked to give gifts; she and her husband, Dean, had money, and their gifts were expensive, the most surprising and useful things, small household appliances or pieces of art. Last year they'd given Lynnie a new telephone and answering machine, things she hadn't thought she needed but now truly appreciated. John Gamble's portable compact disk player had also come from Natty. But it was not true that Natty didn't care about receiving something in return. She *needed* nothing — finding a gift for her was nearly impossible — yet she expected the token. And John Gamble refused to provide it.

Family terrorism, Lynnie thought, and then she realized that Natty would have gotten their parents a wedding gift, and that she would fault the rest of them for forgetting.

It was like Natty to think ahead, to put the dogs in the shed, to have sandwiches in plastic wrap waiting. She asked if they were hungry while they already could hear John Gamble ransacking the refrigerator, the suction of the door opening, the shift of eggs and condiment bottles. Natty liked to feed people, despite the fact that she never ate, herself. Part of her role in the family dynamic was always to be at least ten pounds lighter than her sisters. Lynnie felt fat around Natty, and she knew Natty thrived on it. When they were younger, Natty used to make herself throw up in order to keep thin. She might still do so; one thing Lynnie kept learning was that grownups were merely large versions of their childish selves.

Lynnie trailed her sister into the kitchen. It was a high-ceilinged room, the stove and refrigerator different colors, the table much too large and jammed beneath a window. John Gamble was drinking from the milk carton; Lynnie watched Natty, who held her tongue.

To give her sister something to talk about as an expert, Lynnie said, "How's Dad's back?"

In answer, Natty pointed at what looked like a metal table with no top. "He's having trouble walking." Lynnie only half attended to the ensuing description of their father's back problems. He'd never really recovered from the tornado; his disks were surgically fused over the years, there was a progression of paralysis up his spine. The walker reminded Lynnie of hospitals and death. So she watched John Gamble, who studiously ignored Natty's articulate explanation, the ins and outs of new drugs, of acupuncture and water therapy, her knuckles grinding together to illustrate the missing cushion in her father's spinal column. John Gamble now leaned over the sink, eating English muffins and shredded cheese from a plastic sack, then opened the back door and sniffed the air. He closed it behind him as he left, and reappeared a minute later with the dogs. Three were familiar: the new Scottie, McWard; Natty's golden retriever; and, of course, Rebel. But the fourth, a large brindle beast, Lynnie had never seen before.

"Dammit, Gamble," Natty said, interrupting herself, slapping away Rebel's nose from her crotch. It was a habit Lynnie had not had any success in discouraging. "You're going to wake the whole fucking house!" Lynnie always forgot how profane her sister was when her children weren't around.

John Gamble ignored Natty and sat on the kitchen floor and encouraged the dogs to skitter around him, McWard emitting a low proprietorial growl, the brindle animal with his hackles raised.

"What is *that?*" Lynnie asked.

"Joanne's beast," Natty said. "Hateful thing, another orphan from the pound. He's already tried to bite Amanda, didn't you, you shit? Going for her throat."

John Gamble scooted crablike through the other dogs to get close to the new one, who growled.

"What's his name?" Lynnie asked.

"Mephistopheles."

"He's a jackal," John Gamble said as the animal snapped at him.

"Leave it to Joanne," said Natty. Joanne was Natty's project, her theme, her bane. "Bringing him home was just another example of classic passive-aggressive behavior," Natty went on. "The most hostile brute she could find, just like that punk."

"That punk" was TV Mitchell, Joanne's adopted son. Lynnie had met him the previous Christmas, a ten-year-old boy whose natural mother was in prison for killing her father, the boy's grandfather. Joanne had found TV in the psychiatric ward where she'd interned as a nurse; last year, at age thirty-seven, she had adopted, just as she had taken in strays and outcasts and misfits her whole life.

"Why," John Gamble said, "do you suppose we keep bringing home male dogs? They fight, they pee on everything, they run away, they attack. Females are much more civilized, and yet . . ." He held out his hand toward the four circling dogs, each one with a nose in another's privates.

"I guess we're just stupid," Natty said. "Isn't that what we're supposed to deduce?"

John Gamble scratched his ribs, refusing the bait. "What does one *do* in Dukeyville?" he asked her instead.

Natty had begun tidying up, putting away food, slapping at surfaces with a sponge. "Well," she said, "there's four churches, six bars, a thrift store, some junk shops, two groceries —"

"But what do you *do?*"

"We've been teaching Dean bridge," Natty said. Her husband was a lunk, sweet and handsome and capable of earning a great deal of money, but not entirely bright. When Natty had asked her mother what she thought of him, Dorothea had hesitated, then replied, "Well, he's no intellectual," and that was all.

John Gamble yawned expansively, revealing his three gray teeth, the small yellow flecks of food between the rest, their ragged surfaces. Natty literally gasped, which made Lynnie instantly want to jump to her brother's defense. This was what kept her edgy around her family — the way her feelings for them ran the gamut in a matter of seconds. It was such *work* to be with them.

"I'm crashing on the lawn," John Gamble told them suddenly. "You got any blankets or ground cloth or drapes or something?"

Natty blinked. "We had you on the couch," she said, but John Gamble was already heading through the swinging doors to the living room in search of covers. She followed, whispering, "We had you out here on the long couch because TV is on the other." Lynnie, following, looked down at TV, the strange boy who'd recently joined their family. His mouth was open as he breathed, the lips full and heart-shaped. A dark downy fuzz showed where his sideburns would be; a flush of pink that would become acne and a braided tail of hair lay across his cheek. Lynnie vowed to be open-minded about him, to try to like him. Last Christmas he'd walked in on her in the bathroom, stood gawking before pulling the door closed as he left.

Natty went on in a whisper to John Gamble, "You don't want to sleep outside. It's freezing —"

"Can I take this?" John Gamble held up an army blanket Lynnie could remember from Kansas — its scratchy texture, its too-hot heaviness, its odor of cedar.

"You don't want —"

"Can I take it?"

"Yes!" Natty grabbed her retriever, the dog she could

safely presume upon, and dragged him out the front door. "Go pee!" she commanded, then said to Lynnie, "John Gamble's going to try hard to ruin this wedding, isn't he?"

TV turned in his sleep at the sound of her voice, his body long and manlike beneath the blankets, the couch squeaking under his weight.

"Am I my brother's keeper?" Lynnie asked.

Natty gave her an appraising look. "Basically," she said.

*

Despite deep fatigue, Lynnie had trouble falling asleep. This was always the case in any house where her parents also slept. The room designated as hers was nothing more than a large closet on the second floor with a seventy-five-watt light bulb hanging overhead, dowel rods for clothes hangers, and high shelves on either side lined with extra bath towels and toilet paper. Her bed was a rollaway, and every time she turned it creaked, threatening to dump her out. Through the wall on one side were her parents; on the other were Natty and Dean and their youngest daughter, Thea, who had never slept anywhere but beside her mother. Lynnie recalled her own pleasure in sharing a bed with her parents, the tremendous heat, the impenetrable safety. Theirs was not a physically demonstrative family: Lynnie had used to fake tears simply to earn a hug or stroke. A bad dream was adequate reason to visit her parents' hot bed. Folded in, Lynnie could trace her fingertips over her mother's scarred arms, the little sewn cuts from the tornado, which looked in daylight like harmless white slugs crawling from wrist to shoulder.

Across the hall slept her oldest sister, Joanne, with Natty's other two girls. Though the group assembled here represented the whole of her immediate family, Lynnie felt as if someone were missing. It was always this way: she had, as a child, set an extra place at the dinner table, not to be funny, she didn't think, not to call attention, but to make concrete her sense of someone's absence in the face of irrefutable wholeness. In other houses — her own apartment in Dallas, for example — she often fell asleep envisioning the wide expanse of the United States, her parents and siblings in their homes, the dark rooms in which they steadily breathed, their distant sleeping forms a comfort. But now that these same people slept all around her, their places pegged and inhabited, Lynnie could not rest. This anxious emotion was one she could never recall when separate from her family. They were its cause, they were its very name.

*

Hours later Lynnie woke to whispers and giggles. Her three nieces were standing over her while she lay on the rollaway bed.

"Aunt Lynnie," they said to her, trying the name on their tongues. They were nine, six, and three years old; John Gamble claimed that Natty and Dean only fucked every three years.

Lynnie pulled herself up on an elbow, happy to have slept in a T-shirt instead of naked, happy to have slept and somehow lost her sadness. Fortunately, she could not reconstruct her dreams. "Go look in the yard," she told the girls.

They ran across the hallway to the window. "That's a man!" yelled Thea, the three-year-old. "A man in our flowers!"

"Field clover," her oldest sister corrected her. "They're weeds, not flowers."

Lynnie joined them, looking down at the dark green bundle in the middle of the side yard, John Gamble's red forehead and mussed hair poking out of the cocoon. Rebel wandered nearby, sniffing at the fence. When Lynnie had tried to coax him upstairs with her last night, he had whined until she led him to her brother, on the lawn, where her dog settled, groaning, on John Gamble's feet.

"Are those your pajamas?" asked Betsy, the six-year-old, scrutinizing Lynnie.

Lynnie looked down at her cutoffs and shirt. "You like them?"

"No," Betsy said. "They're like a boy's. I like mine better. See?" She tucked her head to read her pink nightgown. "'Some Bunny Loves Me.'"

"It doesn't say that," Lynnie told her. "It says, 'Some Bunny *Bites* Me.'" She leaned down and gently bit Betsy's shoulder, breathed in the scent of child. The nightgown was of a thin synthetic material Lynnie associated with lightning-like static electricity and tiny black nubs that could be picked off to pass time. Through the nightgown Lynnie could see Betsy's panties and skin, her round bottom. The elastic at the wrists cut into her plump hands.

Amanda, nine, wore a large cotton T-shirt and saggy men's athletic socks; she had no baby fat left. Lynnie noticed with a shock that Amanda had the tiny beginning of breasts, little stopper-sized nipples that she crossed her arms to hide. Lynnie could remember the horror of those sudden lumps, though they hadn't come to her until she was eleven or twelve. John Gamble had told her yesterday that eating steroid-laden beef caused premature puberty.

"Do you eat a lot of red meat?" she asked Amanda, who responded by curling her lip.

Lynnie turned back to the window. Lewisburg appeared smaller in the daylight; from where she stood, Lynnie could see farmland and forest, gloomy hills just at the edge of town.

"Who *is* that man?" Betsy asked.

"Who?" echoed Thea. Her toes protruded from the torn feet of her Dr. Dentons.

"Uncle John Gamble," Amanda told them quietly, watching him, presenting Lynnie with her profile. Amanda had become more than a generic child since she'd last seen her, more complicated and touchy. The dark circles under her eyes were like thumbprints. She was unsmiling, like her mother, but without Natty's smug busyness. Amanda would be called *sensitive* by her teachers, the catch-all word they would use to denote her unnerving silence, her easily hurt feelings, her frequent tears, her unpopularity. Lynnie wanted to hug her close and give her advice. She had a premonition — or perhaps a hope — that someday Amanda might come to her for help.

The girls led her downstairs, pausing at the sofa to inspect TV.

"His feet stink so bad," Betsy whispered, "he has to leave his shoes on the front porch."

Thea giggled, then kissed her fingers and blew across her palm in TV's direction.

"Don't make me sick," said Amanda, slapping Thea's hand.

TV grunted, burrowing into his pillow, and Thea shushed away in her footed pajamas to tell on Amanda.

"Oh, you're in *trouble*," said Betsy.

"No, I'm not," Amanda said confidently. "Mom hates him."

Everyone had gathered in the kitchen, which smelled of scorched coffee and the porky haze that floated near the ceiling. The dogs leapt to their feet when Lynnie entered, skittering and slathering, including the jackal. Instantly he began barking at her, his tongue purple and black, as if he'd eaten ink.

"Shut up, Messy!" three or four voices chorused.

Lynnie's mother herded the dogs out the back door, past Joanne, who was smoking a cigarette and blowing the smoke out the screen, fanning the air with her free hand. "Does this bother you?" she asked Lynnie, smiling nervously.

Lynnie told her it didn't. Between them, they'd taken all the available nervous habits, Lynnie a nail-biter, Joanne a smoker and teeth-grinder. But bad habits looked better on Joanne than they did on Lynnie. Joanne was the only beautiful child, a fact Lynnie might have resented, except that Joanne had always been so ill-at-ease and scared in the world. The surface of her face wore fear like another layer of skin.

"How was the trip?" she asked Lynnie, waving at the smoke.

"O.K. How'd you get here?"

"Rode with Mom and Dad, all of us, me and TV and the dogs in the back seat, just like being kids. I even got carsick. We're going to fly home," she added. "Day after tomorrow."

They stepped apart to allow Dorothea room to pass. On her return, she gave Lynnie a long hug, her bathrobe smelling of coffee and deodorant. All the children resembled Dorothea, round-headed and dark-haired, even the three little girls of the next generation. She had the clear wide blue eyes of someone guileless and young; she would never believe in wickedness. Nothing seemed to have changed about her since her own childhood except her teeth, which appeared to grow longer as she aged.

"Hi, Mom," Lynnie said, pulling away. When she had left for college, eight years earlier, her mother had surprised her by giving her a hug in farewell. Tears had welled up.

Lynnie had consulted with her brother and sisters. "Did she cry when *you* left home?" They confirmed that she had, and they had all expressed similar disbelief. These things were perfectly normal in other families, but in Lynnie's experience, her family did not touch. Now her mother always greeted the children with hugs; this never failed to startle Lynnie, to startle all of them. And it evoked the same feeling she'd had in the night, that mournful, restless sensation relegated exclusively to home.

Her father had stood, with difficulty, and waited for Lynnie to make her way to him along the oversized table. This room was too small for him, the table too crowded in. His chair seat was at the back of his knees, forcing him to bend like a Z. On the table were his large red hands, the spatulate nails. The hands were liver-spotted and covered by skin so prone to tearing, so like parchment, that the slightest scratch would bring blood. As always, a Band-Aid was stuck on one knuckle, and his thumbnail was a ghastly plum color. The things he'd been best at required physical strength or motion: house-building and furniture moving, car repair and yardwork. Now he could hardly stand; his clothes looked handed down from a larger man. Lynnie imagined that inside his rigid body was a swirl of activity, thoughts and desires flying crazily like insects trapped in a jar. The mustache he'd grown over his lip made him look like he might tell a joke. Lynnie hugged him and he patted her back lightly.

"You find the place O.K.?" he asked, for something to say.

"Nice place," Lynnie answered.

"We like it," he said simply, sitting stiffly and slowly down.

Lynnie sat beside him to eat pancakes, which her

mother supplied every few minutes. Joanne refused food, disappearing into the dark living room with her coffee cup and cigarette pack. Lynnie's nieces argued over the chair on Lynnie's other side, Betsy winning, leaning her head on Lynnie's shoulder. Her hair smelled sour, faintly of urine or sweat. Lynnie marveled at her own capacity for instantaneous amnesia: the sad feeling was gone again.

*

Her family discussed itself; that was their topic. When Lynnie had finished breakfast and been invited shopping by Natty, their subject was first (walking down the steep hill to Main Street) Joanne and then (circling the stale little mercantile under the curious eye of the saleswoman) John Gamble.

"His teeth are so goddamned grotesque," Natty declared. Lynnie trudged slightly behind her as usual, wondering what in the world she would find in Lewisburg to give her parents for a wedding gift.

"What did you buy them?" she asked Natty once more.

"It's a surprise, something practical that I'm sure they haven't thought of getting for themselves."

"But what?"

"None o' yo beeswax."

The store they were browsing in was a curious mix of antiques and hardware, little useless knickknacks — kitties, shepherdesses, teacups — among watering cans, paint rollers, flashlights, protective eyewear, insect poison, batteries, and copper plumbing.

Lynnie stopped to finger a package of steel wool scrapers. "I could buy Mom a lifetime supply."

Natty snorted, then resumed her tirade on John Gamble's teeth. "If my teeth looked like that, I'd be at a dentist in a heartbeat."

"I'm not going to find anything in here for them," Lynnie said. "Did Joanne get them a present?"

"Doubtful."

They left the mercantile and crossed the street to the grocery. People stared openly, nodding after they'd gotten over the shock of seeing strange faces in town. Lynnie followed her sister along the aisles of food, admiring as Natty tossed things confidently into the cart. Cheerios, macaroni and cheese, broccoli, grapes, saltines with no salt, two quivering gallons of milk (one whole, one skim), two chunks of cheese, a cantaloupe, ginger snaps, Scotch tape, diaper wipes. Natty didn't even consult prices, didn't carry a list. She'd grabbed her purse on the way out the door knowing there was adequate cash in it. Lynnie had never in her life shopped this way. Her sister's efficiency, her obvious triumphant passage into the world of Wife and Mother, still astonished Lynnie, who sometimes had to collect stray single dollar bills from coat pockets and pennies from dresser drawers in order to buy supper, which might be a carton of ice cream or a can of Tom's Tamales.

"You're not going to eat that?" Natty was saying. Lynnie had picked up an apple and was about to bite into it. "You've got to wash it — with soap — to get the chemicals off. Sometimes I peel them for the kids." Lynnie bit into the apple and was still gnawing at it in the checkout line. "Oh shit," said her sister. "Could you run find cherry yogurt for Thea? I promised her." Lynnie turned without thinking, without consciously resenting the command. Natty had offered to purchase whatever Lynnie might want to eat, had in fact touched a variety of Lynnie's favorite foods, remembering them the way no one else ever would: canned Bartlett pears, rubbery Colby cheese, Brach's —

only Brach's — candy corn. But Lynnie had turned down these offers, she didn't know why, and could only rankle in retrospect at being sent on an errand to the dairy case.

"Maybe I'll offer to pay for a dental exam," Natty went on about John Gamble as up the hill they trudged again, Natty with two bags while Lynnie, a step behind her, carried one.

"He won't want you to do that," Lynnie said. "He said they don't bother him."

"Honey, teeth don't go gray for no reason. Hell, we forgot frozen juice for the punch tomorrow."

"What punch?"

"For the wedding. Remember the wedding?"

"With alcohol?"

"I certainly hope so." Natty ascended the steep front porch of the green house and kicked the door with her shoe. Dean opened it and took the bags from her arms. "Put those away," she told him as she dashed back down the steps. "I gotta get what I forgot." And away she jogged down the hill, leaving Dean and Lynnie together on the porch, Dean smiling amiably. He was the most comfortable person Lynnie knew, happy and complacent and completely unperturbable. Even his smile existed without laugh lines, a big permanent crease on his face.

The wind blew, making the air feel like country air instead of town air. Lynnie shivered. She'd seen a rock shop downtown; maybe she'd go buy her parents a big geode or something. Inside, her father coughed. Little McWard bounced at the screen.

"Whirling dervish," Dean offered, concerning his wife.

*

Lynnie tried to avoid being caught alone with her mother. Dorothea had a clumsy way of eliciting information that embarrassed Lynnie, a supposed-to-be-casual tone that always belied extreme concern. Dorothea was highly shockable. She fretted constantly about all her children, believing over and over again that their temporary trends — in friends, haircuts, lifestyles, lovers — were irreversibly, tragically enduring. She clipped and mailed newspaper or magazine articles she thought pertinent — on nail-biting, in Lynnie's case, or the dangers of living alone in a large city. For a while, when they were children, she'd required family meetings, where they would all sit with their eyes lowered, listening to her try to describe — carefully, withholding judgment — a mysterious disappearance of cash from her purse or a faint odor of marijuana smoke she'd noticed in the car. She wanted to know about her children's lives, and then she wanted to give advice — not only give it, but exact promises that her advice would be taken — whether they had interest in her thoughts or not.

"Tell me about your trip," Dorothea said to Lynnie in the kitchen. Her mother was always busy — cleaning, repairing, reading, playing. Now she sat in a turquoise sweatsuit beneath the sink, scouring a cupboard.

Lynnie began with the tornadoes, enjoying her mother's alarm at her description of the storm. Next she described John Gamble's sagging home, omitting the curious artworks, and the journey, omitting the hitchhiker, the burials, and the bong. "It was fine," she said. Her mother's head disappeared beneath the counter again.

"I'm worried about your brother," she said.

"What?" Lynnie's heart quickened. She didn't want to talk about John Gamble. "What?"

"Your brother," Dorothea said, standing now with a handful of old rubber bands. "We don't hear from him anymore."

"He's just busy with his church. He's got some pea-cocks."

"Your father would like to hear from him more often." This was her mother's way, placing her hurt feelings on someone else. Lynnie now wondered whose idea the wedding was, whether her mother or her father had proposed. It had been Natty who had called to tell Lynnie, beginning a kind of chain reaction: Lynnie had had to persuade John Gamble to come along; Joanne had decided to take time off when she heard the rest of the family would be there.

"Maybe John Gamble will go with your father on his drive tonight to look for animals," Dorothea was saying. "He gets a kick out of seeing moose." From beneath the sink came the sound of scratching, Dorothea's trademark puff of steel wool rasping away. "Nobody's been under here for ages," she said, her voice strained by the angle of her neck. Lynnie was relieved not to discuss John Gamble any further.

"Look at this." Dorothea held out a Folgers can that belonged in a museum. "Projects," she called her daily activities, these endless useless chores. Lynnie had postulated to Natty, who loved analyzing behavior, that busyness made their mother less likely to think about things, though now Dorothea said, in a thoughtful way, "My theory is that this family just up and left one day — got tired of living here. The house stood empty for ten years before we bought it, and nothing appears to have been touched in all that time. This thing" — she held up the can — "was for bacon grease." Much of what she said was prefaced with "My theory," followed by a cheery postulation only remotely realistic. She tossed the coffee can out the back door, the screen of which was propped against the wind, shaking.

"Go wake your brother," she told Lynnie. "I want him to paint something for me."

Their mother used to call John Gamble in a high seductive voice when she wanted him to help her. She would have him hold or lift or move or hammer or adjust something upstairs, a trifling but harassing tendency she had for making repairs or improvements, harnessing her only son into the endeavor. It probably had had appeal for the children when they were six or eight years old, activities meant to instruct them in thriftiness and self-sufficiency, but it was now supremely irritating.

"Get the duct tape," Lynnie said, standing over John Gamble outside, watching his closed eyes. Flies landed on him and his skin went into tiny spasms as they walked from cheek to nose. Sleeping, he looked harmless and pure. Lynnie kicked him. "Mom wants you," she said.

"Not a *project*," he said after a moment, groaning and turning away from the sun. "Where are those girls, anyway? I sent them for food hours ago." He sat up, and Lynnie had to step back, his stench was so strong. Beneath his pillow, which was a pale green couch cushion, was a Baggie of pot and his stained little corncob pipe. "Don't you think I ought to plant a tree out here?" he asked her. "The place is just so scorched-looking."

Lynnie glanced at the grass and field clover. It had not occurred to her to miss a tree, though it was true there wasn't one. Their yard in Kansas was purely trees, not a blade of grass anywhere. In the neighborhood it had stood out like something haunted; their father claimed he was providing chlorophyll for a four-block radius.

"First thing I'm going to do is find a tree," John Gamble told her, pulling his army blanket around his shoulders and wiggling, under it, into his cords. "Then I'm going to build a fire pit. This is the kind of town that'll let you make a fire in your yard, don't you think?"

"I think they'd encourage it. But Mom wants you to paint."

"Yeah, yeah," he said, pulling on his plaid flannel shirt, the elbows of which were worn through. Lynnie wondered what he had done between Christmas and now that would account for the frayed condition of his clothes. Every year she gave him a new identical flannel shirt, eighteen dollars at JCP, red and yellow and blue, size medium; it was all he ever asked for from her. His parents gave him money, his sister Joanne a new pair of pants, also from JCP. Natty always surprised him, excessively, and he never gave her a thing, though he usually remembered her children.

The same information, the same arrangement of facts, wandered around Lynnie's head all the time, and she never knew what to do with any of it. For a while some part of it would make sense and then it would pull loose and float with the rest, one emotional oddity among many.

"Natty got them a wedding gift," she told John Gamble.

"Then there'll be one more star in her heavenly crown," he said, standing and zipping. "Can I borrow your car?"

John Gamble had inherited an offshoot of his mother's tendency to *do* things — Natty's strain of that tendency was to be occupied constantly in practical ways — but he wanted to choose those things, a fact Dorothea hadn't yet figured out. She wanted him to do what she wanted. And none of these things *needed* doing. Why a tree? Why a fire pit? Why paint anything?

"What about Mom?" she asked.

They looked toward the house, where their mother stood at the window, watching them. It was a tall, low window. Before her stood Thea, the baby, the one named after her. Their mother was virtually unchanged since Lynnie's childhood, and Lynnie could so clearly feel her mother's hands resting on *her* shoulders, it was as if she were standing in Thea's place, watching two strangers in the yard folding a blanket and stuffing drug paraphernalia in pockets. If she were her mother, she would feel mournful that her children were grown and secretive. And she would wish that they were small again, and that their problems were manageable, and that she was the one they would come to first for help.

"She was a good mother when we were little," Lynnie declared, loyalty blooming in her throat for no good reason.

"You want to go with me to find a tree?" John Gamble asked.

"Don't you think she was a good mother?"

"Sure. I never said any different. I'll be right back." He jogged to the porch with the blanket and pillow, and Lynnie watched Dorothea turn to talk to him, little Thea slipping between her legs, away from her strange uncle. When he returned he had the other two girls with him. "Natty won't let them go unless you come too," he said flatly.

"O.K.," Lynnie agreed, secretly flattered that Natty might think her worthy of trust, and at the same time angry with her sister for wanting to punish John Gamble by withholding that trust.

*

They drove into the Bitterroot Forest, looking for a tree to steal. John Gamble sat in the back with Betsy, eating the box of crackers Natty had just bought. "No fucking salt," he said, sputtering crumbs for Betsy's amusement. "*Salt*ines without *salt*." Betsy laughed hysterically, crunching up a cracker in her mouth and repeating after him. Amanda

wore her shoulder belt tight across her budding breasts and
held firmly to a chicken handle in the front. Lynnie asked
if her driving was making Amanda nervous. Amanda turned
to look at her, then said no.

The forest was not what Lynnie had imagined a forest
in Montana would be like. For one thing, it kept being
interrupted by farms — ranches, she supposed they were
called out West — and for another, it was unbelievably
sparse. A river ran through it, but it was hardly a river, and
the mountains were merely hills, dotted with cows. They
kept encountering intersections, with stop signs.

"Not a very impressive forest," she said to John Gamble,
who asked her if she'd thought she would see a big bad wolf.

"Tunes, please," he said, clapping his hands once in her
direction, "and then I want these girls to tell me the things
Natty won't let them do."

Lynnie switched on the radio and found country-western twanging.

"Well," Betsy said, "she won't let us have Fruit Stripe
gum. I'm going to buy it when I'm a grownup and eat it
all the time."

"Gum, eh?"

"Actually, it's the sugar."

"And the NutraSweet," Amanda added.

"What else?" John Gamble asked.

"No cartoons with commercials," Betsy went on. "No
clean water for a bath —"

"What?" John Gamble shrieked. "Natty won't allow
clean water?"

Amanda explained. "We recycle bathwater. First Mom
takes a bath, then me, then Betsy and Thea."

"Natty's bath is clean?" John Gamble asked, grinning
savagely.

"It's hottest," Amanda said simply. "Then it cools down for us."

"No guns," Betsy went on, "no makeup, no boys in our house, only in the yard, especially not in our rooms —"

"Why no boys?" Lynnie asked.

"I dunno," said Betsy.

Amanda clarified once more. "Because the last time a boy was in her room they took all the clothes off the Barbies, and the prince was sexing Midge."

"'Sexing'?" Lynnie checked the rearview for John Gamble's expression.

He grinned, asking, "What's that?"

"You know," Betsy said impatiently. "The *love* game. When a mommy and daddy rub tummies together to make a baby."

"Uh-huh," John Gamble said. "I get it."

"It was TV anyway," Betsy went on. "He's kind of rowdy."

"He steals stuff," Amanda added. "He stole our VCR remote and Dad's little headphones. Now we have to get up to pause our movies."

"And money," Betsy said.

"Yeah, money." Amanda nodded.

"TV stole money?" Lynnie asked, thinking of her own wallet, left on the cot at the house.

"I'm sure it was justifiable," John Gamble said.

Lynnie asked him why he thought so but he ignored her, insisting instead that the girls tell him more things their mother wouldn't let them do. His feet, in their cheap tennis shoes, were up toward the gear shift beside Lynnie.

Betsy, warming to the topic of TV, said, "TV also once put a pillow on my face and I couldn't breathe for a long time."

Amanda said, "We didn't tell Mom about that."

Betsy said, "Amanda is TV's girlfriend," then began laughing so hard she couldn't talk.

"You're so stupid," Amanda said calmly. "And if you don't shut up, I'm going to say something you don't want me to."

The four of them rode in silence for a moment, until Betsy said, "Mom won't let us drive the car, not even in the driveway with the engine off. She thinks it will roll in the street. Right, Amanda? Even though we live on a dead end and no one would be there to crash into us and besides, Dad always leaves the emergency brake on."

"Mom's just scared," Amanda said.

John Gamble leaned forward and put his chin on Lynnie's right shoulder to make a request: "Let them drive."

Betsy scrambled up beside him, her seat belt off, her lips dotted with cracker crumbs. "Yeah! I can steer. Can I steer?"

"They need to have some fun," John Gamble said. "They may never have any fun. Their fun may be finished before it's begun. Stop, and let's put them behind the wheel."

Lynnie pulled over. It was John Gamble's nature to subvert. He had taken Lynnie herself hitchhiking when she was only thirteen. They'd gotten a ride downtown to a concert and then back home, the two of them on the street with their thumbs out, then riding in the bed of a pickup truck with a hot-water tank. He'd introduced her to beer and vodka and marijuana and psychedelic mushrooms. It was his *Penthouse* she'd stolen to figure out sex. She'd always been grateful to him, but now she wasn't sure she wanted to participate, no matter how small the transgression. Natty wouldn't approve, and Lynnie understood that. Whatever her fears, rational or not, oughtn't Lynnie to honor them, concerning Natty's children? She and John Gamble would have to tell the girls not to tell Natty. This would unsettle Amanda, who had already begun to understand the ways of family. But Lynnie also didn't want to be a wet blanket, especially around John Gamble. He would continue to subvert, whether she was there or not. What would keep him from taking them out later, doing something worse, something truly dangerous?

"Would your *father* let you drive?" Lynnie asked Amanda, looking for the weak link in their nuclear family.

"He might," Amanda said.

"Yes, he would!" Betsy insisted. "And we won't tell him, anyway."

John Gamble laughed. He climbed out with his spade and dug up a small tree they'd stopped near, an evergreen of some sort, a mere twig. "Fast-growing," he explained, dropping it on Lynnie's floor, dirt scattering around the frail, veiny roots. "Maybe I'll steal a whole stand of trees." He wandered away from them, head lowered, searching for easily removed trees. The girls watched him, Lynnie unwilling to join him. When he was out of sight, she knew he was getting high. A few minutes later he returned with two more, slightly larger trees, his eyes watering from the Visine. Lynnie could smell pot beneath his strong body odor when he climbed back in. The car itself reeked of Christmas, dank pine.

In the end, she let the girls sit on her lap and steer over the empty dirt roads, Betsy giggly and wild, swinging the wheel from side to side as John Gamble threw himself crashing around the back, and then Amanda dead earnest to keep the vehicle aimed straight. "Don't you tell Mama about this," Amanda ordered Betsy as they approached the blacktop to Lewisburg. She had to threaten a few things before Betsy would cross her heart, swear to die, stick a needle in her eye.

Beside the highway back to town was a cat, orange striped, big, and freshly dead. John Gamble leaned forward and motioned with both hands for Lynnie to stop, directing her with chopping signals like an air traffic controller, his cheeks bloated with air that he let squeak out like a balloon. He leapt from the van without a word. The two girls turned to Lynnie with their eyebrows raised.

"He takes care of dead animals," Lynnie told them. Both girls then joined him. They watched him pour a shovelful of dirt over the cat, then say his prayer.

"Say it again!" Betsy said, stepping in place as if she had to pee.

John Gamble repeated himself, all three of them with their heads bowed to mutter his prayer, Betsy's hand over her heart. Inside again, both girls decided to sit in the back with him. He closed his eyes and rested his head on the seat, a girl on either side of him. How could they not trust this man? "Home, James," he said to Lynnie.

*

Joanne, as the first-born, seemed to have gotten all the good genes. She was undeniably lovely. But she was also slow, not exactly stupid — as an employed psychiatric nurse, she was the only one of the four children to have a full-time job — yet dull and languorous. She liked to listen to music by universally acclaimed second-rate musicians like Neil Sedaka and Barry Manilow. Her clothes came from all the wrong decades.

On the front porch of the house, she and Natty worked, snapping beans and husking corn, Joanne wearing a long-sleeved black sweater with tiny silver stars dotting it. Amanda and Betsy trailed John Gamble in from the van. He breezed past his older sisters with his trees, whistling a song, leaving a trail of dirt like coffee grounds.

"It would never occur to you to go around back, would it?" Natty said after him. "Stomp your feet, girls, so you don't track in Dot's house. Men make messes," she told her sisters. "All I do all day is pick up crap Dean leaves around. You'd think he could throw away his own goddamn gum wrappers."

Joanne said of her adopted son, "TV keeps a weasel in his room." Natty and Lynnie squinted their eyes at her. She was frequently oblique.

"Why a weasel?" Lynnie asked.

"Well, his snake died."

Lynnie wondered what it was like to live at Joanne's apartment in Wichita. As a child, Lynnie had had each of her sisters as babysitters. When Natty sat, you couldn't do anything but watch television and go to bed early. The doors were bolted tight, and you always took a tour of the house, checking under furniture and in closets for intruders. You couldn't even have a bath because she worried about drowning. But when Joanne stayed, anything might happen. She used to take John Gamble and Lynnie out for drives in her VW bug, sneaking them from the house in the middle of the night, meeting strange boys over on Douglas Avenue, buying bottles of liquor or Sucrets tins of multicolored pills, cruising the city looking for parties, screeching her tires when she turned corners. Joanne always had a lot of friends. She was the most social of the Links, and this was why it surprised Lynnie that she would end up with such a malevolent household — a sullen, spooky little boy and a hostile, paranoid dog that moved constantly back and forth, as if behind bars. "Pissing," little Thea said, to everyone's delight. "He is pissing back and force."

Clouds were rolling in from the east, high lumpy ones with gray undersides, autumn clouds. The song John Gamble was whistling was for his mother's benefit, a song from the forties called "Elmer's Tune," which Dorothea despised and which John Gamble introduced like a virus into her consciousness so that she would be unable to be rid of it for days at a time.

Ten-year-old TV had slept through breakfast and then disappeared afterward, leaving a foul nest of blankets on the couch. Joanne stared up and down the street as if it might help. Her burning cigarette had an inch-long ash on it. "Luckily, he has Mephistopheles with him for protection."

Natty snorted, then said she was glad she hadn't let Amanda go. "I worry he's a bad influence," she said frankly.

Joanne was so accustomed to having her family criticize her that she had lost the ability to be miffed by it. Both the dog and her new son made Joanne nervous, Lynnie could tell. Joanne had no confidence in her authority over either one. From a lifetime of being ordered around by Natty, Joanne was reluctant to try to tell anyone what to do. Children — and dogs, for that matter — sensed this about her and took advantage. So did men, who continued to break her heart and steal her belongings.

Lynnie fell onto the glider at the end of the porch and shut her eyes, her hands still shuddering from the van's vibrations.

"Did you know a movie star lived here?" Joanne asked her.

"No," Lynnie said without opening her eyes, although she seemed to recall someone mentioning the fact a few months earlier. It wouldn't matter; Joanne liked to talk about strangers. She was like John Gamble that way, happy to have a subject besides family gossip. Her own take on the members of the family was one of pure acceptance. She didn't have a critical bone in her body. You could discuss her in her presence.

"He and Mom and Dad are the only people in years to buy property here," Natty told Lynnie.

"He was in that movie about a cattle drive," Joanne said. She couldn't remember its title. "Him and his brothers," she added dreamily. In two years Joanne would be forty, a fact Lynnie couldn't quite believe. Joanne still fingered her hair like a teenager, touched her own breasts. She still confused the words *scratch* and *itch*.

"*Cows Across America.*" Lynnie guessed at movie titles. "*Begin the Bovine.*"

"His brothers visit here, too," said Natty. "I saw it in *People*. They have a sister who's a dwarf."

"A dwarf!" Joanne said.

"I like Mom and Dad's house," said Lynnie, sitting up. "I wish we'd come here when we were little."

John Gamble pushed open the screen door with his foot while carrying a plate full of food, singing now, "Listen, listen, there's a lot of things that you been missin'," once more taking a song Lynnie had thought peppy and making it doleful. He appeared in time to hear Lynnie's last remark and cut off his song to say, "Live in Dukeyville? Yikes."

"Isn't it weird," Lynnie said, "how this is exactly like a small town is supposed to be? Like the locals all wear overalls, and anything even a little bit exotic at the grocery, like croutons, is kind of stale?"

Joanne had drifted away from her shucking job and was now sitting on the porch railing, leaning against a post, her silhouette unconsciously graceful. She was still scanning the street for her son and dog, twirling a denuded cob in her hand. "This *is* a small town," she said.

"Isn't it the cocktail hour?" John Gamble asked, mouth full of watermelon. "Shouldn't someone bring us a margarita?"

"It's only two," Natty told him. "Cocktail hour is, at the earliest, four. And aren't you fucked up enough?"

John Gamble sat on the steps eating loudly, slurping and spitting, ignoring her. Dean and Thea joined them on the porch, Thea with her middle finger in her mouth. "Hey, Dean," John Gamble said in greeting, "I just figured out who you remind me of."

"Who's that?" Dean asked good-naturedly.

"Ernie," John Gamble said. "Ernie of Ernie and Bert. Doesn't he look like Ernie?"

"Ernie!" Thea said.

Joanne said, of the actor, "He drinks at the Thirsty Dog."

"Who?" John Gamble asked her.

Joanne said wistfully, "We could go down there and see if he came in."

Lynnie studied her sister, who seemed to be wandering the empty rooms of her mind. "I'll go with you," she told Joanne.

"Go where?" John Gamble asked.

"Where?" Thea echoed.

The last thing Lynnie heard from the porch was Natty instructing Dean to check Thea for deer ticks. "Lyme disease is really common in Montana," Natty was saying.

*

The Thirsty Dog was one of six bars on Main; its sign showed a frothy-mouthed canine with bug eyes. Lynnie and Joanne sat at the bar but turned their chrome and vinyl stools to face a dirty front window, their view the VA secondhand store across the street, where two old women sat in lawn chairs on the sidewalk among used baby furniture, automatic swings, and wicker bassinets.

"There's us in forty years," Lynnie said.

Joanne giggled. She had only ordered a Coke, but encouraged Lynnie to get whatever she wanted.

"Why Coke?" Lynnie asked.

"Oh." Joanne faltered, blushing. "I'm on this medication, and there could be a reaction, but probably not, it's only like one in a hundred people who take it, but I'm just more comfortable not drinking very much. Our family kind of drinks a lot, you know?"

"What is their bad reaction?"

"Whose?"

"Number one hundred, the one in a hundred?"

"Oh, well, I don't know, coma."

"Huh." Lynnie drank her beer quickly, enjoying the first rush of happiness it gave her. She felt generous toward Joanne, glad to be sitting in a cheap bar with her. And it was cheap. The bar itself was a simple counter with worn, multicolored floor tiles stuck on its front and top, little flecks of gold pattern in most of them. Corners of the tile had lifted, exposing a sticky black mastic dotted with crumbs. The ceiling was sagging, stained, and cardboard-looking, and against the far wall was a tiny dance floor, backed by a big mirror which was supposed to make the very small room appear larger.

Lynnie asked her sister, "Why do you think he would come to this bar?"

"I've been wondering why he comes to this town. But sometimes rich and famous people do strange things, like I go to this astrologer who's really reasonably priced and she used to do long-distance readings for a singer in L.A."

"Who?"

"Well, I can't remember his name, he was with that band that had that video a few years ago at Stonehenge?"

Lynnie shook her head. Under other circumstances it might have frustrated her to have such a haphazard conversation, but she decided to try to go with Joanne's flow.

The girl behind the bar, the one who'd brought them their drinks, looked like she was sixteen, a plump, gullible type who didn't have a clue what to do about her hair. She kept smiling at Lynnie, a failed attempt to hide the fact that she was staring. Lynnie felt like a star herself, popular and mysterious. The girl now made a little gesture with her swelled hand and Lynnie responded by nodding. Soon another mug of beer sat before her. She slugged it down and ordered a third.

Joanne was talking about a massage she'd gotten recently from another person who'd had some circumstantial tie to Hollywood. "He stood right at my head — my face was in a hole. You ever get a massage? Your face is in a hole, afterwards you have a big oval dent around your nose like a moat — and he rubbed my shoulders for a while and then I felt him get an erection, right on the top of my head. It made me very uncomfortable."

"No kidding."

"But I wish it had worked out, because he was a masseur-psychotherapist and he claimed he could read your body, all your tense muscles and facial expressions and scars and whatnot, everything, and tell you where your problem was, and then sort of flog at it. Wouldn't Mom have a heyday with something like that? Somebody squeezing your glutamus maximus because your boss is a pain in the ass?"

"Gluteus," Lynnie corrected without thinking.

"Gluteus," Joanne agreed, taking a swallow of Coke and chewing an ice cube. "But then he got an erection and that was the end of that. I just flipped — here we are, the only two people in the *bowels* of this huge abandoned building in downtown Wichita, me naked, him with a hard-on."

"What'd he say?"

"Oh, he asked me out or something. I don't know."

"Did you go out?"

"Yeah, I really have a difficult time saying no, I don't know why. We ate sushi. I decided if I ever got another massage I'd go to a woman, though this fellow did have a good idea for therapy and he told me some interesting stories."

"Like what?"

Joanne sighed. "Oh, I can't remember any, offhand. I think he used to dive for pirate loot in the Atlantic, you know how *National Geographic* or somebody was all into finding pirate treasure? Even though it's worthless — where could you sell pirate loot? Hey, look, there's John Gamble." She pointed across the street. "Hi!" she shouted, as if her voice might penetrate the walls or door.

Through the window, in the tenuous heat of the late afternoon, Lynnie watched as her brother entered the thrift store. The two women outside who'd been sunning themselves stirred, fighting their way out of their lawn chairs to follow John Gamble's ratty figure into their store.

Joanne said, "He's always looking for bargains, just like Mom. John Gamble is king of the yard sale. You know what Mom gave me once?"

"Deodorant?" Lynnie guessed. Her mother had left deodorant in Lynnie's stocking last Christmas.

"Worse. She gave me her diaphragm."

"Uck. Why?"

Joanne smiled sadly. "Well, it was after her hysterectomy . . ."

Only their mother would allow frugality to outweigh humiliation. "Unbelievable." Lynnie shook her head, then laughed. Joanne joined her. This was the compensation for all the heartache siblings could bring: with them, you had someone to share the preposterous news of your parents.

"Maybe he's buying a wedding gift!" Lynnie said. "He told me he wasn't, but that would be just like him."

"A gift," Joanne said speculatively. "Wow. I didn't think about that."

"Natty did," Lynnie told her. "As usual, Natty's on top of the gift scene." Across the street John Gamble emerged from the thrift store with a long thin box. "What do you think he bought?"

Joanne squinted. "Rifle?"

He turned the corner toward their parents' house, his feet slapping the pavement like a duck's.

"There he is!" Joanne whispered suddenly. Outside the Thirsty Dog a thin man with a blond beard stopped under the awning to pat his hair. Sure enough, it was the actor, smaller than in his movies, his hair more mousy than blond, his face acne-scarred. He came in slowly, letting the door ease itself shut, the jangling bell quiet, and then sat two stools away from Joanne, turning to her and Lynnie and nodding.

"Hey," Joanne said amiably. She was a good flirt, Lynnie recalled. Joanne always had boyfriends. She had probably slept with more people than the rest of the family had, combined. "I really like your movies," Joanne told him. "I really do, especially that one about the cattle drive."

His faint, superior smile turned to a frown, his eyes swinging upward as he tried to identify the movie she could mean. "Which?" he asked.

"With your brothers, about the cattle drive through

Kansas? It was from a book I read, remember that book, Lynnie? What was it called?" Now all three of them tried to remember what she was talking about.

"Oh, never mind." Joanne laughed, banging her empty Coke glass too heartily on the bar. "We're from Kansas, so maybe I just got stuck on the idea of Kansas. Maybe it was a cattle drive in Idaho. I *do* really like your work. I heard you were on Broadway last year."

"Yep," he said. "That I was. You all from here?"

"Kansas," Joanne repeated, not the least bit irritated that he appeared not to have been listening. "Just here for a wedding. My parents are getting married."

He laughed. "Of the free-love generation, eh?"

"No, they were divorced. Now they're back. It's romantic, isn't it?"

"Sure."

The girl behind the bar had listened to the conversation in the manner of a child eavesdropping on grownups, her head moving back and forth, her expression rapt. When the actor asked for a shot of Cuervo, she took a moment to register that it was her responsibility to provide it.

"I'm Joanne," Joanne said, "and this is my sister Lynnie."

"Billy," the actor said, extending his hand as he leaned over the seats between them.

"Billy," Joanne repeated, now frowning herself. "Huh." She sipped her Coke. "I was thinking you were named Nick. Doesn't he look like that actor Nick, oh, what's his last name, you know?"

Lynnie shook her head. She had no idea who Joanne might be talking about. She ordered a fourth draft and listened to Joanne try to convince Billy he'd been in a movie about cows. He didn't mind; in the end he was trying to remember what family of actors *had* made the movie. Joanne's scatterbrained manner did not offend most people.

When it turned out that the Thirsty Dog had no func-
tioning restroom, Lynnie had to excuse herself and run up
the hill to her parents' house — the town white and hot in
her tunnel-visioned drowsiness, the need to pee a heavy
crux — leaving Joanne and Billy at the bar. Instead of
joining them again, she collapsed blissfully on the front
porch glider and shut her eyes for a nap, the sound of her
own circulating blood thick in her ears. This was her favorite way to fall asleep: instantly, intoxicated.

*

"Your father didn't give you enough attention," a boyfriend
had recently told Lynnie. He was explaining why he was
leaving her — that she hung on his every word too much,
that she didn't have an inner life to fall back on, that she
depended on his opinion. Even then, as he pegged her
personality exactly, she was unable to break from her habit:
"You're right," she'd said, crying as he kissed her in an
unsexual, pitying manner on the forehead. Later she got
pissed off, but what good had that done? Moreover, what
good would it ever do, to get pissed off after the fact, to
have to *decide* that anger was called for?

In the late afternoon doldrums in Lewisburg, Montana, Lynnie woke with flies on her face. "Shit!" she cried,
scratching them away. She fell from the glider to the wood
porch floor. Her brother-in-law, Dean, was thumping up
the steps, carrying bags that clanked. Liquor. The thought
made her queasy.

"What?" he asked.

"Damn flies!" Lynnie told him, sitting up with her legs
straight ahead of her like a plastic doll.

"They call it Big Sky Country, but I think of it as Big
Fly Country." He banged the door shut.

Inside, her father was playing cards with Amanda. This

was something he would never have done when his own children were small; then, it was an adult game of bridge or nothing. He refused to learn any of their games, refused even to allow them onto his lap. "Too much like kinfolks," he would say cryptically, pushing them off, not unkindly but firmly. Now he sat at the dining room table with Amanda, playing, peering over his glasses at his cards, his back achingly stiff, his whole upper body turning when he looked from side to side, bringing a slow thumb to his mouth to touch it daintily with his tongue.

Amanda's absent-minded, mildly impatient manner with him told Lynnie the most: he did not exert force in her life. Because it had been so rare, his participation in a game would have thrilled Lynnie and her siblings, would have been cause for celebration. When Lynnie was a child, he had occasionally flown into fits, which never involved hurting the children but instead were more like bad weather — he would thunder, he would rage and blow, he would storm out the back door and leave a swaying dizzy-calm aftermath; in the air you could feel a shared temptation to giggle. Was that his power, Lynnie wondered — his tempestuous unpredictability, the simultaneous wariness and relief one felt at his departure? Whatever the power had been was now gone. Her father was an old man playing children's card games, a wisp of his dry brown hair standing straight up on his head. In a solid tumbler beside him was his martini, two fat stuffed olives on the bottom like pickled eyeballs.

Natty was reading a mystery in a recliner across the room, looking up occasionally to watch the game. Instead of focusing her anger on her father, Lynnie turned it to Natty, who was smugly elated at her father and daughter's playing together. Lynnie crossed the room and dropped herself heavily on the couch where TV had slept (and left his dirty socks). She said, in an undertone her father could not hear, "He never played games with *us*." Napping always made her disagreeable; she didn't know why she let herself do it.

Natty studied her a second, then removed her reading glasses and swung them by one stem in a slow circle. Lynnie noticed her sister's enlarged breasts, the way they stood unnaturally firm inside her shirt, like grapefruits. Since her surgery, Natty had never had to wear a bra. "He was an awful perfectionist," she said softly, leaning toward Lynnie. "I can remember him teaching me to draw, telling me I didn't understand the vanishing point when all I was trying to do was make houses." She snorted. "He showed me how to shade areas, but I just cried because I didn't want the color black anywhere on the page."

"I don't think it's funny," Lynnie said, her anger with Natty growing, her anger with her father something separate from the man across the room. He was not the same person, and she did not hate him. What *did* she hate? she wondered. There was hate in her, but she couldn't properly affix it. It appeared like a bitter taste in her mouth, then faded.

"He never played with us," she complained once more, halfheartedly.

Natty leaned forward — she was ever ready to discuss the family's shortcomings. "You know what I realized recently? I realized that he didn't *have* to be gone all day every day. Dean comes home constantly. Dad could have done that. He didn't have to be gone all the time. He chose not to see us. At our house, Dean spends at least as much time with the kids as I do."

"Well, you guys are the model family," Lynnie told her sister, a statement Natty accepted without comment.

Their father had been a building inspector for the city, a job that had become increasingly flexible as time passed. Lynnie could remember visiting construction sites with him occasionally, walking through half-finished houses or high-rises wearing a hardhat that was too large for her, that stank of someone's sweat, watching her father lean close to other men's ears and shout over the noise of circular saws and cement trucks, gesturing in the manic way one did amid deafening noise. He'd always been the only man there wearing a necktie, carrying a clipboard, driving a white city vehicle, which Lynnie had preferred to their family station wagon. Lynnie had liked his solemn silence as he evaluated situations. On the job he was calm, honorable, capable of finding things funny. The long, secret affair he'd had with another woman had taken its largest toll on him, returning him to the family an aged and subdued man. Lynnie could not bring herself to feel rage toward him; his punishment outweighed his crime.

Natty was making one of her famous metaphors, a talent she'd developed during college at Bryn Mawr: "He understood the structure of a house, all the things to make it stand up, but he had no interest in the living stuff inside it."

"Oh, fuck off," John Gamble would have said, but Lynnie could only nod as if she believed the thought formidable. And if she considered it long enough, she could find a plausible metaphor in almost anything: her family as a house, as a seven-course meal, as a social disease, as a war zone. But so what?

"Did you miss the cocktail hour?" Dean asked, coming up beside Lynnie with a water glass fizzing full of champagne. Lynnie took it gratefully. It was civilized and wise to drink now, in the unhappy late afternoon hours before dinner, before dark, when everything seemed worn out and difficult. In Dallas she only drank to get drunk, and only with friends at bars or parties, never at home. She rarely bought liquor; wine turned to vinegar before she could finish a bottle. But she would always go along with other people's daily rituals; she'd joined Joanne at the Thirsty Dog, she'd toast now with Dean, at dinner she'd have a beer when her mother did, and afterward she'd continue with cheap chianti, John Gamble's beverage of choice.

"Come see the trees," Dean said, smiling his big Muppet smile at them. "John Gamble's made himself a little *glen* out there."

"In a minute," Natty said vaguely, the way mothers always did, resting her glasses on her nose, turning back to her book.

Lynnie and Dean went outside, passing through the kitchen, where Dorothea patted a head of lettuce with paper towels while humming the odious song John Gamble had infected her with earlier. Before Lynnie could reach the door, Dorothea had requested that she turn on the oven to four-fifty and that Dean open a jar of mustard.

"She always has to make you do something," Lynnie complained to Dean in the yard. "Always."

"I don't mind." Dean hitched his pants under his sagging belly.

"I guess I must, but I don't know why. Except maybe she thinks we owe her something, like all these little favors are payback."

"She's a good egg, your mom."

What Lynnie liked best about Dean was his approval of most anything. He had no imagination himself but was admiring of the capacity in others. For a living, he sold cars, using what John Gamble called the Columbo approach: acting befuddled and confused, dressing badly, scratching his head and seeming to agree with the buyer, constantly talking about his daughters and wife, happy to play the role of dumb guy among girlfolk. John Gamble's last real job had been at Weiner Ford, and Dean had had to fire him, but there appeared to be no ill will between them.

Dean's two youngest girls were bringing rocks to ring around the evergreens while John Gamble knelt, thumping the ground with the flat end of his shovel. Dean said to him, "So would you call this a glen or a dale?"

"Well, Dean," said John Gamble, who punished Natty by being extra-friendly with her husband, "I'd call it a stand. Or maybe a spinney."

"It's the six pine trees," Betsy told her father, dropping a rock at her feet. "Like in *Winnie-the-Pooh?* Except there's only five." She put her hands on her hips to illustrate annoyance with this fact.

"Miss Thea." John Gamble pointed at the three-year-old. "Get me the hose."

"La," she said, complying.

Across the alley behind the house three neighbor children, all of them in cowboy boots, scruffy and tough-looking, stood watching the family. When John Gamble waved them over, they fled like wild animals. Small parts of the periphery of Lewisburg gave Lynnie the creeps, and this was one of them, people watching her.

"Boy," Dean addressed John Gamble, laying his big meaty hand on his brother-in-law's shoulder, "you're right ripe."

"He stinks," Betsy agreed.

John Gamble lifted an arm above his head and sniffed beneath it, letting out a large "Whooeee" for the girls' benefit. Then he took the hose Thea had laboriously wrestled across the yard and doused himself, shaking like a dog under its cold spray.

*

Joanne's son came home with a deep diamond-shaped cut just below his ear. Though he was no longer bleeding, TV's stiff chocolate-colored shirt established that there'd been a heavy flow earlier. He closed his eyes, as if he could make the family disappear. While Dorothea squatted beside him, tamping the cut with a washrag, cooing in her reassuring way, the tip of her tongue resting on her upper lip in concentration, Joanne took a nervous survey to see if she could get a consensus about taking him to the emergency room.

Dorothea, as usual, gave them more information than they needed. She said, "The Lewisburg hospital is actually a nursing home with a doctor on call, maybe twenty residents of the home and a nurse or two. I had to get a prescription there. It's just such a pleasure to find a place with some integrity, where the employees feel some direct responsibility for . . . I'm sure they can do stitches," she finished when Joanne looked at her open-mouthed, confused.

Dorothea made the boy turn sideways, then front, studied his pupils, pulled at the skin gently to see how wide the cut was.

"Should I take him?" Joanne asked Natty, who, as the only other mother of young children, seemed to be the logical person to ask.

"I would," she said, "but of course scars on boys and scars on girls are two different things."

"How are they different?" John Gamble asked without

looking up from a jigsaw puzzle, his clothes still damp from his hose bath. Amanda, also at the puzzle table, stared at TV's face.

"With boys it doesn't matter," Natty told him. "On boys, scars are nothing."

John Gamble shook his head, his opinion of his sister confirmed once again. But Lynnie understood what Natty meant, and though she wished it were otherwise, she knew it was true: on Amanda, to Amanda, a scar would mean something. TV himself argued for staying home.

"I don't want to go," he told Joanne, told everyone in his unfamiliar honking voice. "I'm *fine.*" He'd claimed to have fallen on a rock. Lynnie and John Gamble raised their eyebrows at each other. Lynnie thought he'd been in a fight. His shirt was torn in the back, and both knees of his jeans were greasy black, as if he'd been pushed to the ground in a dark hidden place. Of which Lewisburg appeared to have many, the town slowly emptying as mining and logging dried up. TV's hair was longer than any boy's in town, tied in a ponytail with a fluorescent orange shoelace; he had a dangling skull earring in his right earlobe and a T-shirt bearing an obscure joke: VISUALIZE WHIRLED PEAS. His attitude was sullen; his big unlaced hightops nearly asked to be stepped on. So it wouldn't have surprised Lynnie to discover he'd been pummeled by a gang of humorless locals, kicked by their cowboy boots. She shivered at the thought, quite happy she was no longer anywhere near his age.

Amanda said, "There's blood right there," touching her own chin to illustrate. TV swiped the spot away.

Lynnie's father, silent until now, advised Joanne to go, turning with a quiet shrug. He hated accidents, which he called "stunts," and was bitter at their financial cost — the fender-benders, the broken leg or cracked rib, the blood on the white living room rug. It had been difficult to gauge how much of his reaction was fear and how much anger; perhaps, Lynnie thought, they were the same to him.

"O.K., we're going," Joanne declared. "Just to let the doctor have a look." She pulled a reluctant TV out the front door and then had to return to borrow her parents' car keys and receive directions to the hospital. Only after they'd driven away did someone notice the absence of Joanne's dog, Mephistopheles, who'd been with TV in the morning.

"Should we look for him?" Lynnie asked her mother.

Natty laughed. "Or should we take bets on when — and *if* — Joanne notices he's missing?"

Dorothea sighed. She'd spent the late afternoon making a roast with several fresh vegetables for dinner. The house smelled wonderful; candlelight wavered warmly over the table, the flames reflecting in the white plates and spoon hollows. "We should find your sister's dog," she told them, cupping her hand and blowing out the candles, pulling on her jacket and snapping a leash at McWard's neck.

"The martyr," John Gamble said about their mother as he took Lynnie's car keys from her.

Lynnie went on foot with Amanda and Rebel, figuring that any dog would respond to its kind. Walking uphill from her parents' house, they came upon the town cemetery. The grass was lush here, the markers tilted and out of line, as if there were no plan or plots but simply holes dug when townspeople died. Lynnie shivered; in the slanting late summer light, the air was suddenly cool.

Amanda didn't say a word as they walked. As a child, Lynnie never would have guessed how intimidating it was for grownups to talk with children. One of Lynnie's familiar daydreams was to be restored to her childhood self, this time complete with adult knowledge.

She said to Amanda, "I learned to drive in a graveyard in Wichita. John Gamble used to make me speed around the plots." Her words sounded dopey to her, and Amanda greeted them with silence.

After a few moments, Amanda announced that her parents had bought plots.

"They did?"

"Not for them," Amanda clarified. "For Grandma Dot and Papa."

Lynnie abruptly stopped walking when she figured out what she was being told.

"Why?"

"Because Dot and Papa will need them," Amanda said.

"That's the wedding present," Lynnie said. "Isn't it?"

Amanda nodded. "It's a surprise," she said.

"That's a terrible gift," Lynnie said without thinking. She felt a second of dizzying dislocation: where would her real home be, once her parents had died? To whom would she report her headway in the world?

"What's wrong?" she asked Amanda, who had begun to cry.

"They're all dead," Amanda told her, pointing at the cluster of gravestones before her: a family named Knight, mother, father, beloved sons and daughters, infant, assorted spouses — a big sprawling Montana clan entombed together. "Papa is going to die," Amanda said simply to Lynnie. "He's going to die."

Lynnie bit back the stupid assurance she had been about to give her niece. She reached to embrace Amanda but was aware of her own clumsiness as she felt the child's bony shoulder beneath her hand. Lynnie had no doubt that this awkwardness was a genetic deficiency.

"Papa's going to die, and that's why he and Grandma

Dot are getting married again, that's why," Amanda said between breaths.

Lynnie couldn't refute the logic; Amanda had done better than she at making sense of the wedding. Lynnie told her, "Papa's had a good life."

"He told me it was a long road."

Lynnie pictured an empty road like the one in the forest, her father stepping slowly down it, away.

"Messy!" Amanda suddenly called out, furiously wiping her cheeks. "Here, Messy, Messy!" She slapped her thighs, which made Rebel come sniff her crotch.

"Why won't he come?" she demanded of Lynnie. "I hate that dog! It won't come when you call it and it bites people." She lifted her shirt to show Lynnie her ribs, a skeletal bunch of small bones. "He tried to bite me once, right at my heart."

"Maybe he found a better home," Lynnie offered lamely. She hadn't a clue as to how to protect Amanda, who seemed to be at a stage Lynnie was very familiar with, a stage she'd yet to outgrow herself: the one of knowing both too much and too little to be happy in the world.

*

The family returned without the dog, John Gamble red-eyed and starving. He'd gone off in Lynnie's VW by himself, and from the cemetery she'd watched her red and white van as it, and he, drove out of Lewisburg and into the hills where the mine had been. He brought back a green glass bell that had once sat on a telephone pole. During dinner, it served as centerpiece on the table, an overdone roast and soggy vegetables alongside it. Underneath the table, hidden by the long yellow tablecloth that draped nearly to the floor, sat McWard — there was always a Scottie beneath the Link dining table — waiting for dainties to fall his way.

TV had eight black stitches in his neck, little pieces of thread sticking from the clear tape. His hair fanned out like a rooster's comb, stiff with blood, and it was Natty who told him he had to change his shirt before he sat down to eat with the rest of them. Her three girls looked up at him from their places as if he were a living cautionary tale.

"I'll help you," Lynnie volunteered, jumping up to locate a fresh T-shirt for the boy. In the upstairs bathroom she dampened a washcloth and sat on the bathtub rim to work on his hair.

"We went looking for your dog," she told him.

"He won't come to you," TV said in his broken voice. "He won't come to *me*. I lost him at the school."

"The high school?"

He nodded. Lynnie rinsed out the first rusty mess and began pulling through his brown hair once more. He had tiny moles all over his face like dot-to-dot, small eyes too far apart, and beautiful heart-shaped lips. With the right attitude — cocky and happy — he would be a handsome boy. Otherwise, he was always going to be treated like someone with a bad temper. Better that, Lynnie thought, than a dishrag.

"What were you doing at the school?" she asked.

"Just looking around. I found an open door, but Messy wouldn't come with me, so I left him outside on his leash. When I got back he was gone. I fell down looking for him."

Lynnie thought if he'd fallen, he'd been pushed, but she didn't pursue it. She said, "Does Joanne know he's missing?"

TV shook his head. Lynnie said she wouldn't tell, then added, "It's *good* she was so worried about you she forgot the dog."

"I guess."

"It *is* good," Lynnie insisted.

"When we were at the hospital, she showed me her scars," TV said shyly.

"What scars?"

"The ones on her arm." Lynnie frowned. It was her mother who had scarred arms, from the broken car glass in the tornado.

"What scars?" Lynnie repeated.

TV held up his own olive-brown arm and drew with his finger a series of marks inside the wrist, a crisscrossed staccato of motion. "Lots of them," he said.

"From what?" she asked him, breathing shallowly.

"I don't know."

But Lynnie knew — abruptly and absolutely. *Aren't you hot?* she'd asked Joanne that afternoon on the way to the Thirsty Dog, pointing to her long-sleeved black shirt. Lynnie thought she might cry — the urge was a bright spark in her chest she could barely suppress. Instead, she swiped at TV's earlobe one last time, and they joined the others at the table, TV wearing a Grateful Dead T-shirt of Lynnie's that she decided he could keep.

Now Lynnie wondered for how many years Joanne had been wearing long sleeves. She considered her sister as if she were a stranger, a beautiful stranger who sought astrologers and masseurs, a woman with a son for whom she must care deeply. At the table directly across from Lynnie, Joanne sat with her dark hair hanging in waves around her pale face. The candles shone in her large eyes, illuminating her superior features. Why had someone so lovely been given such tough luck? Was it all her own making? The rest of the world — that is, the world outside her family — had taught Lynnie that the heart was a muscle, subject to strengthening by its own peculiar calisthenics, made resilient and tough with use. But her family always let her know the truth — that her heart was actually made of porcelain — by continuing to break it in incremental measure, one hairline crack at a time.

Around her began the ritual of meal: John Gamble bowing his head for a quick private blessing, Natty insisting that the girls eat a little of everything, her father moving meticulously around the table, pouring the wine, a scant slosh at a time, Dorothea leaping up to get bread, milk, juice, spoons, Dean slicing the roast so thin you wanted to scream. John Gamble rudely began to eat before everyone was served.

Wanting to show the tenderness she felt toward Joanne, Lynnie said, "Remember how fun Joanne was as a babysitter? Remember how she used to let us stay up late and jump on the beds and talk on the phone?"

John Gamble stopped chewing long enough to say, "She phoned Gran long distance for us, remember, when we had chicken pox and thought we might die?"

Joanne blushed. With his mouth full, TV squawked out, "She forgot to pay our bill last month so we don't even *have* a phone!"

"Hear, hear," John Gamble said, reaching across the table to shake Joanne's hand, his shirttails dragging across his plate as he did.

Their father said, "Why didn't you pay your bill? You have money." He sat like a judge, with a fork in one loose fist, a knife in the other, as if he were going to bang the table.

Joanne looked nervously away. "The bill got lost in the papers by the front door, all that junk mail and whatnot, I can never keep all our papers straight, do you guys have that problem? By the time I found it, Ma Bell had axed me."

John Gamble said, "You don't need a phone. I don't have one."

"You don't have children," Natty told him.

"You don't have a job," his father added, resuming eating.

Lynnie said, "You don't *like* talking on the phone, John Gamble."

Joanne said, "I *do* like talking on the telephone. I seem to have more to say, I just feel more relaxed and chatty when I know the person I'm talking to can't see me."

"You can be naked in the tub, if you want," Lynnie said.

"I hate talking on the telephone," Dorothea said. "I feel so trapped."

"I hate it too," John Gamble said.

"Yes, we know," said Natty. She made long-distance phone calls every Sunday night, broadcasting the family's news from Kansas.

The little girls were surreptitiously dropping bits of broccoli beneath the table for McWard, whose movements Lynnie felt, his curly fur brushing against her bare ankles, his whiskers grazing her shoes. When TV noticed what was happening, he too began dropping undesirable food, which made McWard move to the other side.

"Oh!" Joanne exclaimed, jumping back from the table. "What is that?"

A burst of spontaneous laughter erupted as McWard scurried away to the kitchen with TV's roast scraps between his teeth. But the dog made Joanne realize that her own dog was missing, and she slammed out of the house to search for him, leaving TV alone with his new family.

After an uncomfortable moment during which Dorothea

began to circulate the food again, John Gamble abruptly burped a word out — "Hey!" — then said, "I have a surprise for you, TV." He tilted his chair back in the way that used to make their father snap at him and, reaching behind him, pulled out from the bookcase the box Lynnie and Joanne had watched him carry from the thrift store. It was not a wedding gift for his parents; the box held a telescope, an old one, the box's illustration showing suited scientific types from the 1950s pointing up excitedly toward the heavens. TV handled the telescope gently, then stood and attached the tripod, setting the three legs among the serving bowls. He pointed the telescope at the window and looked through it timidly.

The three girls clamored for a look, their half-eaten dinners forgotten. Soon Betsy asked, "Where are *our* presents?" to which John Gamble replied without meanness, "You don't need any."

Natty said to her daughters, "John Gamble doesn't know about presents, girls. He doesn't know you have to be fair."

"Fuck you," John Gamble said amiably to her, stuffing another stem of broccoli in his mouth.

"Say, now," Dean said. But he simply sighed, stretched, and made a lazy attempt to hide a belch.

Amanda had stepped away, and it was she that Lynnie watched, her dark-circled eyes that Lynnie followed from TV to John Gamble to her mother. Natty's anger communicated itself in the clinking her fork tines made against her plate as she stabbed at her salad.

"He'll share it," John Gamble said mildly.

TV grabbed the telescope like a club. "Let's go look at stars," he said to the girls.

*

After dinner, Lynnie's father rustled to his feet and asked if someone wanted to take him for a ride into the hills to look for animals. Wilderness began right at the edges of the town; John Gamble had installed chicken wire around his trees to protect them from porcupines, which, according to local rumor, wandered the streets freely after dark, feasting on tree bark, especially pine. It was not unusual to see deer or moose in town, now and then a bear. Every night Lynnie's father went on a ride, and every night he saw something. But this evening, with Lynnie driving, the animals were nowhere in sight.

They rode along, he with his binoculars, she holding tightly to the steering wheel because this driving at dusk, with her father, in his Toyota, made her nervous.

As of this summer, her father could no longer drive a car. Twenty-six years ago he'd been injured in the tornado, disks in his spine had splintered and herniated; a progressive chain of intolerable pain had moved up his body. Now the disks were nearly all fused, and they kept him from having adequate reflexes behind the wheel of a car. The last time Lynnie and he had sat like this, she driving while he rode as passenger, had been when Lynnie was learning how. Then he was constantly sucking in his breath, hissing, grabbing for the chicken handle, stomping at an imaginary brake pedal on his side of the car. It hadn't taken much to convince him that John Gamble should teach her to drive.

Her father's rigid back meant that he had to fold himself into the car like an ironing board. Lynnie had noticed at breakfast that Dorothea brought him his walker and then lifted him up to it. His body had turned angular, and his clothes hung on him the way they would on a piece of furniture. Something warm and supple had left him forever.

They wandered aimlessly in third gear, peering into the trees and brush, asking each other to identify brown dots in the distance. But the only animals they saw were dead ones, and those were small — raccoons, possums, skunks.

"If John Gamble were here," she told her father, "he would want to bury the road kill."

"What?" Her father hadn't heard her, and he leaned his whole upper body slightly toward her as if to catch her next utterance more carefully. But Lynnie regretted the mention of her brother: John Gamble irritated her father. He didn't seem to care that his daughters had started late, or not at all, on careers, but John Gamble's laziness — of course it would appear as laziness — irked him. When Gran had stipulated how her money would be divided, Lynnie's father had been the one to assign thirty as an age of reason. Lynnie changed topics.

"You know what I think of sometimes?" she asked him. She wondered why she felt a need to confide in him — exactly the polar response she had to her mother. But he wouldn't pounce on her the way her mother would, nor would he be automatically curious about what she thought.

"No," he said. "I don't know what you think."

"I think of the tornado, even though I wasn't there. It's so incredibly lucky we didn't die."

He said, "Whole parking lot full of empty cars, and it picked up ours, the only car with people in it."

"I guess that's not lucky."

"No," he said, "not in the least. Spun us around like cats in a clothes drier." Then he added, "I thought we would die. Sometimes when I hear rocks under the oilpan, like on this dirt road, sometimes I can still feel us flying in that storm."

Lynnie recalled another tornado anecdote — in Kansas, there was no end to them — about a family who'd fled to their basement and emerged later to find their whole house gone, not one thing left but the cellar itself and, miraculously, the front door and frame intact. Despite the absence of walls — nothing separating them from the plains around them — they had walked through the front door to leave the place, or so the story went. Lynnie imagined them even closing the door behind them. She liked the image, the puzzling indelible habits of humans.

Her father now said, "Fear of death is not the way to live."

Lynnie couldn't think of an answer to that, but knew immediately that his words would stay with her, a shadow accompanying the knowledge that his gravesite had been purchased, that a hole in the landscape had been set aside for him.

She stopped the car on a bridge and they climbed out, his sticklike movements reminding Lynnie of a praying mantis, to stare up and down Rock Creek. The vista was dry and silent except for the trickle of water. In other times, her father would have fished this stream, would have walked directly up it in khaki-colored waders, right arm arced over his head, left hand feeding line that snapped and then delivered, gently, a homemade fly to its target. At home, in the basement beneath the plumbing and wires, beside the monstrous asbestos-coated furnace, had been her father's desk, on it a wonderful black box full of hooks and feathers and small animal pelts and metal vises and tiny scissors: his fly-tying kit. The air there was hot and smelled of the nail polish he used to finish his delicate flies. She could see his wide yet deft fingers wrapping thread around a fine barbed hook.

Lynnie stared into the wilderness, annoyed that the animals weren't cooperative tonight. It seemed the least they could do, to saunter out and show themselves. Her father rotated from side to side like a beacon, his gaze falling on the comforting sweep of tree-dotted hills, a huge uninhabited place. He did not seem afraid.

"Lynnie," he said, "I want you to do something for me."

"Sure. What?"

"Take me to the motel on the highway."

Lynnie nodded as if she could understand why without his telling her. They took in the view for a moment more, then he directed her as they drove back toward Lewisburg. Once, up in the darkening brushy hillside, Lynnie thought she might have seen an animal, the shadowy shape of its haunch, the confident, peaceful way it occupied the woods.

At the Snowshoe Motel parking lot, her father asked her to wait outside. "Diane is here," he said simply. And Lynnie nodded again, the wavering image she had of her father's mistress in her mind once more after a long absence. Her father swiveled his way from the front seat, then had to push the lightweight door twice to close it. He was so weak, Lynnie thought, so clearly afraid of pain. His gait, without his walker, seemed stiff, splay-footed like a mime's. Everyone had assumed that his affair with Diane was over years ago, although now Lynnie wondered if on other evenings he'd been delivered to the motel by Joanne or Natty. Somehow that seemed unlikely, Natty being judgmental and Joanne weepy. Should Lynnie be honored or annoyed by his trusting her this way? Was it trusting her, or was he taking advantage? She did not know how to feel, as usual.

At the door to Room 14 he knocked, and then disappeared, as if the room had sucked him away. Lynnie imagined that Diane might be peeking through the door's surveillance lens at her.

In the twenty minutes he stayed, the sky presented its finale, blue turned to orange turned to yellow turned to a mild green, then purple, stars like bright pinholes. Lynnie tried out a few scenarios for Room 14: her father allowing Diane to undress and seduce him, or his steadfast silence driving her to fierce irritation; or possibly they were sitting quietly on the motel bedspread, nothing in the world to do or say. They might stare blankly, stunned, the way Lynnie did, marveling over whatever compulsion had brought Diane these two thousand miles.

Her father at last emerged from Diane's room, and Lynnie jumped out to open his car door for him. His right leg would not pull itself in, so Lynnie knelt to do it, clasping his calf and tucking him inside, shutting the door the way one might pat a blanket under a child's chin. She tried to see if his clothing looked rumpled or refastened, to detect an exotic fragrance, but he seemed unperturbed, poker-faced.

"You O.K.?" Lynnie asked when they had returned to the road.

"Oh, yes," he told her. And then: "Well, that's the end of that."

*

At home, the rest of the grownups were playing bridge; Dorothea was drinking espresso, a sludgy harsh brew, made in an old heavy pot, that she'd never persuaded any of the others to share.

All the Link children had learned bridge early; they had all started out sort of enjoying it. But as they grew older, their enthusiasm for the game went in different directions. Joanne could only be coerced into playing; she could never remember how to bid or play. She always had her mother make her a little diagram of points and strategies, and consulted it constantly. John Gamble played carelessly. He could have been quite good — he'd been a bridge shark when he was younger — but now had turned his back on competitiveness and seemed consciously to slack off, giving up tricks, underbidding. Natty was nearly a pro; she'd read books, surpassed her parents, sometimes played duplicate at a club in Wichita. Lynnie was ambivalent about bridge. Her parents had already taught the other three children — two partners and an alternate — how to play by the time Lynnie became interested, so they hadn't required her presence to have a game. As a result, she had remained a beginner, not bad, not good.

And bridge reminded Lynnie of failure, of her ineptitude. She joined the children in the yard, where mosquitoes were biting despite the chill.

Soon John Gamble stood beside her. "Cloud cover," he said. The little stars Lynnie had seen earlier were blinking out above them.

TV crouched behind the telescope, whose tripod was balanced on a stump. Betsy and Thea ran to and from John Gamble's trees, shouting, "On your mark, get set, go!" every few moments, the nippy air invigorating them. Amanda stood with her hands in her pockets, watching TV. Next door, at the police station, country-western music could be heard; a square of light shone from the window. Up high was a tower the children in Lewisburg might believe had once held a hanging noose.

A big militaristic vehicle came rolling down the quiet street, stopping but not parking in front of their house. The dark glass of the driver's side window glided down and let out the smooth sound of a saxophone.

"That's the actor," Lynnie told John Gamble. "Hey," she called.

Billy peered into the yard. "Joanne here?" he said. "We're supposed to have a drink."

"She's gone looking for her dog," Lynnie said. "He disappeared."

"Lost her pal, did she?" Billy said. "Dog gone, is he? Maybe I'll just cruise in the Rover here and see what I can find." He raised his hand and the window slid up, cutting off the music.

"I should have introduced you," Lynnie said to John Gamble.

"Drive me to the gas station," he replied.

"What?"

"You need to go to the gas station." He'd grabbed his shovel up from the yard, nodding his head toward Lynnie's parked van.

"I'm sick of driving . . . ," she started. She was sick of going places, of learning things. She wanted to lie on her cot and think. Or cry.

"Come on," John Gamble insisted. "You need gas."

They called out to Amanda and TV where they were going, then got back in the VW, John Gamble in the driver's seat. "I'm already carsick," Lynnie complained. "You should have let me drive. It's my car."

"The dog is dead," John Gamble said as they zoomed off.

"What?"

"On the highway. I found him earlier, but I didn't have my shovel. We gotta go bury him. I mean, really bury him."

"Oh, man, Joanne's cursed."

"No, she's not. A famous person is seeking her."

"True. I guess. But that actor could be an asshole. I mean, he's *probably* an asshole."

"The dog was definitely an asshole."

Mephistopheles lay lifeless on the road John Gamble

had taken to the abandoned mine. In the headlights Lynnie could see no blood, no visible damage. His eyes were black, reflecting the van's lights. She swallowed back sadness; dead, he did not menace her.

Off the road, John Gamble scraped the ground with the tip of the shovel, trying to find a soft spot, while Lynnie pushed the animal toward him with her feet. Later there would be his bristly variegated hairs to brush off her clothing. "I didn't like this dog," she said.

"Did anyone?" John Gamble said breathlessly. He'd begun a hole and was already sweating. They needed to hurry.

"Joanne did. I can't stand how pathetic her life is, can you?"

He didn't answer, continuing to dig.

The highway was empty but for them. How had Mephistopheles managed to get himself killed on a road this desolate? "John Gamble," Lynnie said, "what if TV killed the dog?"

"What would be the point of that?" he asked, breathing hard.

"I don't know. Just general badness, maybe."

"He's not bad. His mother's the one in jail for murder, not him."

"How'd this dog get run over on a road like this?"

"He was big and vicious and probably stupid. That's how. And don't start believing all that bullshit Natty feeds her kids about TV. He's O.K."

From the distance came two headlights, high off the ground, the rumble of a truck or van.

"Those halogens can only mean the Rover," John Gamble said, placing himself squarely in front of the dead dog, blocking him from sight. The vehicle pulled alongside them. Joanne rolled down her window.

"Look who found me!" she called to them. "This is a

much better way to search for Messy, way up high, and there's four-wheel drive, too. And a CD player."

"Any luck?" Lynnie asked her, wondering how a CD player was helping out the search.

"Oh, that old dog's chasing himself a rabbit," Billy called from the driver's seat. He was busy playing with his gear stick, chewing a toothpick. Lynnie thought his patience seemed too businesslike, like something he might have method-acted himself into, knowing it would someday prove useful.

"What are you guys doing?" Joanne asked.

"Digging trees," John Gamble told her, brandishing his dirty spade. Mephistopheles had been pushed far enough off the highway to be invisible from Billy's truck.

"Watch out for Smokey Bear," Billy cautioned. "These forest fellows don't like you taking their wildlife."

"Huh huh huh," John Gamble laughed insincerely.

"Well," Joanne said as Billy's engine roared, "see you back at the ranch."

They left in a draft of exhaust. "He's an asshole," Lynnie told her brother.

"Find rocks," he instructed her.

Afterward, when the dog was covered by dirt and stones, he muttered his prayer, and Lynnie let the refrain follow her home: *God help those animals who must cross the road.*

"Do you ever think Joanne might feel so bad she'd kill herself?" she asked John Gamble as they stopped outside the house.

He took a last hit from the joint he'd lighted, swallowed back smoke, and spoke from the top of his inhalation, a gasp that reminded Lynnie of gangster imitations: "I think we're all closer to suicide than we'd dare ever admit."

Lynnie frowned at him. Was he warning her? But he exhaled calmly through his nose and smiled at her.

"Diane's at a motel here," Lynnie told him.

"Who?"

"Diane. Dad's Diane."

John Gamble sighed in a burdened, exasperated way. "It's not our business," he said. "Really. There's nothing we can do."

"I shouldn't tell Mom?"

"You shouldn't even tell me. Everyone ought to be able to have some secrets."

They got out of the car. Lynnie chewed up a Breath Saver, standing in the cold outside the house for a few moments to air the marijuana from her clothes.

"If we play bridge," John Gamble told her, "you be my partner, O.K.?"

She nodded. Inside, her mother laughed, then Dean. Her mother and Dean were jolly drinkers, good sports. Around them, you thought you might be having fun. Lynnie started up the steps behind John Gamble, drawn toward the laughter as toward warmth.

Before entering the house, John Gamble reminded her, "Remember — Mephistopheles is lost, not gone," and Lynnie consented to his kindhearted lie.

*

McWard and Rebel overturned the trash in the night. Both of them were hiding in the downstairs bathroom when Lynnie discovered the corncobs and oily lettuce all over the kitchen floor in the early morning. "Bad dogs!" she yelled at them, striking each on the nose. "Goddamn stupid animals!" She picked everything up and threw it back in the can, then opened the door to kick the dogs outside.

Her fury was larger than their misbehavior, an outrage they seemed to understand as they tucked their tails between their legs and scuttled away.

In the yard, John Gamble and TV lay in the circle made by the new little trees, only their heads visible beneath the single blanket, TV burrowed up under John Gamble's chin. The sky was gray, although it was too early to tell if it was from clouds or mere sunlessness. Perhaps to keep warm, perhaps simply out of need for comfort, John Gamble and TV had snuggled into each other in their sleep, and John Gamble's arm was thrown over the boy protectively. While Lynnie watched, they suddenly stirred, turning in opposite directions simultaneously, pulling the blanket taut between them as they lay back to back, butt to butt. The telescope still sat on its stump, aimed directly skyward like a rocket.

Lynnie returned to the house, where Natty and Dean were up, trudging sleepily about the kitchen in matching bathrobes. Dean asked Natty if she was experiencing morning sickness.

Only now, after having been in Lewisburg two nights, did Lynnie learn that Natty was pregnant again. "Pregnant?" she said, remembering John Gamble's line on the subject: *They only fuck every three years.*

"She's nauseous," Dean said.

"Nauseated," Natty corrected him, and then said to Lynnie, "I thought you already knew," and sniffed.

"How would I know?" Lynnie moved awkwardly to hug her sister. Natty's chest was rock-hard, her breasts completely ungiving.

"Everybody always knows everything in this family. It's our trademark."

"Well, I didn't know."

"Nobody in this family ever congratulates anybody," Natty complained.

"That's because we never know what's going on, contrary to what you think."

Dean, sitting at the table, hunched over his instant coffee like a gargoyle, commented, "The problem in this family is that no one prefaces news so that others will know how to take it. When you call one another, you should start out by saying, 'I have some good news.' Then you say, 'I'm pregnant.' Or, 'I'm coming home for a visit.' What this family does is call up and just blurt news, like the person you're calling is supposed to know how to take it. 'I'm pregnant,' Natty might say, and of course your mother says something like 'Do you *want* to be?' in a meek little voice. What hint have you given her?" He hadn't even looked up, had just sat chatting away while Lynnie and Natty stared, dumbfounded, at him. No one ever expected Dean to say anything intelligent.

"Mom said, 'Do you want to be?'?" Lynnie asked.

Natty nodded. "I told her she'd be the last to know if I was pregnant and didn't want to be. Everyone gets all wide-eyed and horrified about it."

"Congratulations," Lynnie said. "I bet you want a boy this time." When Natty leaned over to retrieve scallions and green pepper from the hydrator, Lynnie could see a ridge in her cleavage, a straight raised line like a long pencil beneath her skin.

"That's the other thing everyone thinks, that we'd want a boy." Natty located cheese and sour cream and eggs. "I want another girl. I like girls."

Dean added, "We love girls. If it ain't broke, don't fix it."

Dorothea entered the kitchen in her bathrobe, her hair flattened in the shape of an anvil. "I had the most hideous dreams," she said.

"Me too," said Natty, pushing the refrigerator door shut with a slippered foot.

"I dreamed your father fell," Dorothea said. "I took him to the mall, on the second floor by the Chick-Fil-A, and suddenly there weren't any balcony railings." She looked directly into Lynnie's eyes, yet beyond, recalling her terror. Lynnie, for an instant, felt exactly how her mother loved her father. He was her project, his disability her new baby to protect. Lynnie fought her impulse to sneer at this care-taking kind of love; after all, it was the kind her mother had proved best at. She did it well.

"Scary," Lynnie said.

Her mother nodded absently, then focused on Lynnie, who had to look away.

"The dogs got in the trash," Lynnie said, hoping to avert any further discussion of dreams, the competition for most nightmarish. Really, she hated hearing other people's dreams unless she appeared in them.

Her mother shook her head. "That McWard is a perfect gentleman until other dogs come around. Then he gets in his pack mentality. Perfectly horrible."

"Just like all of us," said Natty as she cracked eggs into a bowl. The shells she crammed together into a single cupped structure, her movements quick and contentious. "I believe all animals have a vicious pack personality."

"Except me," said Dean. "I love a crowd, the more the merrier, bring on the pack."

"I have good news for you, Mom," Lynnie said brightly, sitting down beside Dean and nudging him. "It's your wedding day."

"Thank you," her mother answered, while Dean laughed.

The fact that her parents had not been married for the last six years had sat like a spare worry in Lynnie's body, no more troublesome than the rest. In college, when the breakup had become final, and even now, she sometimes spent the odd fact like currency. Later she would undoubtedly talk about this wedding the same way. "I went to Montana," she would say casually, when asked. "My parents got married."

*

It was late morning, and TV still lay on the lawn, rolled tight in John Gamble's army blanket.

Lynnie's father had gotten dressed early and now sat confined in his suit, sitting erect on the couch and lecturing Natty on the subject of McWard, who had climbed onto the table and eaten the yellow wedding cake frosting when Natty had turned her back. "You all wanted us to replace Geronimo when he died, oh, everyone was so sad, 'Get a new dog, Dad, isn't it lonely without old Mo?' Then you *give* us a dog, *this* very dog" — the Scottie sat down happily, hanging his tongue out, semiaware that the conversation concerned him — "and now all anyone can do is complain."

"Doorknob!" John Gamble cried approvingly. The household Scotties were always called either Doorknob, because they were dumb, or Scum, because they inevitably spent their lives skimming around the kitchen for leftover nibbles.

"Oh, I wish Mephistopheles would come back!" Joanne moaned from the window seat, where she sat as if posing, an unlit cigarette between her fingers. She hadn't been home last night when Lynnie had finally gone to bed.

"Maybe you want to wake TV?" Dorothea said as she passed through. Despite its being her wedding day, Lynnie's mother had dressed in her jeans and sweatshirt and was hustling from room to room, setting things down and picking them up, humming a song.

"He needs to get his sleep," Joanne said. "He waited up for me last night, poor thing. I'll wake him before the wedding."

Dorothea's busyness tired Lynnie — her mother was so competent, so superior at preparation that Lynnie frequently fell into a limp defeat in her presence. She sat beside her father on the couch, wondering if he'd dreamed of Diane last night. Had his love for her disappeared? Or had it simply reattached itself to Dorothea, a habit reacquired? Truly, the thing that mystified Lynnie was not the affair but the revival of the marriage.

Natty and Dorothea stopped to look around, their expressions identical. There was a punch bowl full of pink punch, a basket of crackers, empty platters waiting for cold cuts, small bowls for condiments, upturned glasses for proposing a toast, festive yellow napkins, and the pretty cake. The groom had shaved — his face was streaked, with red tracks here and there — and Natty's girls were already dressed, sitting sweetly in a row watching *Barney and Friends* on the snowy black-and-white television. Their dresses were matched, peach floral frocks Natty would have sewn herself. Their knees were lined up, four white-stockinged knobs and Thea's pudgy dimples on the end.

But sitting with them was John Gamble, stinking of pot. Dragging at him, the girls had begged him to join them. You could almost make out the cloud his presence seemed to cast on Natty's image of her parents' wedding. He laughed uproariously as Barney the purple dinosaur simpered and pranced, the girls covering their faces as they giggled with him, and Lynnie remembered his once telling her that certain children's shows on PBS were *designed* for doing drugs.

"Don't rile them up," Natty warned her brother. "You know how you always rile up the girls and then leave them

for the grownups to calm down. Girls, you behave yourselves until after Dot and Papa's wedding."

John Gamble didn't appear to listen to a word of it.

The windowpanes shook as a hard wind blew, a distinctly autumn wind. A hubcap rolled tinnily down the
empty street out front. Lynnie and John Gamble would
leave tomorrow morning, possibly this afternoon. She had
a headache, a response, no doubt, to the simultaneous stress
and relief at the prospect of leaving.

"Mom," she said to Dorothea, "I'm going to send you
and Dad your gift later on, O.K.?"

"Oh, honey, we didn't expect wedding gifts." Dorothea
laughed. Lynnie wondered how she would cover her alarm
at receiving grave plots from Natty and Dean. True, they
were necessary things, plots, and extravagantly expensive,
and undeniably practical. But also macabre, and their purchase most certainly ranked among the vast array of activities you could label, in a family, terrorist.

A half-hour before the ceremony was to begin, the four
women in the family took over the upstairs bedrooms and
bathroom to dress. In another family the doors might have
been open and they might have wandered from room to
room half-dressed or even naked, helping each other zip up
dresses or select shoes. But in this family, the doors were all
closed. As far as Lynnie knew, they'd never been naked in
a room together. She herself hurried, as if someone might
burst in on her.

When they emerged, they awkwardly complimented
one another's clothes.

Natty said, "Think John Gamble will put on a tie?"

Joanne said, "He might if he has a girlfriend. Girlfriends kind of keep men on top of manners, have you
noticed that? Does he have a girlfriend anymore?"

"You don't care if he wears a tie, do you, Mom?" Lynnie wobbled around on her heels, enjoying the silky slide of her hose and slip.

"Not really," Dorothea said, fixing a wide hat on her damp hair. "I don't care what anybody wears," she continued cheerfully, though Lynnie thought that it wasn't really true.

Natty turned to Lynnie. "You don't have to defend him, you know. It wouldn't kill you to admit he's a mess."

"Who says I defend him?"

Joanne said, "I'd like to meet his girlfriend, if he has one. No matter how weird John Gamble was, he always brought home the nicest girlfriends."

Lynnie said, "I thought they were all really dumb."

"That's because you thought he was too good for them," said Natty.

"He was," Lynnie said. "He probably still is." She tried to imagine the girlfriend her brother would have nowadays. She shivered. Her dress was far too sheer for the weather, and she'd forgotten to bring makeup to Montana. Joanne's wedding outfit was a tight maroon dress with long tubular sleeves and a very low neckline. It would have been more appropriate at a piano lounge, but she looked beautiful in it, somehow beyond the reproach of conventional fashion. Natty's dress matched her daughters' and made her look like the maid of honor. *Matron* of honor, Lynnie amended.

"Lipstick, anyone?" Natty said as they tugged themselves into shape. Lynnie agreed to wear a bright red lipstick, far more garish than anything she would ever dream of purchasing herself. She and Joanne shared the silvery-threaded mirror in the bathroom, Joanne's lipstick a deep liver color, Lynnie running the candy-apple red over and over her own mouth, enjoying the tawdriness.

At the top of the stairs their mother held out her stubby-nailed hands. "I hope the ring still fits," she said as they headed down.

*

Dorothea asked John Gamble to wake TV, and Lynnie to put away her dog. Lynnie took Rebel by the collar out to her van so he wouldn't be a nuisance and left him there to breathe patches of fog on the window as he whined, sweeping his tail winsomely.

The chill wind blew violently; someone had heard that snow flurries were in the forecast. Lynnie's eyes teared and her skirt billowed up into her face as she hurried on her heels to the house; she pushed it down to see John Gamble wrestling with TV on the lawn, the two of them rolling like dogs, like children or lovers. John Gamble's legs flailed, TV's braid flipped around his face, the blanket unraveled and, caught by the wind, sailed a few yards away.

It occurred to Lynnie then, for the first time, that her brother wasn't going to get any easier to be around, that he would most likely borrow money from her, that he might end up living with her, that forever he would be her obligation in some way. It did not frighten her. In fact, she almost welcomed the responsibility, realizing he was something like a pet himself, a being whose temperament and behavior she had little control over, a being she would love even when she felt like cursing and kicking him.

Other kinds of love existed, and then there was this kind.

Lynnie was on the porch stairs, hanging on to the railing against the wind, when she heard TV squeal, a high animal sound. Lynnie stumbled back down the steps and crossed the grass, her heels sinking in the soft earth. TV and John Gamble sat on their knees on the lawn, facing each other, TV's hand at his cheek.

"Lynnie," John Gamble said urgently, his face a shocking white.

"What? Are you O.K.?" He looked as if he might fall forward into the grass; Lynnie wondered if he could possibly have OD'd on something. He reached out toward TV, who flinched. Lynnie knelt, gently pushing TV's hand away from his cheek, turning his face so that she could see a large bite mark just under the boy's eye.

"Oh my god! Was that from one of the dogs?"

TV shook his head quickly, tossing Lynnie's hand away as he did. It was a new wound, one Lynnie had not seen yesterday when cleaning him up. The circle was red, indentations of teeth showing along with tiny dots where blood had risen. The skin had not been broken but had been bitten hard enough to leave a blossoming impression. "What happened?" she asked.

"It was an accident," John Gamble pleaded, as if she'd accused him. His hands were moving at his neck. "Nothing happened. We were just wrestling around. It isn't what you think." But what *did* she think? Lynnie attended to the fact of his rambling more than his actual words. Now his fingers moved between his shirt buttons, as if scratching a sudden rash on his chest. The shirt, she noticed in a kind of mental aside, was new, its creases remaining from the cardboard it'd been folded around.

They all stood up, and TV swallowed, frowning, looking not at Lynnie but at something to her left, far away, off where the animals were hiding in the forest. She'd had little sustained interest in knowing about his life before reaching her family; her assumption had been that he would be safe with them, that things would become easier, equitable.

Frightened and not at all certain about what had happened, Lynnie said to John Gamble, in an effort to convince herself, "You couldn't have meant to hurt him. You wouldn't hurt him."

Her brother shook his head quickly, like an admonished child eager to receive adult benevolence.

Lynnie would be haunted by this mystery of John Gamble's biting TV; she would fall into it often, and without warning, yet fail ever to do more than rediscover it as a yawning empty space in her allegiance to her brother, the blank hole you might label *loyalty* or *love*.

"It's O.K.," Lynnie told him now, trying to sound reassuring. To TV she said, "Are you O.K.?"

The boy shook his hair from his eyes, took a step back, and lifted his chin in a way that effectively closed Lynnie out. She had to admit that she did not want in. She did not love him, and she probably never would. It was her brother's murky bewilderment that concerned her, not TV's. Such was the predicament, the utter unfairness, of family.

"What can we do?" her brother asked, his breathing visible, his chest rising in his shirt. "It looks terrible."

"You have makeup?" TV said in his broken voice, focusing his distant gaze on Lynnie, getting more directly to the point. "I think makeup, that cover-up stuff."

John Gamble's face was miserable, unlike TV's, which looked merely defensive, an expression he had undoubtedly cultivated during his natural mother's crime and incarceration. Lynnie blinked a few times to provide some sort of transition, some opportunity to move from shock to pragmatic action. Then she leaned forward, in spite of TV's reflexive cringe, and, grasping the back of his head firmly, kissed him with her abundantly lipsticked mouth, leaving a brighter, cheerier circle over the present one.

"There," she said, running her fingers around her mouth to tidy up.

TV reached tenderly, not touching his wound. Now it was a badge of happy lips, not teeth, as if the affection had been of an acceptable nature.

John Gamble said, "Thank you."

*

At noon the judge from the courthouse across the street walked over during her lunch hour to perform the ceremony. She was a pear-shaped fortyish woman wearing square-framed glasses on the end of her nose, holding a folded paper in her hands, and smiling distractedly at the family as they pulled themselves together. Her eyes ran over them in a perfunctory manner, idling only briefly, nearly imperceptibly, at John Gamble's shabbiness, Joanne's cocktail dress, TV's long hair, his red cheek. She did not ask why Dorothea and John were marrying, did not ask why here, in a town that had never known or cared for them, asked little really except for their preferred forms of address.

The family made a wobbly circle around the bride and groom, Dean stumbling over a chair leg and landing against the bookcase, his daughters and wife looking at him icily. Dorothea wore a wide straw hat with a dangling green ribbon that kept falling into her eyes. Her dress was plain, drop-waisted, striped horizontally with fat bands of bright color like a kindergartner's. She wore beads made from rolled triangles of paper — the smudgy gray of newsprint and glue — that Amanda and Betsy had created for her. Dorothea chatted energetically with the judge while everyone else stood, as maladroit as strangers. Finally there was a silence that the judge felt comfortable speaking into: "Is this everyone?"

They all looked around, counting; Lynnie felt the familiar sense of someone's being missing, felt herself glance out the window as if the straggler might come running over the yard to join them, happy child or kind adult, perhaps her Gran, or simply someone to make her feel she belonged, someone almost exactly like Lynnie herself: she felt distinctly like the family understudy, an apprentice to each and every one of them. But she saw nothing outside except clouds pouring over the distant hills like churning water, John Gamble's little trees blowing sideways in the high wind; the house would fly away, and they would depart stupidly through the still-standing door. But for the moment they were a family, complete, reconvened, shoulder to shoulder.

"Let us now witness this union," the judge began.

Lynnie's father, rigid in his old wool suit, wore a Band-Aid on a left knuckle. When he was asked to take Dorothea's hand in his, his fingers quaked, and the peach-colored Band-Aid seemed absurdly small against his large dark red flesh. Her parents looked like a pair of children to Lynnie, wearing costumes complete with hat and heels, clasping hands as if for the first time, standing in a circle learning the rules to a silly game.

Lynnie did not think she belonged to an ordinary family. Nor were they extraordinary — simply knocked about and scarred by the world, and the weather, and themselves, and each other, flawed on their surfaces in ways they could hide, and broken inside in ways no one would ever excavate. Their ritual was as crude as they were; one dog was scratching at the closet door, another whined from outside, a third thumped his tail beneath the table where the cake sat. Another lay buried in a shallow grave just outside town. This small ceremony, this clumsy rendezvous, was as close as her family was going to get to grace.

Her parents were encouraged to kiss each other. Lynnie's inclination was to look away — but shouldn't it be simple to behold their affection for each other? Her father fumbled with Dorothea's hat, bending formally to find her mouth with his. Now Lynnie let tears pop into her eyes, where they beaded and fell, beaded and fell, like a fountain of tiny pearls. She had learned a hundred things over the last few days, and she was destined to forget them all. This knowledge of her own forgetfulness, forgivingness, was what Lynnie had to seize on to, to take with her, this and her imperfect heart.